E. F. (Edward Frederic) Benson

Limitations

A Novel

E. F. (Edward Frederic) Benson

Limitations
A Novel

ISBN/EAN: 9783337032685

Printed in Europe, USA, Canada, Australia, Japan

Cover: Foto ©Andreas Hilbeck / pixelio.de

More available books at **www.hansebooks.com**

Limitations.

A NOVEL.

BY

E. F. BENSON,

AUTHOR OF "DODO," ETC.

THIRD EDITION.

LONDON:

A. D. INNES & CO.,

BEDFORD STREET.

1896.

LIMITATIONS.

CHAPTER I.

TOM CARLINGFORD was sitting at his piano, in his rooms at King's College, Cambridge, playing the overture to *Lohengrin* with the most indifferent success. It was a hot night in the middle of August, and he was dressed suitably, if not elegantly, in a canvas shirt, a pair of flannel trousers, and socks. He had no tie on, and he was smoking a meerschaum bowl of peculiarly spotted appearance, through a long cherry-wood stem. The remains of a nondescript meal laid coldly on the table, and a cricket-bag on the hearth-rug, seemed to indicate that he had been away playing cricket, and had got back too late for hall. The piano was almost as disreputable in appearance as its master, for it stood in a thorough draught, between the windows opening on to the front lawn and the door opening into the smaller sitting-room, and the guttering candle was making a fine stalactite formation of wax on D in alt. Several good pictures and college photographs hung on the walls, and between the windows stood a small bookcase, suspiciously tidy. Tom played with the loud pedal down, and treated his hands in the way in which we are told we should bestow our alms. D in alt had stuck fast to C sharp and C, and the effect, when either of these three notes was played, was extremely curious. However, he finished the overture after a fashion, and got up.

"This is a red-letter day for Wagner," he remarked. "What do you do with pipes when they get leprous, Teddy?" he asked, looking dubiously at the meerschaum bowl.

"I sit down and do Herodotus," remarked a slightly irritated voice from the window-seat, behind the lamp.

"I don't think that's any use," said Tom.

"Perhaps you've never tried it. I wish to goodness you'd sit quiet for ten minutes, and let me work!"

Tom walked up to the lamp, and examined the pipe more closely.

"It is as spotted and ringstraked as Jacob's oxen," he remarked. "Teddy, do stop working! It's after eleven, and you said you'd stop at eleven."

"And if you inquire what the reason for——" murmured Teddy.

"I never inquired the reason," interrupted Tom. "I don't want to know. Do stop! You're awfully unsociable!"

"Five minutes more," said Ted inexorably.

Tom took a turn up and down the room, and whistled a few bars of a popular tune. Then he took up a book, yawned prodigiously, and read for the space of a minute and a quarter, lying back in a long basket-chair.

"What the use of my learning classics is, I don't know," he remarked. "I'm not going to be a schoolmaster or a frowsy don."

"No, we can't all be schoolmasters or frowsy dons, any more than we can all be sculptors," said the voice from the window-seat vindictively.

Tom laughed.

"Dear old boy, I mean no reflection on you. You'll be a capital don, if you succeed in getting a fellowship, and it will always be a consolation to you to know that you probably won't be as frowsy as some of your colleagues. I can't think how you can possibly contemplate teaching Latin prose to a lot of silly oafs like me for the remainder of your mortal life."

"You must remember that all undergraduates aren't such fools as you."

"That's quite true; but some are much more unpleasant. They are, really; it's no use denying it."

Ted shut his books, and looked meditatively out on to the court through the intervening flower-box, filling his pipe the while, and Tom, finding he got no answer, continued—

"And I suppose, in course of time, they'll make you a dean. That's a jolly occupation! Eight a.m. on a winter's morning. And the warming apparatus of the chapel is defective. Furthermore, you must remember that those are the dizzy heights to which you will rise, if you are successful; if not, you will have spent the six best years of your life in writing about the deliberative subjunctive, and, at the end, have the consolation of being told that the electors considered your dissertation very promising, but unfortunately there was no vacancy for you. They will also recommend you to publish it, and it will be cut up in the *Classical Review*, by a Dead Sea ape with bleary eyes and a bald head, who will say you are an ignoramus, and had better read his grammar before you write one of your own. Oh, it's a sweet prospect! It is grammar you do, isn't it?"

"No; but it doesn't matter," said Ted. "Go on."

"How a sensible man can contemplate spending his life in a place like this, I cannot conceive," said Tom. "It's the duty of every man to knock about a bit, and learn that the outer darkness does not begin at Cambridge Station. There is a place called London, and there are other places called Europe, Asia, Africa, and America."

"And Australia. Do you propose to go to them all?" asked Ted. "It's a new idea, isn't it? Yesterday you said that, as soon as you went down, you were going to bury yourself at home for five years, and work. Why is Applethorpe so much better than Cambridge?"

"Why?" said Tom. "The difference lies in me. I shall continue to be aware of the existence of other countries, and other interests. Great heavens! I asked Marshall to-day, in an unreflective moment, if he knew Thomas Hardy, and he said, 'No; when did he come up?' And Marshall is a successful, valuable man, according to their lights here. He's a tutor, and he collects postmarks. That's what you may become some day. My hat, what a brute you will be!"

Ted Markham left the window-seat, and came and stood on the hearth-rug.

"You don't understand," he said. "It's not necessary to vegetate because you live here, and it's not necessary to be unaware of the existence of Hardy because you know Thucydides. I don't want fame in the way you want it in the least. I haven't the least desire to make a splash, as you call it. It seems to me that one can become educated, in your sense of the word, simply by living and seeing people. It doesn't really help you to live in a big town, and have five hundred acquaintances instead of fifty."

"No, I know," said Tom, "but as a matter of experience, of men who settle down here, a larger proportion are vegetables than should be. They want to be the authorities on gerunds, or Thucydides, or supines in *-um*, or binomial theorems, or acid radicals, and they get to care for nothing else. If there were only a dozen fellowships reserved for men who didn't mean to work at anything, it would be all right, but when every one cares for his own line more than anything else, you get a want of proportion. Collectively they care for nothing but lines, individually each for his own line. And, after all, lines are a very small part of life. What difference would it make to any one if there was no such thing as the deliberative subjunctive?"

Markham did not reply for a moment.

"No one supposes it would," he said, after a pause, "but you must remember that grammar is not necessarily uninteresting because it doesn't interest you. In any case let's walk down to the bridge."

"All right. Where are my shoes, and my coat? Ah, I'm sitting on it!"

Tom's rooms were on the ground floor on the side of the court facing the chapel. The moon had risen in a soft blue sky, and as they stepped into the open air they paused a moment.

The side of the chapel opposite them was bathed in whitest light, cast obliquely on to it, and buttresses and pinnacles were outlined with shadows. The great shield-bearing dragons perched high above the little side-chapels stood out clear-lined and fantastic from their backgrounds, and the great crowned roses and portcullis beneath them looked as if they were cut in ivory and ebony. The moon caught a hundred uneven points in the windows, giving almost the impression that the chapel was lighted inside. To the east and west rose the four pinnacles dreamlike into the vault of the sky. In front of them stretched the level close-cut lawn looking black beneath the moonlight, and from the centre came the gentle metallic drip of the fountain into its stone basin. Towards the town the gas-lit streets shot a reddish glare through the white light, and now and then a late cab rattled across the stone-lined rails of the tramway. From the left there came from the rooms of some musically minded undergraduate the sound of a rich, fruity voice, singing,

"I want no star in heaven to guide me," followed by "a confused noise within," exactly as if some one had sat down on the piano.

Tom murmured, "I want no songs by Mr. Tosti," drew his hand through Markham's arm, and they strolled down together towards the river.

"Of course I don't mean that you'll become like Marshall," he said, "but it does make me wild to think of the lives some of these people lead. They don't care for anything they should care about, and even if they do care about it, they never let you know it, or talk of it. Oh, Teddy, don't become a vegetable!"

"And yet when I came up," said Markham, "my father used to write me letters, asking me about my new impressions, and this fresh world that was opening round me, and there really wasn't any fresh world opening round me, and I didn't have any new impressions of any sort. It seemed to me like any other place—and I was expected to feel the bustle and the stir, and the active thought, and temptations, and I don't know what beside."

"O Lord!" sighed Tom. "I know just the sort of thing. I don't know if there is any bustle and stir, and active thought, but I certainly never came across them. Doesn't the *Cambridge Review* call itself the 'Journal of University Life and Thought?' Meditate on that a moment. As for temptations, the only temptations I know of are not to be dressed by eight, not to go to Sunday morning chapel, and not to work from nine till two. But I've been acquainted with all those temptations all my life, except that one had to be up by 7.30 at Eton.   The temptations, in fact, are less severe here."

"I don't know how it is," said Ted, "but whenever people write books about Cambridge, they make the bad undergraduates go to gambling hells on the Chesterton Road, and the good ones be filled with ennobling thoughts when they contemplate their stately chapel.   Did you ever go to a gambling hell on the Chesterton Road, Tom?"

"No; do you ever have ennobling thoughts when you look at the stately chapel?   Of course you don't. You think it's deuced pretty, and so do I, and we both play whist with threepenny points; and as a matter of fact we don't fall in love with each other's cousins at the May races, nor do we sport deans into their rooms, nor do deans marry bedmakers.   Oh, we are very ordinary!"

"I feel a temptation to walk across the grass," said Ted.

"Yes, you're the wicked B.A. who leads the fresh, bright undergraduate—that's me—into all sorts of snares.   What fools people are!"

Tom sat on the balustrade of the bridge and lit a pipe.   The match burned steadily in the still night air.

"Now, Teddy, listen," he said, and he dropped it over into the black water.   There was a moment's silence as it fell through the air; then a sudden subdued hiss as the red-hot dottel was quenched.

"I wonder if you know how nice that is," said Tom.   "I don't believe you enjoy that sort of thing a bit."

"Dropping matches into the river?" asked Markham. "No, I don't know that I care for it very much."

"Oh, it's awfully nice," said Tom. "Here goes another. There—that little hiss after the silence. Fusees would be even better. No; you haven't got an artistic soul. Never mind; it would be dreadfully in your way up here. Teddy, stop up here till the end of the month, and then come and stay with us a bit. You needn't shoot unless you like."

"Yes, I shall stop up till the end, but I don't know whether I can come home with you. I ought to work."

"What rot it is!" said Tom angrily. "You've been working for six months quite continuously, and you think you can't spare a week to be sociable in. What on earth does your wretched work matter, if you do nothing else? What is the good of a man who only works?"

"More good than a man who never works. But I agree with you, really."

"Well, but you behave as if you didn't think so," said Tom. "The other day you said you sympathized with that wretched grammarian in Browning, who spent his whole life in settling the question of the Enclitic $\delta\nu$, or some folly of that sort, and caught a cold on his chest in consequence, and had integral calculus and tussis, and a hundred other things. Very right and proper. Have you got any syphons? I wish for whisky. Well, will you come home with me or not? I'm not going to press you."

"No, I don't want pressing. Yes, I'll come. I

should like to very much. You leave one alone, which is the first quality of a host."

They strolled up again, as the clock began to strike twelve.

"I'm sure I've done you much more good than you'd have got in an hour out of your Herodotus," said Tom. "There is one really good point about you, and that is that if you are told something you think about it. I shouldn't wonder if I found you dropping matches into the Cam some night soon."

"It's quite possible. Let's see, what is the point of it?—the sudden splash at the end of the silence, isn't it?"

"Yes, it is like so many things. It's like a mole burrowing silently in the earth, and then suddenly coming out at a different place. You needn't examine that analogy. It's like what I am going to do. I'm going to work very hard and quite silently for several years, and then suddenly I'm going to make a splash."

"But are you going out immediately afterwards—like the match?"

"I don't know; perhaps I shall—who knows?"

"Tom, are you aware that we are talking exactly like the people in books about Cambridge—the two friends, you know, who walk about on moonlight nights, and meditate on life and being?"

"God forbid!" said Tom piously. "But we'd better go indoors, just to be safe. Those people are so ridiculous only because they are always the same. Of course we all *do* meditate a little on life and being, but we do other things besides. But they come out in the evening like rabbits out of their burrow, and disappear again till the next evening. I'm going to play cricket to-morrow. They never do that."

"And drink whisky now. They never do that."

"No. To drink whisky is next door to going to the gambling hell on the Chesterton Road. Don't go to bed yet. Come to my room."

"I thought you wanted a syphon."

"Yes; go and get one, will you, and bring it round."

"Any more orders?" asked Markham.

"Oh yes," said Tom—"some tobacco. I've run out."

The Long Vacation Term was, so Tom thought, a really admirable institution, and it might have been invented exclusively for him. None of the colleges are more than half full, there are no lectures, and no need of wearing caps and gowns. The usual things go on as usual, but in a less emphatic manner. Those who wish to work do so, but not with any sense of being ill-used if they are interrupted; college matches take place, but they are not matters of first-class importance, or of first-class cricket. There is a country-house atmosphere about the place, an atmosphere of flannel trousers in the morning, of never being in a hurry, of a good deal of slackly played lawn tennis, and going on the river in canoes. This suited Tom very well, for he was more than anything else an ambitious loafer, who might turn out a loafer without ambition or an ambitious man. Successful loafing is not a gift to be despised; it requires a certain amount of ability, for the successful loafer must never be bored with doing nothing. Tom had quite enough ability to be thoroughly successful in this line; he was clever, artistic, original, and full of many interests, and in consequence he loafed from year's end to year's end without ever wishing to do anything else, though he meant to do other things often enough. He played games well, but amateurishly, not taking them seriously enough to be pre-eminent in anything from rowing down to chess, but finding amusement in them, often playing a good innings at cricket when it was not wanted, and given to slog at dangerous balls when it was particularly important that he should keep his wicket up. "College matches in the Long," as he explained, were about his form.

He was for ever coming into harmless little collisions with the arm of the academic law, being found in the streets after dark without cap or gown, not from any wish to transgress the regulations which the accumulated wisdom of generations had framed, but from considering in a genial way, on each particular occasion, that it was a matter of no importance. In the same way, if he more frequently walked across the hallowed grass than he went round by the path, or if Mr. Carlingford's name was more often conspicuous by its absence than its presence from the boards that told how many undergraduates attended lectures, he evinced such frank surprise when the matter was brought home to him, was so ready to express regret for what had happened, and so identified himself with his tutor's wish that it should not occur again, that the offence seemed at once to appear in an almost wholly unobjectionable light. He was now at the end of his second year at Cambridge, and the prospects of his getting through a Tripos with any credit either to himself or his teachers were small. His teachers regretted this more probably than Tom himself, for they were quite aware of his ability, or at least his power to do better than badly, while Tom was supremely unconscious of it. He had been told that a Tripos was a test of merit, and he accepted the fact cheerfully, even when coupled with the assurance that he would probably only get a third. Tom drew the inference that he was therefore a fool, and neither wished to dispute it nor disprove it. He was, perhaps, conscious of a feeling that a great many men who seemed to him to be extraordinarily dull took brilliant degrees, and supposed that he was wrong in thinking them dull, or at any rate that the abilities which ensured good degrees were compatible in the same man with the extremes of social deficiencies. Meantime he made admirable little sketches of his friends in the margin of his books, and on sheets of paper during lecture hours; settled down to the belief that his mission was to be a sculptor, and was almost surprised that the hour had passed so soon. For the rest he was a young man of twenty-one, of rather more than medium height, with an extraordinarily pleasant face and a pair of honest brown eyes, which looked quite straight at you, and always seemed to be glad to see you. He looked intensely English, and preeminently clean among that race of clean men. Even Mr. Marshall, about whom Tom has already hazarded an opinion, had been heard to say that Carlingford. was an uncommonly pleasant fellow, though he hardly ever came to have his Latin prose looked over.

It was nearer ten o'clock than nine when Tom emerged half dressed from his bedroom next morning, to find two or three cold pieces of bacon waiting for him, which he inspected with an air of slight but resigned curiosity. It really seemed so odd that this world should contain things so undesirable as pieces of cold crinkled bacon; the reasons for their existence were as unintelligible as the causes which produced centipedes or deliberative subjunctives. Markham came in at this moment, for Tom had said he was coming to work with him at half-past nine, but his face expressed no surprise.

"Come in, old man," said Tom. "I hate people who say 'old man,' don't you? Have you come to breakfast? That's right. Sit down, and help yourself. I've breakfasted ages ago, and I'm afraid the tea's quite cold. Never mind, I'll make some more. You may think I'm foolish, but it's not so. As a matter of fact, I didn't wake till half-past nine. Make tea, Teddy; I'll be ready in a minute."

"I didn't come here to make tea for you, but to work," said Markham, lighting the spirit-lamp.

"Well, you're late, then," said Tom; "you said you'd be here at half-past nine, and it's close on ten. And I wish it was eleven."

"Why?"

"Because I should have shaved, and have eaten a little cold crinkled bacon. Also perhaps have done a little work. But about that I can't say.

By the way," he called out from his bedroom, "Teddy!"

"Well?"

"I'm going to study the antique this morning in the Cast Museum. Come too?"

"Rot!"

"What?"

"Rot!"

"Oh! This is rather a brilliant conversation, isn't it? Well, I'm going there really. Do come. You'll see some pretty things. I wish I'd done the Discobolus. I should have, if some one hadn't thought of it first. I shall do a man shying a cricket-ball. Pull the string and the model will work."

Tom emerged from his bedroom and sat down to the cold bacon.

"I shall complain of the cook," he remarked. "This bacon is cold. I didn't order cold bacon. I'm not a hedger and ditcher. What are hedgers and ditchers? Anyhow, they eat cold bacon in hedges and ditches. I've seen them myself."

"Perhaps you didn't order your breakfast at three minutes to ten."

"Don't be snappy, Ted. But you're quite right. I don't know what they mean by it. Was it you who came in here about half-past eight, and knocked at my door?"

"No. I shouldn't have stopped there. But I thought you said you didn't awake till after nine."

"Oh, that was afterwards. I didn't awake that time till after nine. You see it was quite an accident that some one came in here at half-past eight, and

I couldn't conscientiously count that. I'm sure you must see that no one with any sense of honour could have taken advantage of that."

"No, it would have been hardly fair, would it?" said Markham dryly. "A tricky sort of thing to do. Where did you say you were going to spend the morning?"

"At the Archæological Museum. I went there yesterday for the first time. They've got no end of casts. All the best Greek things, you know."

"It won't help you much in your Tripos, will it?"

"No, of course it won't," shouted Tom. "Good heavens, to hear you talk, one would think that a man's place in heaven was decided by his Tripos, not to mention his place on earth! I'm not going to be a don or a schoolmaster, as I told you last night—— "

"Frowsy don," said Markham.

"All right, frowsy don, and I don't care a blow whether I get ploughed or not. I don't feel the least interest in any of the books I have to read, so why should I read them?"

"Then why do you ever read at all?"

"Because dons and other people, like you, for instance, make such a fuss if I don't."

Markham walked to the window and pulled up the blind, letting a great hot square of sunshine in upon the carpet.

"I wonder at your considering that sufficient reason. Of course I'm grateful for the compliment. Personally I should never think of doing a thing because you would make a fuss if I did not."

"Oh, go home, Teddy," said Tom in cordial invitation. "You talk like pieces for Latin prose. Look here, I'm going to the museum for an hour, and then I shall come and work. This afternoon we play some college—John's, I think—on our ground. You said you'd play. We shall begin at two sharp. Mind you work very hard all the morning, and try to finish the fifth book of Herodotus—or whatever it is—before lunch. I hope you always mark your book with a pencil, and if you find any difficulties, bring them to me."

Tom laid a paternal hand on Markham's shoulder, and blew a smoke-ring at him.

"And now I'm going to study the heathen antique. I wish you'd come. It would really do you good. For me of course it's necessary, as I'm going to be a sculptor. Teddy, will you be my model for 'The Academic Don'? I'm going to do a statue of the academic don, a mixture of you and Marshall and a few others—a type, you know, not an individual. That's always going to be my plan. I shall do a pedimental group, 'Typical Developments of Modern Dons.' In the centre the don stands upright, looking more or less like an ordinary man : then you see him beginning to stoop, then sitting down, getting more and more like a vegetable at each stage, and in the corner there will be two large decayed cauliflowers, with fine caterpillars crawling all over them. In ten years you shall sit for the cauliflower. Good-bye."

Tom banged the door after him and went off to his museum, and there was nothing left for Ted but to follow his advice and begin working, which he did in a savage spirit. Like many rather silent, rather serious people, he found a great stimulus in the presence of some one who, like Tom, was hardly ever serious, and never silent. He made periodical attempts to take Tom in hand, but, like most people who had tried to do so, his efforts were not very successful. Tom had loafing in the blood, and his ambitions did not run in the lines of Triposes. At the same time it was owing to him that Tom had not at present failed very signally in college examinations, for Ted had succeeded in making him work, if not steadily, at least intermittently. Tom's fits of intermittent work had not, it is true, occurred very often, but when they did occur they lasted sometimes for a week, of eight-hour days, and left him idler than ever. But, from Ted's point of view, a widely supported and seemingly rational one—that men came up to the university partly at least to work, and that examinations were the criterion whereby the success of nine terms of residence was judged— these intermittent fits were better than nothing, and when they were induced just before an examination they led to results which, though superficial, were, according to the standard he measured them by, tolerably satisfactory. Tom never professed to feel the least interest in what he was working at, but pressure would sometimes make him work; and a very vivid memory, though one of short range, enabled him to reproduce the results of his week's cramming.

But Tom's influence over his friend was of a much more personal and vital kind. Ted looked on to the time when Tom should go down, and leave him, as he hoped, to a permanent university life, with blankness. He formed few friendships—and he had never been intimate with any one before. Tom's healthy, out-of-door sort of mind, coupled with his artistic and picturesque ability, and his personal charm, had for him a unique attraction. You may see an even further development of the same phenomenon sometimes in the lower animals. A staid senior collie will often strike up an intimacy with a frisky young kitten, though it is hard to understand what the common ground between them is. The collie is not happy without the kitten, but unfortunately the kitten is quite happy without the collie—in fact, it would find the continuance of its exclusive society a little tedious.

CHAPTER II.

TOM came back from his museum about twelve, in an unusually sombre mood: the Discobolus apparently had not proved inspiring; and he took his books to Markham's rooms, tumbled them all down on the floor, lit a pipe, and took up his parable.

"Those things are no good to me," he said; "they may have been all very well when the race of men was a race of gods, when all the best athletes went to the games naked, and wrestled and boxed together; but it is out of date. Of course they are awfully beautiful, but they are obsolete."

"Do you mean that you prefer Dresden china shepherdesses?" asked Markham.

"No, of course not; they are out of date too, and they are not beautiful. They are only clever, which is a very lamentable thing to be. No one was ever like that. An artist must represent men and women as he sees them, and he doesn't see them nowadays either in the Greek style or in the Dresden style. Yet how are you to make knickerbockers statuesque?"

"You aren't; or do you mean to say that the artists of every age must reproduce the costume of every age? Surely, if we all dressed in sacks, you couldn't represent them."

"Yes, but we never shall dress in sacks," said Tom; "that makes just the difference, or rather there will be no sculptors if we do. To look at a well-made man going out shooting gives one a sense of satisfaction: what I want to do is to make statues like them, which will give you the same satisfaction. Somebody wrote an article somewhere on the incomparable beauty of modern dress. I didn't read it, but it must be all wrong. It is the ugliest dress ever invented. How can you make waistcoats statuesque? I haven't got one on for that reason."

"Tom, do you mean to do any work this morning?" asked Markham.

Tom shook his head.

"No, I've got something more important to think about. Do you see my difficulty? I want to make trousers beautiful, and women's evening dress beautiful, and shirt sleeves beautiful."

"Shirt sleeves are not beautiful," said Markham; "how can you make them so, and yet be truthful?"

"My dear fellow, it is exactly that which it is a sculptor's business to find out," said Tom. "I don't mean I shall make them beautiful in the same way as the robes of the goddesses in the Parthenon pediments are beautiful, but I shall make them admirable somehow. I shall make you feel satisfied when you look at them. Think of that boxer's head in the British Museum: he must have been an ugly lout, but what a masterpiece it is! That is a much greater triumph than the Discobolus, simply because it represents an ugly man."

"Tom, don't pretend you belong to the school that

says that everything that exists is worth representing. No one wants to see drawings of dunghills."

Tom rose from his chair and began to walk about
the room.

"I don't know," he said, "I can't be sure about it.
Before I judge I shall go and see the best things
that are to be seen. I shall go to Rome, I shall go
to Athens—Athens first, I think. I don't want to
be influenced by any modern art, and if you go to
Rome you must fall in with some modern school or
other: there are too many artists at Rome. Yes, I
shall go to Athens the autumn after I have taken
my degree. But I expect to be disappointed. It
will all be beautiful, but it will be all obsolete, and
that will be distressing. Greek statues are in the
grand style, like the Acropolis, I expect. They
were perfect for that age and for that people, but
I don't think they would do now. We're not in the
grand style at all. We wear cloth caps and Norfolk
jackets. Fancy the Discobolus in a Norfolk jacket,
or Athene in a bonnet and high heels. I shall go
and talk to Marshall about Athens. He's been there.
You play this afternoon, Teddy, you know. Two
sharp. I'm going to lunch in hall at one."

Tom gathered his books together, preparatory to
leaving the room. "I wish I hadn't gone to that
Museum," he said; "it's put me out of conceit. You
can't do anything good unless you believe in yourself. People talk of humility being a virtue; if so,
it's one of the seven deadly virtues."

Tom met Mr. Marshall going across the court,
and assailed him with questions about Athens. This

eminent scholar was a small man, with a quick, nervous manner and weak, blinking eyes. He had a nose like a beak, which completed his resemblance to a young owl.

"Athens, yes. I was there six years ago," he said. "I remember it rained a good deal. The Acropolis, of course, is very fine. There is, as you know, a beautiful temple to Minerva on it. I calculated that the blocks composing the row of masonry above the pillar must have weighed fifteen or twenty tons each. I was very much interested in speculating how they got them into place. Yes."

"I'm going to work there," said Tom, "after I've taken my degree. I suppose they've got masses of things there."

"The museums are very considerable buildings," said Marshall. "I was very much struck by the size of them. I should be most pleased to be of any use to you, in the way of recommending hotels and so forth."

"Many thanks," said Tom. "I shall ask you again about it, if I may."

Tom went to his rooms, and addressed his piano dramatically. "That is a tutor," he said.

He went up rather late to cricket, being the captain, and having warned every one that the match was going to begin at two sharp, won the toss, went in himself, and got bowled during the first over, in trying to slog a well-pitched ball over long-on's head.

"I vote we declare the innings closed," he said, as he returned to the pavilion. "To close our innings for one run would be so original that it would be really worth while just once. Hit them about, Teddy, and make a century!"

Tom had the satisfaction of seeing his side make between two and three hundred, but however gratifying this was to him as a member of the team, it was tempered with other feelings. He went and bowled at the nets for half an hour, watched the game a little, and felt that his applause was hollow. Markham was playing characteristically ; that is to say, he left dangerous balls on the off alone, hit hard and well at badly pitched ones, and played good-length balls with care and precision.

" There's no fun in that," thought Tom to himself ; " any one can do that. All the same any one can get out first ball, like me, if they play the ass."

Markham was in about an hour, and when it was over he and Tom went to get tea.

"I wish you'd had a decent innings instead of me," said Markham, as they walked off to the pavilion.

" Nonsense, Teddy ; you played very well."

" I mean you enjoy it much more than I do."

" Well, that's your fault. Hullo, there's Pritchard out!"

Pritchard came up to them, dangling his glove in his hand, with much to say.

" It's a beastly light," he began, as soon as he was up to them. " I played the ball all right, but I simply couldn't see it. Besides, it shot."

" Well, it was just the other way with me," remarked Tom. " I saw the ball all right, but I couldn't play it, and it didn't shoot."

"Oh, you tried to slog your first ball," said he, walking away.

Tom and Markham sat down under the chestnut-tree and drank their tea.

"Shall I come to you as soon as term is over?" asked Markham. "The last day of term is Saturday week, you know."

"Hang it! so it is. Yes, come at once; it will be the twenty-ninth, won't it? Thirty days hath—no there are thirty-one. Tuesday will be the first. You may come and carry my cartridges if you won't shoot."

"That will be charming. I can't see what the fun of hitting little brown birds is."

"Oh, well, you may always miss! But if you come to that, what's the fun of hitting a little red cricket-ball?"

"Well, you may always miss that," said Markham, "just as you did, Tom! Besides, if you hit it you score runs."

"Well, if you hit the little brown bird twice, you score a brace of partridges. Besides, you have a nice walk over turnips and mangolds——"

"Well, you can do that in August."

"Oh, Teddy, there's no hope for you!" said Tom. "When you die and go to hell, they'll make you shoot all day until you love it, and then they'll send you to heaven, where there is no shooting at all. I don't suppose there are such things as rocketing angels, are there?"

"Tom, the only excuse for being profane is being funny."

"All right. But I don't see why there shouldn't be. There is such a thing as a shooting star."

" What *do* you mean ? "

"I'm sure I don't know," said Tom. "Of course there was some connection in my mind, or I shouldn't have said it."

"Do you mean that no one, even you, can talk sheer drivel ? "

"Don't ask so many questions, Teddy. We shall be all out in a minute; there's the ninth wicket down. Come on, we'll give those beggars a chance. You know it is all nonsense saying that trousers and shirts are not beautiful. Look at Harold bowling there. Do you see how the wind blows the shirt tight over his shoulder? That's an opportunity for a sculptor which the Greeks didn't use—you get all the shape of the arm, and that look of wind and motion which the loose flap of the sleeve gives."

"I should advise you to do a statue of a man bowling in a high wind," said Markham.

"I'm going to—just at the moment when the ball leaves his hand, one leg right forward, with the trouser loose on it, the other leg back with the trouser tight. It's all nonsense about momentary postures not being statuesque. They are statuesque above all others. I don't call those knights in armour on Gothic tombs statuesque. Sculpture represents life, not death. There! why the deuce Hargrave tried to hit that ball, I don't know. Of course it bowled him."

"Thomas Carlingford did the same," said Markham.

"I know he did. That's why he has every right to express his opinion, as it is strictly founded on experience. Look sharp with the roller! We'll go out at once."

The remaining fortnight of the Long passed away quickly and uneventfully, and by degrees the colleges began to empty themselves. In King's hardly any one was left except Tom and Markham, who played tennis together when there was no longer a cricket team available, and spent the mornings, Markham working, Tom doing anything else by preference. The latter got hold of a lump of modelling wax, and made the prettiest possible sketch, as he had intended, of a man bowling. The figure was charmingly fresh, and had a certain masterly look about it which showed through all its defects. Tom lost his temper with it twenty times a day, and twice crushed the whole thing into a shapeless mass, was sorry he had done so, and set to work again. He had never had any teaching, but there was no doubt that he had got the artist's fingers, which are of more importance than many lessons. Lessons you can obtain in exchange for varying sums of money, and artist's fingers are a free gift, but they are given to the few.

Meantime Markham bent his grave, black-haired head over his Herodotus, and sat on a cane-backed chair at the table, while Tom lolled in the window-seat, and poured out floods of desultory criticism on every subject under the sun. At times Markham gathered up his books impatiently, and left the room, declaring that it was impossible to do anything if

Tom was there ; but after a quarter of an hour or so he always wished that Tom would follow him, and at the end of half an hour he usually went back, finding that the wish to be with him was stronger than the wish to get on with his work. Tom apparently was quite unconscious of all this. He was always very fond of the other, but in a breezy, out-of-door manner, and he would always have preferred playing cricket, with or without his friend, to his undivided company at home, while Markham had been conscious on several occasions of being glad when it rained, making cricket impossible, but making it natural for Tom to come to him to be supplied with other amusements.

Once during this week the two had settled, in default of other things to do, to go up the river and have tea at Byron's pool, bathe, and come home again in the evening. But during the morning a note had come for Tom, asking him to play for an inter-college club against a town club, and he accepted with alacrity, and went to Markham's room to tell him that he couldn't come with him.

Markham said, " All right," without looking up from his books ; but for some reason Tom was unsatisfied. He paused with his hand on the door.

"You don't mind, do you ? " he said.

"I don't want you not to play," said Markham coolly.

" What's the matter ? " asked Tom in surprise.

Markham got up and went to the window.

" Nothing.   Mind you make some runs."

But Tom still lingered.

" Look here, I'll come up the river if you are keen

about it.   I only thought we settled to do it if nothing else turned up."

Markham recovered himself.

"Yes, it's perfectly right, Tom.   Bring your books in here and work till lunch."

"No, I can't; we're going to begin at one.   I shall go and have some lunch now.   You can get some one else to go up the river with you, you know; no one is doing anything this afternoon."

"No, I don't think I shall go; I don't want to much.   Are you playing on the Piece?   I shall stroll down there after lunch."

Markham's father was the incumbent of a small living about ten miles from Cambridge, where he spent a happy, and therefore a good life, doing his parish work with great regularity and no enthusiasm, reading Sir Walter Scott's novels through again and again, looking after a rather famous breed of spaniels, and editing, at intervals of about three years, an edition of some classic, adapted, as he suggested in his prefaces, for the higher forms in public schools. His religion was a matter of quiet conviction to him, and his other conviction in life—two convictions is a large allowance for an average man—was his belief in the classics.   Ted had been brought up in the same convictions, and at present had shown no signs, outward or inward, of departing from either of them. The nearest approach he had had to abandoning either was due to Tom's frank inability to find amusement or interest in classics, for Markham, recognizing his undoubted ability, could not quite dismiss his opinion off-hand.   The father's wish for the son was that he should be a great Christian apologist, in Orders as a matter of course, and a Fellow of his college. At times, Markham suspected that Tom's religion had no greater place in his interests than classics; but of this he knew nothing, for nine young men out of ten do not talk about their religion, even if they know about it, and Tom was emphatically not the tenth.

Ted left Cambridge to go home two days before the end of term, for Chesterford was on Tom's way, and he wished to pick up some books at home, and leave others there.

His father met him at the station, driving a neat, rather unclerically high dog-cart, accompanied by two spaniels and a horsey-looking lad, who was coachman, gardener, and organ-blower in church. Mr. Markham was a tallish, distinguished-looking man, in whom the resemblance to his son could be traced; he wore a straw hat and a grey coat, so that, had it not been for his white tie, you would perhaps have been at a loss to guess what his profession was.

"Well, my boy," he said heartily, "I'm glad to see you, though it is for such a short time. Have you got all your luggage? Jim will put it in the cart for you. I've got a thing or two to do in the village," he continued, taking the reins. "Wroxly tells me he's got some wonderful stuff for the distemper, and Flo is down with it, poor lass! She's a bit better this morning, and I think we shall pull her through."

"Which is Flo?" asked Ted, who thought dogs were uninteresting.

"Flo? She's one of the last lot, born in April—don't you remember? She's the best of them all, I think. Wonderful long silky ears."

"That's no clue to me, father," said Ted. "I always think they are all just alike."

"Ah, well, my boy, they aren't so important as classics. I read that note of yours in the *Classical Review*, and it seemed to me uncommonly good. How has your work been getting on?"

"Oh, fairly well, thanks. I haven't done much lately, though. I've been looking after Tom Carlingford."

"That's the boy who was here a year ago, isn't it? You're going to him to-morrow, I think you said. Get him to come here again, Ted; we all liked him so much. Not much of a classic, I should think—— "

"No. Tom doesn't care for classics," said Ted, "and there's no reason why he should work at them, you see. He's awfully rich, and he's going to be a sculptor."

"A sculptor—that's rather an irregular profession."

"Yes. Tom's irregular, too."

"Has he got any ability?"

"I always think he's extremely clever," said Ted with finality.

"Dear me, he didn't strike me as clever at all," said his father. "I remember he spent most of his time skating, and sitting by the fire reading old volumes of *Punch*."

"I dare say I'm wrong," said Ted. "You see, I'm

very fond of him.   Ah, here we are, and here's May
coming down the drive to meet us!"

If Tom had spent his time skating and reading
Punch when he might have been talking to May—
always supposing that May did not skate and did not
read *Punch* with him—he was a fool.   That, however,
is probably sufficiently obvious already.   In this case,
Tom's folly consisted in preferring even old volumes
of *Punch* to the society and conversation of a typical
English girl of the upper classes, tall, fair, slim, just
at that period of her life when the blush of girlhood
is growing into the light of womanhood, a girl whose
destiny it clearly was to be a wife, and the mother of
long-limbed boys who yearn all their boyhood to
be men, and who become men, real men, at the proper
time.

Ted jumped down off the dog-cart as it turned
up the steep drive, leaving his father there; and
the brother and sister walked up to the house
together.

"Yes, it's always the way, Ted," she said; "you
come here one day and go off the next.   And you
promised to be here all September!"

"Well, I shall be here nearly all September," said
he.   "I'm only going to the Carlingfords' for a
week."

"How is Mr. Carlingford?" asked May, after a
pause.

"He's all right.   He always is.   He has talked a
good deal, and done very little work.   He also made
one century in a college match, and followed it up by
five ducks."

"I thought you were going to bring him here again."

"Yes," said Ted, "I had thought of it. But he asked me to go back with him for a bit."

They had reached the house by this time, and Mr. Markham was just going off to the kennels, to try the effect of the new medicine on Flo.

"Flo's a good deal better, father," said May; "I think she's getting over it."

"Ah, I'm glad of that. But I shall just try her with this. By the way, did you take those books you have been covering to the parish library?"

"Yes, I took them this morning, and brought back some others."

"That's a good girl! And the meeting of the outdoor relief fund?"

"It went all right. Come down to the lake, Ted, and we'll paddle about."

They walked across the lawn, down over two fields, now green and tall with the aftermath, and pushed off in a somewhat antiquated boat.

"Well, May, how have things been going?"

"Oh, much as usual! I've been busy lately. Oh, Ted, isn't it lovely? Look at the reflections there. I do love this place!"

"Could you live here always?" asked Ted.

"Why, yes, of course; what more can one want? I should hate to live in a town! And think of leaving the village, and all the dear dull old people! I like dull old people—I like little ordinary things to do, like covering parish books. That's the life I should choose—wouldn't you?"

Ted did not answer for a moment.

D

"Yes, I think I should. All the same, you know——
No, I like this best."

"People talk of the stir and bustle of London,"
went on May, dipping her hand into the water, and
pulling up a long flowering reed, "but I should detest
that. It would frighten me."

"It's my opinion that the bustle and stir is exaggerated," said Ted. "People are much the same
all the world over."

"I don't think that," said May. "Miss Wrexham
was here last week, staying at the Hall; father and
I dined there once while she was here. Well, she is
quite a different sort of person. She was always
talking, and wanting to do something else. She
couldn't sit still for two minutes together, and she
talked in a way I didn't understand."

"How do you mean?"

"I can't express it exactly," said May. "She
seemed to belong to a different order of woman
altogether. One morning she asked me if I did any
work in the parish. I told her the sort of things I
spend my day in, and she said, 'Oh, that must be so
sweet! just living in a country place like this, and
seeing poor people, and going to early celebrations.
I suppose you go to London, don't you, in the
summer?' Then, of course, I had to explain that
country clergymen couldn't do that sort of thing,
and she said how stupid it was of her, and would I
forgive her. She talked as if all one did was the
same kind of thing—as if covering parish books was
the same thing as going to communion. And why
should she ask me to forgive her?"

"I imagine you didn't like her much," said Ted.

"No, I can't say that I did. I don't think she is genuine."

"Oh, you can't tell," said Ted. "I know several people like that, and they are just the same as we are, just as genuine certainly, but they say whatever comes into their heads."

"Well, that's not genuine," objected May.

"I don't see why."

"Because what you say ought to represent what you are. If you say anything that comes into your head, you make the big things and the little things all equal. Pull round, will you?—there's the luncheon-bell."

CHAPTER III.

Mr. Carlingford lived in an ugly but comfortable house among the broad-backed Surrey Downs, generally alone, for a life of sixty-eight years had convinced him that he found his own society less tedious than that of his friends. He made, however, one exception in favour of Tom, for whom he had a considerable liking. He had married late, had been a widower for twenty-one years—since Tom's birth— and had no other children. He seldom spoke of his wife, so that we have no means of finding out whether he included her in the verdict he mentally passed on his friends, but there is no reason to suppose that he did not.

His house, Applethorpe Manor, he rented from the owner, who was in straitened circumstances; he refused to buy it, for, as he said, he would probably not live much longer, and it was more than possible that Tom would not want to keep it, and would very likely sell it for much under its value. But Tom might have been well content to keep such a place; it stood admirably, surrounded by its own grounds, and a park of some six hundred acres stretched away from halfway up the gentle slope in front of the house to the top of the down.

Behind, the hill-slope declined rapidly away to the bottom of the valley, in which lay the little red-roofed village, overlooked by a church, in which a nineteenth-century architect had accomplished his wicked will, dealing death to early Norman work. On the other side of the village another down rose in gentle slopes of yellowing autumn fields, planted here and there with beech and oak woods. At intervals, the chalky sub-soil came to the surface like the bleached bones of the world, but for the most part a thick loamy earth hid the underlying barrenness.

South of the house lay a level lawn, dominated by a large cedar-tree, the horizontal fans of whose branches formed an effectual protection against sun, and even against rain ; flower-beds arrayed in fantastic patterns, having for the centre of their system an Italian stone vase, stretched out to one side of this tree, while to the other the lawn lay steeped in summer suns, or grew rank and mossy under autumn rains. A terrace festooned with virginia-creeper and low-growing monthly roses bounded the lawn to the south, below which lay a long strip of flower-bed, and beyond, a broad hayfield, stretching down as far as the village.

But on the 1st of September, two days after the arrival of Tom and Markham, there were other guests in the house. Mr. Carlingford's sister had married a peer, who privately considered his wife's brother rather low, but tolerated him for the sake of his partridge-shooting, about which the most fastidious could not possibly be depreciatory. Lady

Ramsden was a tall, sallow, and fretful woman, who literally enjoyed rather bad health, though not so bad as she imagined. In fact, her bad health only manifested itself in intermittent medicine-taking, stopping in bed for breakfast, and not going to church on Sunday. She was one of those women about whom people say, when they are yet in their teens, that they are sweetly pretty, but very delicate-looking; when they are about thirty, that they will not wear well; and when they are thirty-five, " Poor dear." Lady Ramsden was forty, and her cup of ineffectiveness was full.

Her husband was clearly English, almost brutally English. The name of his nationality was, as it were, written in red ink all over his body and his mind, and he dressed, so to speak, in Union Jack. He was tall, well set up, had once represented his native borough in the House of Commons in his youth, and now in middle age, having repeatedly failed to get into the Lower House, had been awarded the Consolation Stakes, and sat in the Upper. He was fond of shooting, but shot badly, had several shelves in his library full of parliamentary blue-books, which he sent periodically to be bound up, but which were never looked at either before or after that operation, spent five months every year in London, and half the day in all those five months in the bow-window of his club, and the other seven months in the country, and told rather long-winded stories. The point of these stories was always well defined, because he himself always began to laugh just before he got to it, which was a very convenient habit.

The other two guests were Miss Wrexham, who had been staying near the Markhams a fortnight ago, and her brother Bob, who was in every respect like a young gentleman from Woolwich. He had been at Eton with Tom, and they had kept up a sort of acquaintance since: Tom had stayed with him, and he with Tom. In the intervals they never wrote to one another, but were extremely glad to see each other again. Tom had, to a superlative degree, the power of picking up a friendship at the point where it had stopped, and of carrying it forward as if there had been no interruption.

The shooters, consisting of Tom, Bob Wrexham, and Lord Ramsden, started soon after breakfast on the first; Markham had claimed the fulfilment of Tom's promise, and had taken himself off to the smoking-room when they went out, and presumably spent a profitable though solitary morning there. The two ladies, Mr. Carlingford and he were going to walk out about half-past twelve, to a cottage some mile and a half off, and join the shooters at lunch. Lady Ramsden established herself at a writing-table in the drawing-room, wrote several unnecessary letters in a tall, angular hand, and Miss Wrexham, who always made a point of doing the paying thing, went out for a short ride with her host, and took an intelligent interest in all he said.

The shooting-party had already arrived at the luncheon-place when the others came, and were clamouring for food. Lord Ramsden, it was noticed sat a little apart, and was smoking a cigarette with an isolated and reserved air.

"Oh, what a sweet little cottage!" said Maud Wrexham, as they entered. "Mr. Carlingford, if I were you, I should come and live here. Why, there's a warming-pan! Do you know, I don't think I ever saw a warming-pan before. How clever it was of me to know it was one, wasn't it? That's what they call intuitive cerebration. I shall write to the Physical Research about it."

Tom considered.

"Is it intuitive cerebration when one crosses the Channel for the first time, and sees the coast, to know that it is France? You have never seen it before, you know."

Lady Ramsden gave a thin monosyllabic laugh.

"No, that's only remembering what you have seen on an atlas," said Maud. "I never saw a map of this cottage with 'warming-pan' marked on it."

"The Physical Research Society are a company of amiable and intelligent lunatics," remarked Mr. Carlingford. "Don't have anything to do with them, Miss Wrexham. Are you ready for your lunch, Ramsden? What sort of sport have you had?"

Lord Ramsden threw away the end of his cigarette, which he had been smoking at the door, and came in.

"Birds very wild," he said. "It's no use walking them up."

"Oh, we've got twelve brace," said Tom, cheerfully. "It's not so bad. However, we can drive after lunch; there are lots of them in the stubble, and we can't get near them any other way."

"Tom's been talking art all the morning,"

remarked Bob Wrexham ; "I draw the line at talking art when you're shooting."

"You can't do two things at once," growled his lordship, who had not pursued the subject of the birds being wild.

"Tom never does less than two things at once," said his father ; "he says there isn't time."

"I can eat and talk at once," said Tom, with his mouth full.

"Yes, old chap, and you can shoot more than one bird at once," said Bob. "It was the most disgraceful thing I ever saw. Tom fired into the middle of a covey which ought to have been out of shot. The worst of it was that he killed a brace. However, it's good for the bag."

Mr. Carlingford was sitting next Tom, and murmured gently to him, "How odd it is that the only way to keep up your bags is to destroy your braces!"

Lord Ramsden was reviving a little under the influence of food. "I never can shoot in the morning," he confessed ; "it was always the way with me. Once at Ramsden I told them to have lunch ready at half-past eleven, so that we could have a long afternoon. And, by Jove, I didn't miss the rest of the day. They were very much amused at it all."

Mr. Carlingford regretted to himself that he was not a friend of Peter Magnus, but received his lordship's remarks with cordiality, and after a quick lunch Tom got up.

"Well, we'd better be off again as soon as we can," he said. "Teddy, you must come with us, and if you won't shoot, you'll see me do it. Miss Wrexham, I'm sure you want a walk."

"I should love to come," said she, "if I shan't be in the way. But aren't women a fearful nuisance when you are shooting? Bob always sends me home after lunch."

"Yes," said Bob, "Tom only asked you out of politeness. He meant you to refuse."

"I don't believe you did," said she. "Anyhow, if you did, you may say so, and I'll go home. I will, really; I shan't be offended. I don't know how."

"May I be permitted to express a hope," said Lord Ramsden, "that Miss Wrexham will grace— ah, exactly, will come with us? You'd better be getting home, dear," he said to his wife. "You don't want to trudge over ploughed fields."

"Gracious, no!" said Lady Ramsden. "I'm sure I shall be tired out as it is."

Miss Wrexham paired off with Markham, who had an ample opportunity of testing his sister's judgment of her.

"It was so delicious, that little peep I had of your sister," she said; "I long for that sort of life myself. She must be so happy with her dear little everyday duties. I'm sure that's why there used to be saints, and why there are none now. People used to live like that in the country, just doing their duty; and then, when men began to herd into towns, they saw at once how beautiful the lives of those others must have been, so of course they canonized them."

"I don't know," said Markham, who treated all subjects gravely; "I expect there is just as much opportunity for becoming a saint if you live in a town. Of course, it's harder. After all, saints were only very good people with the power of making their goodness felt, and it's harder to make yourself felt in London, because every one is in such a hurry."

"Oh dear me, yes, it's fearful to think of!" said Maud. "One is busy the whole day, and yet one gets nothing done—nothing worth doing, at least. I can't imagine a saint living in London—that's to say, doing what we naturally do in London. But if I lived in the country, it would be just as natural to do what your sister does. I'm always supposed to be frivolous, and I don't know what; but it's a great shame. Of course, I talk thirteen to the dozen, but that is no proof of frivolity. I'm sure your sister thought me frivolous, and I thought her so sweet It's not a bit fair."

Ted did not reply, and after a moment Miss Wrexham continued——

"You can't deny it, you see. Do you know, I think some of the saints must have been rather trying. It was St. Elizabeth, wasn't it, who told her husband she'd only got some roses in her apron, when it was bread really? Poor dear! You see he knew it was bread, and she knew it was; and then, when she opened her apron, there was nothing but roses. I hope they pricked her—it really was mean. You know, if I was reading a novel on Sunday, and they asked me what book it was, I should say a novel. St. Elizabeth would have said a Septuagint. I hate her."

Ted laughed.

"I wonder if you really care what my sister thought of you. Why should you care? You've only just seen her."

"Ah, but what does that matter?" asked Maud. "Of course I care. I always make a point of being nice to people in railway carriages and 'buses—I always go in 'buses in London, don't you?—even though I only see them for two minutes. I want to be nice to everybody. I care immensely what every one thinks of me."

"But how can it matter?" said Ted. "Those people whom you meet just for two minutes have no opportunity of judging you. They form their impressions on perfectly superficial things."

"Ah, I see! Your sister formed an unfavourable impression of me, and you excuse her by saying it was superficial."

"I've got a great mind to tell you what she said," remarked Ted.

Maud stopped for a moment, and turned to him.

"Ah, do tell me!"

"She said she thought you weren't genuine."

Maud stared for a moment in deep perplexity.

"Not genuine? Why—why, that is exactly what I am! Why did she think that?"

"I just remember her saying that you talked about early celebrations, and covering books for the parish library, as if they were one and the same thing."

Maud stood still for a moment longer, recalling the scene, and then broke out into a light laugh.

"Oh, I see, I see!" she cried. "Oh dear me, how funny! She had every excuse for thinking that, but she was so wrong. She hasn't got a picturesque mind, I'm afraid. But I saw the whole picture of her in her life there so clearly. You can talk of a Madonna and the little Italian landscape behind her chair in one breath, can't you? She thought I regarded them as equally essential. I'm so glad you told me that. I never take offence; I only profit by such things if they are true, and forget them if they are not. There is an atom of truth in this, although, as I say, she was wrong."

The shooters were waiting, when they got up to them, for a long narrow valley of stubble to be driven down, and Ted and Maud got under shelter of the same tall hedge, which separated the fields, and waited with them.

Markham went up to where Tom was standing. The latter at once began talking in a whisper about the artistic beauty of a drive.

"If you shoot, you are called a barbarian," he explained. "That's so silly. Why, a drive is the most beautiful thing there is! First you wait, hearing nothing—and then you hear little far-away sounds, and you know they are off. Then there comes that flight of stupid sparrows and small birds, and then silence again. Then there's a sudden rush through the hedge, perhaps, and out comes a hare. And then—and then—'Mark over!' and you hear the whistling of wings, which sound as if they wanted oiling. And, best of all, that extraordinary ceasing of voluntary motion. The bird's wings clap down to his sides, you know, but he still goes on as if he was alive. I killed a bird once that was coming towards

me, and it fell slap on me and knocked me down.
You needn't believe me unless you like. There!
They've started! Keep quiet, Teddy; it will all
happen just as I said."

Tom stepped a little way back from the hedge, in
order to get a longer view, almost trembling with
excitement as "Mark over!" sounded from higher
up the valley. The covey came over Lord Ramsden,
and he missed solemnly with both barrels.

"Those birds went on just as if they were alive,"
remarked Ted in an undertone to Tom, who grinned
maliciously.

"He missed eight birds this morning in succession,"
he whispered; and then he said to Bob Wrexham,
"You should see me play lawn-tennis. Look out,
there's another covey coming!"

A big lot approached the tall hedge like a stream,
caught sight of Tom, and wheeled rapidly to the
centre. Two, however, turned a little somersault in
the air, and fell thirty yards behind him in the
stubble.

"There, did you see?" asked Tom, reloading.
"That's another of those things like dropping
matches in the Cam. They came blazing over, then
there's a little pause, and a thud. I'm afraid my
poor uncle has missed again."

Markham meditated.

"Yes, I see. That really was rather nice. There
must be some satisfaction in doing that."

"Of course, half the pleasure lies in not being
certain whether you are going to hit or not. If
I always hit I don't think I should care about it—

not so much, at any rate. It's like gambling with an enormous proportion of chances in your favour if you play well."

Miss Wrexham took almost as much interest in the proceedings as the shooters themselves, and she showed no wish to go back until they all went home. Lord Ramsden met with greater success towards the end of the afternoon, and they all returned in excellent spirits.

Tom and Miss Wrexham were walking a little in front of the others, and in answer to some questions of hers, he was saying what he was going to do when he left Cambridge.

"It must be such a blessing," she said, "to know for certain, as you do, exactly what you want to be, and to be able to be it. Most people never know what they want to be. Bob is going into the army simply because he can't think of anything else."

"The worst of most professions is that they are only ways of making money," said Tom. "Artists and clergymen are the only people who do what they have a passion for. No one can have a passion for cross-examining witnesses."

"Oh, I don't know about that!" objected Maud. "My mother—do you know my mother?—has a passion, literally a passion, for making arrangements. Really her chief joy in life is arranging things quite irrespective of what the arrangements are; but I think people like her are mostly women."

"What is your passion?" asked Tom.

"Making people like me, especially if they hate me naturally. I wouldn't say that it is my vocation, because lots of people detest me. Don't trouble to say you don't believe me. I am sure that sort of speech would come very badly from you."

"Do you mean that I've got such awkward manners, or that I am naturally honest?"

"I mean that when a man doesn't owe a compliment, it is no use his trying to pay one."

"Compliments are a cheap way of paying debts. They are like apologies. I always apologize if it will do any good."

Maud walked on in silence a little way.

"If I wasn't a woman," she said at length very slowly, "I should choose to be a man. No, it's not such nonsense as it sounds. What I really mean is that men have great advantages over us in some ways. A woman can hardly ever become anything else than an amateur, and I want to be a professional artist, and a musician, and she-clergyman, living in the country. But I wouldn't give up being a woman. Women have much more self than men, else they would have all taken to professions long ago. If men hadn't professions they would all bore themselves to death. That is why they take to the Stock Exchange and politics—they do anything to make them forget their own selves. I don't say that women are any better, but they find themselves more interesting than men do."

"But men have to make money or else they couldn't marry and support families," said Tom rather feebly.

"Yes; but don't you see that if women had not been sufficiently interested in themselves to make them not want professions, they would have had them long ago? They would both have worked for their living. As it is, a woman's chief object is to marry a rich man, so that she can't possibly work."

"That's a new idea," said Tom. "What are you going to do with it?"

"How do you mean?"

"You ought to marry a poor man, and help him to earn his living."

"Unfortunately I have lots of money myself."

Tom drew in a deep breath.

"That is a misfortune. I am in the same state. One can't give it all to a lunatic asylum, or else people think you are laying up treasure for your own dotage. I wish I was poor, really poor, you know, out at elbows, having to work for my bread. It must be exquisite to be poor."

"It's a ridiculous arrangement," said Maud suddenly. " My grandmother left me heaps of money, and poor Bob none ; now Bob wants money and I don't. But I expect, if one was poor, one would get to like money."

" No doubt one would," said Tom, "but that would do one no harm. One would get to know what its value was. At present I haven't the slightest idea. That is not being miserly—misers never know the value of money ; they only know the price of things they want, but refuse to buy."

They had reached the front door, and stood waiting for the others.

"One ought to be allowed to change circumstances with one's friends," said Tom. " I would choose Ted Markham's circumstances. He is poor, and he is working at what he likes best. Just think how happy one would be! Success to him means the fullest possible success ; position means opportunities."

" What do you mean by opportunities ? "

" Why, the University Press will consent to publish his editions of classical authors."

" That's narrow," remarked Miss Wrexham. " Providence has spared me that limitation."

" That's what I'm always telling him. But it must be very comfortable to be narrow."

" Until you know you are narrow."

" Oh, but then you become broad," said Tom, "and that's nice too ! "

" We are a pair of blighted beings," said Miss Wrexham solemnly. " We have been made rich and broad, whereas we only want to be poor and narrow."

" No, we should like to be narrow, if we couldn't be broad," said Tom—"just as you would like to be a man if you couldn't be a woman."

" Ah, well, one can't have everything."

Tom looked at her with radiant confidence.

" I mean to have everything ! " he announced.

CHAPTER IV.

Tom went back to Cambridge for his third year with his mind fully made up as regard his career. He was alone with his father his last night at home, and they had talked the matter out—or rather Tom talked the matter out, and his father expressed acquiescence with his proposed arrangements, and mingled a little cynical advice.

"You see, I must be a sculptor, father," Tom had said, "at least, that is my passion. If you wish me to go into the business or go to the bar, I'll go, but that won't be the work of my life. You don't object, do you?"

They were sitting in the smoking-room after dinner before the fire, for October had started with early frosts, and Mr. Carlingford loathed cold weather. He often stopped indoors for two or three weeks at a time in the winter.

"My dear boy," he replied, "I don't object to anything about you at present; I really find you the only satisfactory spot in a—a satisfactory life. There is only one thing I should object to, and that is if you made a fool of yourself. Don't do that, Tom. Many people when they make fools of themselves think that they are being original, whereas

they are doing what nine-tenths of the human race
has done since the beginning of the world—more
than nine-tenths, probably. Adam and Eve both
made fools of themselves, so did Cain and Abel—
Abel particularly. And a sculptor has such unlimited opportunities for making a fool of himself."

"In what way?" asked Tom.

"Falling in love with his models, or still worse,
marrying them. If you are going to the devil, go
to him like a gentleman. Then, sculptors often wear
long hair, and Liberty fabric ties, with gold rings
round them. I knew a sculptor once who wore a
cameo ring. If you wear a cameo ring I shall cut
my throat."

"Oh, I shan't do any of those things," said Tom
confidently.

"No, I think it is most probable that you won't,
otherwise I should make objections to your being
a sculptor. But you can't tell. You haven't had
many opportunities yet."

"One can make a fool of one's self at Cambridge if
it comes to that," said Tom.

"No, not very easily. Public opinion is against it,
whereas in most places the fools themselves consti-
tute public opinion. I'm glad of it, though it is only
putting off the evil days a little longer. When I
was at Cambridge, boys made fools of themselves
earlier than they do now. For instance, people get
drunk much less. It's a change for the better, I
suppose. But I don't know that this generation will
have gone through less dirt when they are forty, than

we did.   There comes a time to every one when they must decide definitely whether they are going to make fools of themselves or not.   I've got very strong views about morality."

His clever, wrinkled old face beamed with amusement.

"Morality is just a synonym for wisdom," he went on, "and immorality is folly.   I don't know anything about the religious side of it all.   I leave that to others, professionals.   But I know a little about folly.   It's quite the worst investment you can make."

"I don't know that I ever thought about it at all," said Tom frankly; "I don't mean to be a brute if I can help it."

"There are no such things as brutes," said his father; "there are only wise men and fools—chiefly fools.   Every man has to settle the question for himself as to which he will be : no one goes through life scot-free of the necessity of fighting inclinations. I haven't ever talked to you before about it, because it is no use giving advice to young men, and the worst thing of all is to tell them to think about such things.   You have to think about it when your time comes; till then it's best not to know it.   The best preparation is to lead a healthy life, and think about cricket, not to read White Cross tracts and go to purity meetings."

Tom rose from his chair and knocked out the ashes of his pipe against the chimney-piece.

"I think you're wrong, father," he said ; "if one has an aim in life, everything gives way to that.   If one has principles, one cannot disregard them."

"Sometimes principles interfere with interests," remarked Mr. Carlingford.

Tom laughed.

"Idle men are the vicious men," he said.

"I haven't done a stroke of work for ten years," remarked his father with amusement. "All the same, I haven't been idle. I find plenty to do in watching other people. But there is one piece of advice I would really like to give you. If you find you fall in love with any unsuitable young person—a model probably—send her about her business. If it's too far gone for that, cut her throat—it is probably her fault—she probably wanted you to fall in love with her, and if you see any objection to that, cut mine, or cut your own. Perhaps your own is best. It is unpleasant, no doubt, for the moment, but that is better than wishing every moment for the rest of your life that you had done it."

"But one can always cut one's throat. Besides, isn't that making a fool of one's self?"

"Not at all : it is the consequence of having made a fool of one's self."

Tom frowned.

"Ah, I don't like people talking about consequences. That is the talk of cowards."

His father laughed.

"Never mind me, Tom," he said ; "I don't expect you to agree with me. I am a vicious coward, am I not?"

"What I mean is, that you can make the best or the worst of a bad job," said Tom. "When people talk of consequences, they seem to mean the worst consequences. When a man has made a mistake, it is stupid of him to sit down and say, ' Well, that is done ; now for the consequences.' There is almost always a choice of consequences."

"Very often there are no consequences," remarked his father. "I don't think I ever did anything which had any consequences. But then, I never remember doing anything either, except making some money. When are you going to marry, Tom?" he asked suddenly.

Tom looked startled.

"When I fall in love, I suppose," he said roundly.

"That's a man's answer. Well, my boy, I'm going to bed. You go to Cambridge to-morrow, don't you? Are you going to do well in your Tripos?"

"I should think it's very unlikely," said Tom. "It seems that I'm a fool."

"That's no reason why you shouldn't do well."

"Then it seems that I'm the wrong sort of fool."

Mr. Carlingford lighted his candle.

"That is very likely. Don't trouble to do well on my account. I really don't care the least what you do."

"I shan't trouble to do well on my own," said Tom, laughing. "We had better prepare for failure."

It was very evident in the course of the next term that Tom was extremely unlikely to do well on anybody's account. The wine of his passion had begun to ferment in his brain, and he lounged his mornings away sometimes in the cast museum, sometimes in his room over a bushel of sculptor's clay. At other times he had fits of complete idleness. He would get up late, perhaps go to a lecture, then stroll up to the tennis court, and play till lunch-time. In the afternoon he would play football, and sit talking over tea till Hall time, and after Hall play whist till bed-time. Markham, who was busy writing a dissertation for his Fellowship, had not time to look after him at all, and those in authority gave him up as a bad job. Tom regarded his own position as an excellent example of a man determining the consequences of his acts.

"I haven't done any work for weeks," he said to Markham one day, "and I ought to be in hot water. As a matter of fact, I am not, because I make up for it by cordially agreeing with all that they say to me, and never being out after twelve."

"Don't you think you are behaving rather idiotically?" asked Markham. "You seem to be rather proud of doing no work. It's very easy; any one can do it."

"Yes, I know it's very easy," said Tom, who was in an exasperating mood, "that's why I do it. At the same time, any one can't do it. You couldn't, for example."

"I hope I should never wish to try."

"My dear Ted, you are incapable of wishing to try. It isn't in you. It's not so easy to be idle—though I said it was just now, because I wanted to make you angry—you must have a great deal to think about in order to be idle. If you don't do something, you must be something, and that requires thought."

"May I ask what you are being just now?"

"You shouldn't interrupt, Ted. I was going to say that of course there are some people, who neither do or are anything, but they are idiots. I'm not that sort of idiot myself; just now I am being an artist."

"I don't doubt it, but what reason have I for believing it ?"

"Oh, none at all," said Tom, "but you asked me. I am meditating. I shall do the better for this some day."

Markham made an impatient movement in his chair.

"Excuse my saying that I want to go on with my work."

Tom laughed.

"Poor, dear old Ted, how you must loathe me ! You can't understand my doing nothing any more than I can understand your doing so much. Is your work of such vital importance? What does it all come to ?"

"You've asked that before," remarked Ted.

"Yes, and you've never answered it. I can understand a man doing archæology ; there's some human interest in that. I like to know what sort of ear-rings the Greek women used to wear. Oh, Ted, do you know the sepulchral reliefs from Athens? there's a cast of one in the Museum. It's wonderful. I shall do one to you when you die."

"I wish you would go to your room, and get on with it."

"Is the deliberative subjunctive going to kill you so soon as that ? Well, I've often warned you.

Good-bye, Teddy. You're not sociable this morning."

Tom departed, whistling loudly, and out of tune.

The Fellowship elections took place in March, and as the days drew near, Markham, finding himself unable to work, and fretting because he could not, very wisely determined to go away from Cambridge for the last week, having made Tom promise to telegraph the result to him. Tom was just returning from the telegraph office, having performed what was a thoroughly pleasing and satisfactory duty, and was crossing the court in the gathering dusk, when he saw a figure standing on the path near the Hall, where the announcement was posted. A sociable curiosity made him tack off a little and see who it was, and to his astonishment he found Markham standing there.

"Why, Teddy, I've just telegraphed to you!" he cried.

Markham turned round to him.

"Quick! tell me quick!" he said.

"You may walk across the grass," said Tom solemnly; this being one of the Fellows' privileges "And you may set to work to become a fossil as soon as you please. Well, I congratulate you, I suppose, though I'm not sure it's the best thing for you."

Markham caught hold of Tom's arm.

"I think," he said, very slowly and deliberately, "I think I've been making a fool of myself. This morning I found I couldn't stop away, and I came back about a quarter of an hour ago. Since then

I have been standing here, not daring to go in and see. Tom, I'm going to chapel."

It was two or three days after this that the two were walking down to the Pitt on Sunday evening. On their way they passed one of the mission-rooms in the town, and the street was almost blocked by a crowd all trying to get in. Tom, who was never so happy as in a mass of surging humanity, insisted on mingling with them and seeing what was going on. Markham tried to dissuade him, but failed, and after a good deal of pushing he succeeded in getting inside.

It was a Revivalist meeting full to overflowing; the room was hung with flaring banners, lit with blazing gas-standards, and warm condensed moisture shone on the walls. Tom looked with wonder and slight disgust towards the platform, where a short, stumpy man with a chin beard was addressing the people. He was describing his own conversion, which transformed him, according to his own account, from a swindling greengrocer into one of the saved. This happy change had also been accompanied with a great improvement in the greengrocery business. Instead of giving short weight and being always in debt, he took to giving full measure and speedily opened an account at a savings bank. He also mentioned that he became a teetotaler at the same time, though the more obvious connection between this fact and the incident of the savings bank did not seem to occur either to him or to his audience. All these sumptuous results were a direct effect of grace.

Tom listened for some minutes with amusement struggling with disgust, until the preacher in a sudden burst of gratitude gave out a hymn of the most militant order, and packed solidly with concrete images of abstract ideas. A young woman in a large poke bonnet was busy thrusting hymn-books into the hands of the congregation, and gave one to Tom. The band struck up a tune expressive of the liveliest devotion, and the congregation joined at the top of their voices.

They were in the middle of the second verse, when a sudden stir ran through the crowd, and from the middle of the hall there ran up to the platform a young woman, smartly—over-smartly—dressed, who burst into a loud fit of hysterical crying, and cried out that she was saved. The hymn was stopped at once, and the preacher led her aside while the congregation waited. In a few moments he led her back to the front of the platform, and gave out another hymn :—

"There were ninety-and-nine that safely lay."

Tom's sense of amusement was gone—a frown gathered on his forehead. What on earth did it all mean? It was clear what sort of a girl it was who had "stormed the gate of Heaven," as the preacher expressed it—he had often noticed her in the streets—and now she was—what? How was she suddenly different from what she was before? Had her previous life been blotted out? What was the change, what did it mean? It could have been no easy thing to make an exhibition of one's self like that; and where was the driving power? He began to be almost afraid. And before the hymn was finished the same thing happened again, this time to an elderly, respectable-looking man, who delivered a short speech to the congregation with tears streaming down his face. There was some strange force abroad, and Tom did not like it at all. He was desperately afraid of making a fool of himself, and he remembered his father's warnings, though they were delivered in a very different sense. The vulgarity, the loudness of the whole proceedings were still very present to him, but he felt that he was in the presence of some force, hysterical perhaps, or perhaps only that force which does exist in enthusiastic crowds, of the nature of which he was absolutely ignorant. For aught he knew it might lay its hands on him next. So he resorted to the most obvious way out of it, and pushing through the crowd, he left the room.

Late that night he strolled into Markham's room, as the latter was just thinking that it was time to go to bed, and proceeded to deliver himself of his impressions at length.

"It made me confoundedly uncomfortable," he commented, after giving a full account of what had taken place. "I didn't half like it, Teddy; I never saw anything like it before, and it was so much more real than I expected. What do you suppose that girl felt, or that man either? How can the singing of a hymn change the whole moral character? It must be hysterical. That's why I went away; I was afraid of becoming hysterical too. Think how flat one would feel the next morning. And oh! the awful commonness of it all. The elect greengrocer was the scrubbiest sort of brute. Fancy announcing publicly that you were saved! Surely, that is the one thing in the world one would be reticent about. What does it all mean, Teddy?"

Markham felt the natural reserve which almost all young men feel in talking of such subjects, and Tom's sudden curiosity about it surprised him. It was like Tom to mix with any crowd to see what was going forward, but it was so unlike him to have waited a single moment after seeing what it was, that Ted had waited in the street for him, expecting him to appear again every moment, and had eventually gone on to the Pitt, in a puzzled frame of mind.

"I don't exactly know, Tom," he said, after a pause. "I believe that that sort of conversion, as they call it, often has permanent effects. I think it quite conceivable that the greengrocer will continue to give full measure."

"But about the savings bank!" burst out Tom; "how can that have anything to do with it?"

"You would put it differently, of course: you would say, 'Honesty is the best policy.'"

"Possibly I should. At any rate, if one can account intelligibly for a thing it is better to do so, than to try to account for it fallaciously."

Markham frowned.

"We've never talked of this kind of thing before," he said tentatively. "I haven't the remotest idea what your religion is, or, indeed, if you've got any."

"That's exactly what I've been thinking to myself all the evening," remarked Tom. "I don't know myself; I was only conscious that I felt no kind of sympathy with those people. I was amused and disgusted, and then I was frightened."

"I wish you had stopped," said Markham, suddenly.

"Why on earth? Do you really think it would have done me any good to have been suddenly 'taken' as those people were? I suppose you will say I am a Pharisee—but what good would it have done me? What should I not do that I do now, or what should I do that I do not do? Early chapels, I suppose——"

"Ah, don't!" said Markham, with sudden earnestness. "Those things may mean nothing; to you, but they do to others—and among others to me."

Tom stared in perplexity.

"To you—do you believe in that sort of conversion? Do you think that something can happen to you suddenly like that which changes you?"

"I can't help believing it. How can I say that such things do not happen? I stake my life on such possibilities."

"The whole thing seems so irrational to me," said Tom. "In anything else, a man's life is not changed by a little thing of that sort. And then the banking account——"

"Well, take an instance in your own line," said Markham. "Can't you imagine a modern artist who looks at a Raphael for the first time becoming a convert to that style of art?"

"That's quite different," said Tom. "These people have probably been brought up in these beliefs; the idea is not a new one to them. No doubt it came home with more force at such a moment. It is like a man who had been looking at Raphaels all his life, and caring nothing for them, being suddenly convinced by one of them. That doesn't seem to me likely."

"You may be right, I can't say, for you know more of the subject than I. But what right have you to say that a thing doesn't seem likely in a matter of which, as you said, you know nothing?"

"That's true," said Tom, "I do know nothing of it. But who does?"

"The probability is, that people who have thought about it know more than those who haven't."

Tom got up, and began to walk up and down the room.

"Well, I want to know, but how can I? If I didn't feel an interest in it, I shouldn't have come to talk about it. But I am altogether at sea. I wasn't brought up in a religious household. My father never speaks of such things. At school I had to read the Bible, chiefly the Acts, like any other school lesson. I was confirmed as a matter of course. If you are not religiously minded, how can you become religious? If a man is not literary, you don't expect him to feel any interest in books."

"But it's a defect that he doesn't."

"Yes, because he naturally moves among people who do," said Tom, "and he necessarily feels out of it. But though you move among religious people you don't feel out of it, because their religion does not come into their lives. I suppose you would call my father an Atheist, but you wouldn't know it, unless you inferred it from the fact that he doesn't go to church on Sundays, and that we don't have family prayers. How is it possible for me to feel such things? Perhaps—you see I never knew my mother, she died when I was a baby——"

"Were you not brought up to believe anything?"

"My nurse taught me to say my prayers. On cold evenings I used to ask if I might say them in bed, and I always got dropped on for it. It was considered a form of profanity. I never understood why. And when the age for nurses ceased, my prayers ceased also. I want to know where the difference between me and religious people comes in. A large number of religious people lose their tempers oftener than I do, because I was born with a better temper than they. You read of clergymen being convicted of theft. I never was, because I never stole anything. Gentlemen don't do such things. It seems to me that we both agree with a certain code of morality for different reasons."

"Did it never occur to you to wonder why you existed, or how you existed, or what was the object of your existence at all?"

Tom looked at him straight in the face.

"No, never. What good would it do me to puzzle my head about such things even if it had occurred to me? Here I am; how or why I have no means of telling. But I mean to make other people know why I existed; one can't do more than that. I am going to be an artist."

Markham felt the hopelessness of making Tom understand. It was like describing colours to a blind man ; for himself he had been brought up in a child-like faith, and he was childlike still. His life had been sheltered, nursed in traditions, and when it was transplanted to the outer air, it was a sapling capable of striking roots, and standing by itself. It had never known what the drenching showers of autumn, or the winds of winter were, till it was capable, not exactly of despising them, but of being unconscious of them. If Tom was blind, he was blind, too, in another sense.

There was a long silence. Tom had halted in his walk by the chimney-piece, and was poking a paper spill down his pipe stem. Markham was sitting at the table, puzzled and helpless. It was a couple of minutes perhaps before Tom spoke. Then he spoke decidedly.

"I'm not going to bother about it," he said. "I don't understand what it all means, but I don't understand what most things mean. If it is a big thing, you may be sure that there are many ways of getting at it. One man can't see all the way round a big thing. You are at one side of it, Ted, perhaps I am nowhere ; but then, again, I may be at the other side of it. I may be meant to come to it by roads you can never guess of. If I am meant to know it, I shall know it some time. By-the-by, we play tennis at ten to-morrow."

"You've got a lecture at ten," said Markham.

"Many things may happen at ten," said Tom "but the probability is in favour of only one thing happening. I don't think the lecture has supreme rights. However, if it has, you won't get a game."

"Oh, but you promised you'd play!" said Markham unwisely.

"I can't go back on that," said Tom. "I never promised to go to a lecture. You shall give me breakfast at nine—or perhaps a little after nine. Let's call it nine-ish."

CHAPTER V.

MAUD WREXHAM was sitting in her mother's room one morning, towards the end of July, after breakfast, telling Lady Chatham her engagements for the day. This piece of ritual was daily and invariable, and her mother spent the succeeding three-quarters of an hour in trying "to work things in," as she called it —in other words, to manage that one carriage should drop two people in different parts of London, and call for them both again at the hour they wanted. These manœuvres usually ended in both parties concerned taking hansoms, after waiting a considerable time for the carriage to pick them up, and driving home separately, while the empty carriage, with the coachman, who was always sceptical about such arrangements, returned home gloomily about half an hour later.

"I think I shall go to Victoria and meet Arthur," Maud was just saying; "he will catch the first boat from Calais, and his train gets in about five."

"Dear Arthur!" exclaimed Lady Chatham with effusion, "I hope he won't be dreadfully relaxed. Athens is so relaxing; I wish he could have stopped at Berlin."

Arthur Wrexham had just spent his first year at

Athens, as third Secretary to the Legation, and was coming home for two months' leave.

"He'll have a lot of luggage, mother," went on Maud; "you'd far better let me take a hansom, and then he and I can come back in one, and send his luggage by a four-wheeler."

Lady Chatham examined her engagement-book with avidity.

"No, Maud, it's the easiest thing in the world. What a coincidence! I've got to pick your father up at Victoria Mansions at a quarter-past five. I will drop you at Victoria, and then go on. If we are there by ten minutes past, it will do perfectly; the boat is sure to be late."

"It will be rather stupid if I miss him," said Maud.

"You'll be in plenty of time—or if you like, I will start five minutes earlier, and go round to see—no, I can't do that. Then, as you say, you can take a hansom. No, you needn't do that. If I take the landau we can all come back together. Five minutes for getting to Victoria Mansions, and five minutes back. He'll take ten minutes getting his luggage out. How much luggage will he have?"

"I don't really know."

"Because we might take the lighter things—I needn't take a footman—and send the heavier ones home by Carter and Paterson."

"I think it would be safer to get a cab, wouldn't it?"

"I'll think about it, and tell you at lunch. Dear Arthur! Well, what else are you going to do?"

"We're going to the Ramsdens' dance this evening, and dining there first."

"Then the other carriage can take us, and if Arthur cares to go to the dance—they didn't know he'd be back, but I'm sure they want him to come—Lady Ramsden told me so, if he was back by any chance —it can come back here, and take him on again at ten. Then you and I will come back in it, when you've had enough, and if Arthur wants to stop, I'm afraid he must find his own way back. Is that all?"

"I'm lunching with the Cornishes."

"Well, then, I'll leave a note for you about Arthur's luggage, as I shan't see you at lunch. Where do the Cornishes live?"

"In Pont Street."

"Then it's the most convenient thing in the world. I'm going to my dentist at half-past twelve, and I shall be back by two. Then the carriage can take you on at once."

"They lunch at two, I'm afraid, mother."

"Well, dear, you'll only be a few minutes late. It will save you the bother of taking a hansom, or walking."

"Oh, never mind! I shall be out, I expect, and shall go there straight."

"Where are you going?"

"Oh, shopping."

"Well, then, I might drop you on my way to the dentist's wherever you liked. If you will be ready at twelve I will take you. Or five minutes to twelve, if you are going out of my way."

Maud got up.

"No, start at twelve as you intended, and if I'm

in, and ready, I'll come with you. Don't wait for
me, mother."

"If you'd only tell me exactly where you want
to go, and when, Maud, I've no doubt I could work
it in."

"I've got to go to Houghton and Gunn's first."

"Very well, then," said her mother, triumphantly,
"nothing can be simpler. I drop you there, and go
to the dentist's. Then I send the carriage back for
you, and you do anything else you want, and come
back to the dentist's at half-past one. Then we
drive straight to Pont Street, and I drop you again,
and go home."

Maud's chief object at this moment, it must be
confessed, was to get out of the room. So she
assented with fervour.

"That's beautiful, mother. How clever of you to
work it all in!"

Lady Chatham heaved a sigh of well-earned satisfaction. "Yes, I think everything is provided for.
Ring the bell, darling, will you? I must send word
to the stables at once."

Lady Chatham felt that she had really deserved a
painless visit to the dentist. She was always regretting that her time was so dreadfully taken up with
little things, and that she never could do anything
she really wanted to do, though what that was is
quite unknown. It is to be suspected that in addition to her daily arrangements, she spent much time
in making plans for Maud's future, which included
far more than the ordinary maternally matrimonial
plans include. She intended, for instance, to send

her out to Athens for a few months during the winter, where she would live with her brother, and see a little foreign life. Foreign life, she considered, was something very mysterious, but very broadening in its effects on the human mind. The fact that you no longer had meat breakfast at half-past nine, and lunch at two, but *café au lait* at eight and *déjeûner* at twelve or half-past, was apparently the door to whole vistas of widening experiences. Breakfast at half-past nine and lunch at two were parts of the organism of life, and the substitution of other hours instead of those was a change the importance of which could not be overlooked. She had spent six months in Rome when she was a girl, with an uncle, who was ambassador there, and she always looked back to that six months as having been something very revolutionary and startling. It had made, she often said, the whole difference to her.

To-day, however, the arrangements, owing to a distinct intervention of Providence, who roughened the seas, and made the train late, went off more satisfactorily than usual, and as they drove to the Ramsdens in the evening, Lady Chatham felt that the dentist really had hurt her more than he should have been allowed to do, and hoped that she would have a pleasant dinner to make up for it.

The Ramsdens lived in one of the few houses in London which do not remind one of barracks, and Lady Ramsden's parties had the reputation, among those who were asked, of being very smart, while those who were not considered her a pushing woman. Four or five times a year her dinners had a little paragraph all to themselves in the *Morning Post*, beginning with a Royal Highness and ending with Colonels in attendance, on the page that announced the movements of nations and the quarrels of kings. Lady Ramsden always snipped these out, and pasted them in an extract book. There was a certain monotony about them, but you cannot have too much of a good thing. But this was not one of her really smart parties; originally it was to have been, but the Highness had been unable to come, and she had to have recourse, not only to mere Honourables, but even a plain Mr., in the shape of Tom Carlingford.

Tom had already arrived when Lady Chatham got there, and Maud was quite surprised to find how glad she was to see him again. Apparently, her mission of being nice to people had been successful in this instance, for he was evidently equally glad to see her. He took her in to dinner, and as Tom's custom was, began exactly where they had left off.

"I'm going out to Greece in October," he was saying. " I've finished with Cambridge."

"I remember your telling me you were going out," said Maud. " I'm going too ; did you know that? My brother is at the Legation there."

"Oh, but how nice !" said Tom. " Are you going soon ? "

"Well, about the beginning of December, for a month or two. You'll see my brother to-night. He's coming to the dance afterwards. Have you taken your degree? By the way, I saw that your friend

Mr. Markham had got a Fellowship. I was so pleased. I nearly wrote to congratulate him."

"Why didn't you quite?" asked Tom.

"Surely it was sufficiently shocking that I nearly did. Are you going to get a Fellowship too?"

Tom grinned.

"Well, it's not imminent."

"Why, aren't you ambitious? It's a pity for a man not to be ambitious."

"My ambitions don't lie in those lines. Besides, I'm a fool. Every one has told me so scores of times."

Later on in the evening the two were sitting out in a charming little courtyard in the centre of the house, open to the air, and walled with banks of flowers. The place was lit up by small electric lights among the flowers, and the air was deliciously cool and dim after the hot glare of the ball-room. The steady hum of a London night came to them clearly in the stillness, that noise of busy people, which never is quiet. The place was nearly deserted, and Maud was fanning herself lazily.

"There, do you hear it?" she said; "that's the noise I love. I like to know that I am in the middle of millions of people."

Tom smiled.

"Ah! you like it too, do you?" he said. "It's the finest thing in the world. But I always want to get at it, to make its heart beat quicker or slower as I wish. That's a modest ambition, isn't it?"

Maud stopped fanning herself, and dropped her hands into her lap.

"Yes; how is one to do it? I'm going to do it

too, you know. We shall have to send word to each other whether its heart is to go quick or slow, else there will be trouble. I feel so dreadfully small in London. I suppose it is good for one, but it's very unpleasant."

"No, it's not good for one, except that if you know you are small, you are already half-way to being big," said Tom. "At any rate, one can never be big without the consciousness of being small."

Maud sat still for a moment, saying nothing.

"Why did you care nothing about what you did at Cambridge, then?" she asked. "Surely you could have made a beginning there."

"I got a third in my Tripos," remarked Tom. "Have you ever done Greek grammar, or Thucydides?"

"No, never; why?"

"It's the sort of thing a parrot could be taught to do."

"And because you are not a parrot, they couldn't teach you. Is that it?"

Tom laughed.

"Well, you needn't believe it unless you like, but I believe I could have done well if I had wanted to enough. I really didn't want to. There's not time for that sort of thing."

"What did you do instead?"

"I enjoyed myself. I've had my holiday, and now I'm going to work. Here's your brother coming to look for you."

Arthur Wrexham was a slight, delicate-looking man, who apparently suffered from extreme languor;

he was very well dressed, and had weak blue eyes, which looked only a quarter awake. He had already roused Tom's wrath by confessing, in answer to certain questions, that he had never been into any of the museums.

"There's such a lot to do, you know," he explained. "One has to go to the Legation every day to see if there are any letters to be written, and then one has to take some exercise, you know, and go out to dinner. Then there are cigarettes to smoke."

"Perhaps you don't care about art?" Tom had said charitably.

"Oh dear, yes, I'm devoted to it! I mean to let all the museums burst upon me some day."

"They won't burst upon you unless you go there," Tom had replied.

Just now, Arthur was peculiarly gentle and *piano;* he dangled his hands weakly before him, and wore an expression of appreciative languor.

"Oh, here you are!" he said. "I wish you'd come home, Maud. I think I shall go, in any case. Do you think there's a hansom about anywhere?"

Maud laughed.

"Poor dear, shall I go and call one for you?"

"I suppose there's sure to be one somewhere in the street, isn't there? Delightful party it's been, hasn't it? No, I haven't danced, but it's so nice to be in London again. I shall go and sit in the Park to-morrow, on a little civilized green chair. There are no green chairs in Athens, you know, and no parks either. It really is a barbarous place; I can't think why you want to go there, Maud."

"Why don't you take a little civilized green chair with you, Arthur," she said, "and put it in the garden? That would do for the park."

"Yes, it's so good of you to suggest that; but it wouldn't do at all. It's not only the little green chair, it's the civilization generally, and the grey sky, and sirloins of beef one wants."

"I thought you hated beef," said Maud. "I'm sure I've heard you say that it was barbarous food."

"Oh yes, I know it is; but I like to know that it's there. I don't want to eat it, but there always ought to be some on the sideboard. Well, won't you come, Maud?"

"No, I'm not coming yet."

Tom grew exasperated.

"Can't you find your way home alone?" he asked.

Arthur Wrexham looked at him for a moment with mild and slightly piteous surprise.

"Oh yes, I shall be all right," he said, "if I can only get a hansom! I suppose there's a man who will call a hansom for me if I give him a shilling. Good night, Maud."

He went very quietly away, bestowing a nod and a tired smile on Tom.

"It's so funny that he should be my brother," said Maud, when he was out of hearing ; "and all he wants to do is to read little French books, and sit in the Park, and have tea on the terrace of the House of Commons. I wonder he didn't mention that."

"I dare say he'll do it in a day or two, when he gets less tired," said Tom ; "he evidently means to begin gently."

Maud drew on her gloves again.

" Here's my partner coming to look for me," she said. " I must go. Mind you come and see us. You are in London for a time, are you not ? "

" Oh yes, till the end of July, or nearly. I don't suppose I ever spent a whole week in London before, but father has at last consented to take a house for a couple of months. He even came to Henley this year, though I must say he was much bored by it, and almost perfectly silent, except once when a lot of dabchicks came swimming round, and he looked up and said, ' The very dabchicks come about me un- awares, making mouths at me.' He likes sitting in the Park, too, and observing the weaknesses of the human race."

" He must have his hands full. Doesn't he observe their strong points as well ? "

" No, I don't think he does," said Tom. " He likes them weak."

Tom, fool though he might be, was wise enough to know that there are a great many interesting things to see in London, and had deliberately set himself to see them, with the result that in two or three weeks he knew more about the town than most Englishmen, and nearly as much as most Americans. Though he meant to specialize in sculpture, he had an " all-round eye," as the saying is, and a great power of reducing what he saw to mental pictures and little dramatic vignettes, and he found food for imagination scattered broadcast. Its extraordinary crude contrasts struck him most, and he often went rather early to theatres or to the opera, in order to stand for a few minutes at the street corner and watch the upper classes going to have their emotions tickled, while the grimy crowd round them hustled and pushed along in a never-ending stream. On one of these occasions a sturdy beggar asked him for money, and Tom, seized by a sudden impulse, showed him half-a-sovereign and asked him what he would do with it if he gave it him. The man's eyes glistened, and he looked Tom full in the face.

"I should be drunk for a week, sir," he said.

Tom broke into a roar of appreciative laughter, and gave it him.

The action was wholly indefensible from every point of view, but it was thoroughly characteristic. Love of life, in any form and in any guise, was stronger in him than the whole world beside. Anything which gave the genuine ring of life, whether made of gold or the basest of alloys, was worth the most valuable metals if they had no currency.

At other times he would go to the British Museum, which is quite worth a visit, and look at the Elgin marbles till his head ached. But he usually came away feeling rather helpless and dispirited. There was often a large number of young men and women copying them in chalks or oils, and Tom had sudden revulsions of feelings when he gazed at these. There was one girl in particular, with a frizzy fringe of seaweed-coloured hair and spectacles, who was making an admirable copy of the Olympos figure. She was dressed in a velveteen body, rather short in the sleeves, a badly cut skirt of green cloth, and wore very high-heeled shoes of antique patent leather.

Somehow the combination of such an artist with such a subject confirmed the impression he had received at Cambridge when looking at the Discobolus figure. The thing was no longer possible. Beautiful nude youths did not now sit on lion-skins at street-corners, any more than Queen Victoria ate Homeric meals like Agamemnon. The grand style was obsolete. And on such occasions Tom would leave the Elgin room with a sigh. If the world was to be conquered it must be conquered with modern weapons of war ; no amount of spears and slings would be a match for Martini rifles, field-guns, and cordite. Spears and slings were more beautiful, no doubt, but they were out of date. Just now that meant a good deal to Tom.

But if the Elgin marbles were out of date, still more out of date was Cambridge with its deliberative subjunctives. He thought with something like horror of the dull steady life there ; of the long mornings when decorous isolation was observed throughout the college; when men sat with dictionaries and notebooks in front of them, and discreetly analysed Thucydides' account of the Peloponnesian war. That was more hopelessly obsolete than the Elgin marbles, for the latter were in the vanguard of their times, whereas Cambridge was painfully crawling back to times long past, and thinking throughout the tedious process that it was in the forefront of thought and advancement. It was the classical branches of that eminent university which seemed to him so woefully retrograde in their tendencies—for the medical, scientific, and even mathematical schools he felt, if not sympathy, at any rate no impatient condolence. " And then they marched two parasangs and came to the River Amaspis . . and after having dinner there and marching two more parasangs, they encamped for the night." The old sentences came back to him, as a Wagnerian may remember bars of Donizetti or Rossini heard in the unregenerate days.

And Markham? Markham came up to town for a few days in July, and worked at manuscripts in the British Museum. He was collating texts of an obscure Greek author, and explaining to a limited section of society how certain glosses crept in. It appeared that the copyist of the thirteenth century had taken unwarrantable liberties with the text, and that he had also frequently copied a word into a line he was writing, either from the preceding or the subsequent line, and this naturally led to a great deal of unnecessary confusion. One of the most vital results of this carelessness, as it appeared to Tom, lay in the fact that a sensible man like Markham should be spending the best years of his life in determining where this deplorable scribe had not taken the trouble to copy exactly what lay before him. And as no earlier copy of the work was extant, there was a field for the most various and lively conjectures, the truth of which would for ever remain in pleasing uncertainty. Markham, of course, was staying with Tom, and one evening the latter waxed quite hot on the subject, to his father's great amusement.

"Did I tell you of that beggar I gave half a sovereign to one night?" he asked. "Well, I consider him to be infinitely your superior. When the

Judgment day comes, he will know much more about his fellow-men than you ever will, and, according to all creeds, he will be in a better position than you when the accounts are settled."

"If you mean that to get drunk for a week is knowing about your fellow-men," said Markham, "I agree with you. But that sort of knowledge doesn't seem to me worth much."

"Oh, Teddy, I really wish you would get drunk once or twice, or be disreputable in some way! It would be the making of you. You are without charity; you don't even know what it means. You have never known what it is to make allowances for anybody."

"On the contrary, I am employed just now in making allowances for my thirteenth-century copyist, whom you gird at so."

"No, you don't make allowances for him in the least," said Tom; "you note down in a cold critical way just where he goes obviously wrong. You gloat over his mistakes because they enable you to make brilliant—I suppose you are brilliant—guesses at what he should have written. You don't think of the poor old man having to copy out dull Greek iambics by the yard, and getting very sleepy over the process. There would be some interest in that; what you do is to rob everything of all the human interest it ever possessed."

Mr. Carlingford had spent his life from the age of fourteen to fifty-eight in learning how to acquire money and in proceeding to do so, and had existed entirely for the business house which he had founded and raised to an important and safe position. But his work had never been a passion to him, and at the latter age he had retired, leaving the management of affairs in the hands of his old partner and his son, who had a few years afterwards been also taken into the business. Mr. Carlingford on retiring had not left his capital merely as a deposit in the business, but remained a partner, though he took no part whatever in the management of the affairs. In his elder partner he felt as much confidence as it was in his nature to feel towards any one, and as, since his retiring, his income had shown no signs of falling off, his confidence had rapidly flowered into a total indifference to all such concerns. His fortune, in fact, was sufficiently large to enable him to feel a profound contempt for money, bred from familiarity with it, and he did not put the slightest opposition in the way of Tom becoming a sculptor or adopting any profession, except that of a clergyman, however unremunerative.

Tom very soon got known and even discussed in a certain section of London society. He was extremely presentable, he made himself uniformly agreeable, except to Markham, and he had the incidental advantage of being the heir of an exceedingly rich man. Lady Chatham in the intervals of arranging about carriages congratulated herself on having previously settled for Maud to go out with her brother to Athens that winter. She even went so far as to allude to it once to her husband, who always saw the darker side of any scheme.

"Well, my dear, I think it very rash of you to

encourage their intimacy," he said ; " Mr. Carlingford has no land, and even land is worth nothing now."

Lady Chatham was rather horror-struck at this very unveiled way of stating the objection to a subject she had introduced so cautiously.

"Tom Carlingford is just as nice as he can be," she replied, "and very well connected, and what investments and land have to do with the question, Chatham, I really don't know."

"But you were saying only the other day that you hoped Maud would marry well."

"I have my only daughter's real advantage at heart, and that only," she replied with finality.

Lord Chatham overlooked the finality, and continued—

"Then did you only mean that you hoped she would marry a nice man, when you said you hoped she would marry well ? "

" Of course it is an advantage to marry a man who can keep her in boots and gloves," said Lady Chatham, stung into innocuous sarcasm.

"Oh, well, I dare say Tom Carlingford could do that, even if his father's business smashed altogether. Mind you send the carriage back for me punctually, dear ; I've got another meeting to go to after the House, and if it isn't ready I shall have to take a cab, and the carriage perhaps will wait half an hour or more, and we shall be late for dinner."

CHAPTER VI.

ToM had spent the latter part of the summer and the earlier autumn at a sculptor's studio in Paris, and arrived at Athens in a decade of summer November days. The fogs and frosts had laid a hand on Paris before he left, and the new heaven and the new earth looked very fair as his ship steamed slowly into the Piræus just before sunrise. The violet crown of mountains round Athens lay in dewy silence waiting for the dawn, and even in the dim half light the air was full of southern colour. He stood on the deck until the sun had shot up above Pentelicus, and was joined by Arthur Wrexham, who had secured a month's extra leave, on a vague plea of debility.

"It's so delicious to be in these classic waters again," said that diplomatist. "England had become quite unbearably foggy. Cook's man will get us a boat."

"What's that mountain?" asked Tom peremptorily—"that one, just where the sun has risen."

Arthur Wrexham looked vaguely in the direction of the sun.

"Oh, it's Hymettus, I think, but I'm not sure. I've no head for these barbarous names. Have you got all your things together? Do you see Cook's man anywhere? They all talk Greek here."

A medley of boats full of picturesque Southerners was waiting below, offering to take any one on shore at a ridiculously low figure, and in wholly unintelligible language.

"It's no use waiting for Cook's man," said Tom; "let's get one of these brown ruffians to take us ashore."

"If you'll talk to him, and tell him we will only pay a fifth part of what he wants, we will," said Arthur Wrexham, "but I can't understand them."

Tom found his way up to the Acropolis during the morning, and suspended judgment. The whole thing was so transcendently beautiful that he could not endorse his own prophecies that it would be obsolete, and since obsolete, disappointing. He planted himself on the Propylæa steps for half an hour, and looked out from between a frame of marble pillars stained to the richest orange with wind and rain over the Attic plain, across the sea towards Salamis and Ægina. The sky, one blue, touched another blue on the horizon, and melted the edges of capes and mountains.

To the right, across the grey-green olive grove far below, rose the swelling mass of Parnes, fringed with pine woods, and a white village nestled on its lower slopes. Close on his right stood the hill Areopagus, with steps and caves cut in its brown-red sides. The wind, blowing lightly from the west, seemed full of dead memories of tiresome books, coming back to life and beauty. After that he sat for a time in front of the west façade of the Parthenon, which stood like some gracious presiding presence keeping watch over the town and the plain. High up on the pediment still rested the figure of a man and woman, she with her arm round him, he leaning against her breast, and behind the first row of columns rose the line of frieze showing the youth of Athens making their horses ready to start in the great birthday procession of the goddess. To the left stood the marble maidens, holding for ever on their heads the roof of the south porch of the Erecththeum, yet bearing it as no burden has yet been borne. One with her right knee bent, and hands loose by her side, stood as if she could have borne the weight of the world, and yet not been weary, and another like her, as a sister is like a sister, seemed just to have shifted her position, to have drawn the right foot back, and clasped her hands behind her. Between the more roughly cut blocks of foundation stones sprang vivid flowers, and the fallen columns of the great temple lay at rest on beds of long wavy grasses. High in the eastern heavens sat Pentelicus and Hymettus, two mountains of marble, and the quarries from which Athens had been built from generation to generation showed only like a couple of tiny scratches in their long flanks. Then looking over the east wall of the Acropolis, he saw the modern town spread out beneath him, with sober, grave cypresses keeping sentinel by the tower of the winds, or a little to the right that sad company of giants, the remaining columns of the temple of Zeus Olympios, standing like strange, tall men from some other land, gazed at by the crowd of inquisitive modern houses, that keep on pushing their way closer to them. After lunch he went to the museums and saw the lines of statues and reliefs, and said nothing. He went to the Street of Tombs, and saw other tomb reliefs standing as they had stood for two thousand years, under the deep blue of the southern sky, so placed that the grasses that sprang from their ashes budded and flowered in sight of the Acropolis ; and the decade of summer days passed away.

An easterly gale and floods of driving rain kept him indoors one morning, and he wrote to Markham. An extract from his letter will give the state of his feelings better than anything else.

"I have been here between a week and a fort-night," he wrote, "and I am no nearer making up my mind than I was at first. If the beauty of the whole place was not so overwhelming, I should have merely, as I expected to do, studied how the sculptors of that day rendered muscles, and examined the *technique* of their work. As it is, I have done nothing of the kind. Now and then when I am tired I suddenly remember the absolute perfection of some detail, but in general I don't consciously notice it. The art is so triumphant that one cannot look at it in pieces. Men *admired* the sun before they peered at him through telescopes and found out sun-spots, and it was not till after that they tried to explain the sun-spots. It is the same with me ; I can only look and wonder. An Englishman has offered very kindly to lend me some books about sculpture. The suddenness of my refusal startled him. I care nothing at present about schools, and the way one man rendered eyes and another rendered hair. I can't judge it yet. But if they will build a temple of Pentelic marble in London, and stain it orange and red with weather, and put a hollow turquoise over it for a sky, and the Ionian Sea the colour of a sapphire in the background, I will do a statue for it. Some one told me once that I was not ambitious! Do you agree with that verdict? To-morrow if it is fine I go to Olympia. There is the finest thing of all there—a Hermes by Praxiteles. I don't think either Praxiteles or Hermes come into your line. One was a god, and I rather expect to find that the other was too."

From an artistic standpoint that visit to Olympia was perhaps the making of Tom; for all financial purposes it was his ruin. When he saw it, he said, "By Gad!" and stopped there half a day. The young god stands with his head a little bent, and a smile on his lips, looking at the babe whom he carries on his arm, half lost in his own thoughts. And the divine fire descended on Tom.

He stopped at Olympia for a day and a half, and then returned to Athens. Another artist had arrived at his hotel a day or two before, rather to Tom's disgust, but he quickly made friends with him, and had left with him several photographs of a couple of statuettes he had made that autumn in England. They were extremely pretty and essentially modern in style. Manvers himself was of the most advanced realistic school, and had got past mere prettiness, and recorded sheer ugliness with the most amazing skill.   He worked a good deal in Paris, but had come south owing to ill-health, and found a cynical pleasure in watching Tom's enthusiasm for a school that was almost comically *passé*, as *passé* as crinoline.   He had been through the same stage himself.

He had looked at the photographs Tom had given him with a good deal of respect, and was turning them over for the third or fourth time, when Tom himself came into the room on his return from Olympia.   Manvers was lying at full length on a sofa, smoking a bitter weed.

"Ah, there you are!" he said.   "Do you know these are devilish pretty?"

Tom strode across the room, and when he saw what Manners was looking at, he frowned.

"Give them me, Manvers," he said, and twitched them out of his hand.

It was a damp, windy day, and Manvers, who hated any temperature but the warmest, had made the hotel proprietor light a fire in the smoking-room. Tom looked at the photographs for a moment with intense disgust, and threw them into the fire.   In a few moments the draught had carried a few fragments of crinkly ash up the chimney.

Manvers took a puff or two at his bitter weed.

"Ah! the Hermes is to blame for that, I suppose," he said.   "I've seen the photographs of it.   That is why I did not go to Olympia with you.   Partly also, because it is cold.   I'm sorry you threw those photographs away; they were very pretty."

"They were abominations," said Tom, and sat down.

"And so you are going to set up a very life-size

'Apollo—six foot four in his sandals—as I did," said Manvers, "and you will gnash your teeth over it every day for a month, and then you will return to your senses."

"For the first time in my life I am fully sane," said Tom. "I have seen perfection, and I know what it means. I shall find out the way to do it. Don't laugh—I shall. It won't be easy, but it can be done. It has been done once, and it can be done again. What a blind fool I have been!"

Manvers crossed one leg over the other.

"Yes, it's delicious to feel like that," he said. "I quite envy you. I felt like it once—and those things don't happen twice. I congratulate you with all my heart, and I shall congratulate you more when you have recovered."

Tom snorted with indignation.

"I am as sane as you are," he said, "but I shan't set up a life-size statue just yet; I have got to study first. I know what the language means, and I am going to read all that exists in it. I have got the key to it all. The whole thing used to puzzle me; it was an unknown tongue, obsolete and dead, I thought it. But now I have the means of finding it all out."

Manvers closed his eyes.

"*Nunc dimittis*," he said piously. "I suppose we may expect a new Greek god every year for the present. What will you do with them, by-the-by? Life-size figures take up such a lot of room in a studio."

"That's so like you," said Tom; "as if it matters anything to me what happens to them. I shall produce them, that is enough."

"So the rest of the world will think, as you will find."

"What ?"

"I mean they won't go a step further, and wish to possess them."

"My dear Manvers, what do I care ?"

Manvers looked at him composedly.

"Yes, of course, it doesn't matter to you just yet. But when the masterpieces are fruitful and multiply (masterpieces breed like rabbits, you know), you will begin to wonder by degrees why they are unappreciated. You will be like a struggling curate with many children. He loves them all, but he cannot help wondering wistfully what will happen to them."

Tom shook his head with an air of benign superiority.

"You don't really think that, do you ?"

"Ah, well, it would be driving the case to extremes. What I expect will happen is that you will get tired of your masterpieces, or rather your first masterpiece, long before the rest of the world has an opportunity of doing so."

Tom looked at him compassionately.

"Poor chap; of course you are *blasé* and disillusioned. It must be very uncomfortable."

"From your point of view, I am, but not from my own. I saw a woman in the streets to-day with high-heeled boots and a parasol with lace round the edge, and the face of . . . well, not of a fallen angel, but an angel who never rose. To you that would mean nothing, but to me it was a solid ingot of inspiration for terra-cotta tossed in my path. From my point of view you are simply blind."

"Long may I remain so!" remarked Tom. "There's the bell for dinner. I am not going to eat no dinner because the heavens are opened."

"Did no manna fall into the railway carriage?" asked Manvers. "How forgetful of the Olympians!"

"No, I had lunch at Corinth," said Tom, laughing.

Whether Tom was sane or not, he was not sufficiently mad to set up a life-size Apollo in his bedroom. The artist's inspiration had descended on him, but not at present the artist's inevitable need of producing. The inspiration had come in a flood, and he bathed in it; there would be time enough afterwards to wade out and devote himself to the task of utilizing a given amount of the water. He wandered about the museums, and sat on the steps of the Parthenon, picturing to himself the two long rows of statues which once led up from the gates, and turning to the long riband of frieze on the west to people the path again with the Panathenaic procession. They were gods, Athens was a city of gods, and gods could not die; they were youth, beauty, enthusiasm all realized, ready to be realized again. It was all very well for Manvers to talk about phases, and developments, and schools that were *passées*, and schools that were decadent, but when you are face to face with perfection. . . .

Such was his creed. He believed in beauty. Even the classics—Xenophon with his parasangs, Thucydides with his Peloponnesian war—were glorified. Those men had been of the beautiful race, they had lived in the country where beauty unveiled had dwelt. They were to him as are, to one seeking for his love, men met by the wayside, men with whom she has spoken, on whom perhaps she smiled. They may not have known how fair she was, but even they were men different from others, for they had seen her, and could not be the same after that.

So he gave himself up heart and soul to his religion, and his religion lay broadcast like manna ; he sat in the Dionysiac theatre, and read Aristophanes ; he spelt out shorter Greek inscriptions with reverence ; he walked to Eleusis by the sacred way ; he sat an hour on the barrow at Marathon that holds the bones of the Greeks who conquered the Persians and died in victory. If this is to be mad, it is a pleasant thing to be mad, but it is a form of madness which is the outcome of youth and enthusiasm, and possibly genius, and is therefore not so common or so incurable as other forms.

Maud Wrexham's anticipations about her visit to Athens were a good deal heightened by the knowledge that she would find Tom Carlingford there. They had met several times during the autumn in England, and she found his company very stimulating. Tom above all things was an enthusiast, and enthusiasts are usually very sympathetic people, because, having seen unlimited vistas opening out in their own line they are willing, even eager, to allow for unlimited vistas in any other. Maud's vista was a wide one, embracing all mankind, just in the same way as Tom's did, the difference lying in the fact that Tom meant to compass his ends by artistic achievement, which would compel admiration and awe, whereas Maud's programme was entirely vague. She had a passion for the human race, and intended that they should have a passion for her.

Tom and she, being already fairly intimate, saw a good deal of each other. Maud, too, had experienced a quite peculiar pleasure in the sight of the Acropolis, and Tom's presence by no means lessened it.

They were sitting one bright winter's day on the steps of the little temple to Nike, which looks over the lower Attic plain, and across the narrow sea to Ægina and Salamis, and Tom was feeling a new-found joy in having some one to whom he could talk fully, being sure of sympathy. Though his artist's nature had not yet insisted on the life-size Apollo, expression of some sort was becoming necessary to him.

He pointed towards Salamis.

" That's where they smashed the Persian fleet," he said, "and our Lady of Victory was standing here where you and I are sitting. She used to be a winged goddess, but when she saw that, she plucked off her wings, and became the Wingless Victory. At least, that is my version. And here they set her temple on high."

Maud's eyes sparkled, and she said nothing for a minute or two.

" I'm afraid I'm a pagan," she remarked at length ; " I believe in these gods and goddesses."

" Why, of course you do," said Tom. " These myths could never have been invented; they were a conviction. And a conviction is the only religion worth having."

" But doesn't it matter what the conviction is ? "

" No, certainly not. One man's conviction may not be the conviction of another man, or of any other man, but it is the true thing for him. A man's conviction is that for which he was made."

"But don't you believe in a time when every one, dead or alive, will have the same conviction?"

"I hardly know. But at any given moment I can't realize that it's any conviction which I don't share at that moment."

Maud flushed ever so faintly before she spoke again.

"What is your conviction at this moment?"

Tom looked at her seriously, and examined the ferrule of his stick without speaking.

"What is yours?" he asked.

"Ah! but my question came first."

"My conviction is that a man can realize either in others, or in some image in his brain which he works out perfectly or imperfectly, ideal beauty. It may be moral or physical beauty. And his mission is to do it."

Maud had waited for his answer with an anxiety she could hardly explain to herself; her heart took upon itself to beat with quick throbs, that seemed to make her whole being alert. But this was only half an answer.

"And what is he to do with it when he has realized it?" she asked, with the same intentness.

"Surely that is enough," said Tom. "He loves it, of course."

He stood up and looked out over the sea. "My God! he loves nothing else!" he added.

For the life of her Maud could not help questioning him further.

"Yes, that, of course. But here one is in this

puzzling world, and how is one to begin? My conviction is—— "

"Yes, I know," broke in Tom; "I remember you telling me perfectly. You want to make the whole world yours. So do I ; and here is my first step ready for me."

"Yes, you are an artist. That is a serviceable tool."

"A tool? It is the end in itself. If you use it rightly, all the rest is there. The mainspring of this civilization which we see here was beauty. They conquered the Persians for the beauty of the thing."

"Oh, I'm not so sure about that! I think their hearths and homes had something to do with it."

"Then why had no one else conquered the Persians? Every nation they had already subdued had its hearths and homes. The Greeks had no more hearths and homes than others, and the biceps of the Greek was no bigger than that of other men. Everything else was only the wire down which the electric current came—and the electric current which killed the Persian was the love of art."

"Then why did they fall before Rome?"

"Because the current had grown weak. Their art degenerated, and they fell."

Maud scratched the cement pavement at her feet meditatively. She felt rather chilled and discouraged. She had expected—well, what had she expected?

" I think you are inhuman," she said at last.

"Yes, I know I am. I believe I have got hold of this tool, as you call it, and I think of nothing else but how to use it. I must go back to England soon, and work."

Maud had stood up, and the least tremor passed over her. Tom noticed it.

"You are catching cold," he said, "sitting here. What an ass I was not to think of it before ! Here's your cloak; let me help you on with it."

"Thanks—it is rather cold. I thought you were going to be out here all the winter."

"I feel just now that I should like to stop here for ever."

They had strolled back into the Acropolis, and Maud felt glad they were moving, for a silence then is less embarrassing than when one is stopping still. Their talk had been a little upsetting to her in some way, and she wanted a moment to steady herself in. They had left Arthur Wrexham sitting in a rather forlorn manner on a large slab of cold Pentelic marble. He refused to come on to the Nike bastion because he was smoking a cigarette, and there was a wind there. So he contented himself with answering in a vaguely appreciative manner, how very classic it all was, and that he should certainly come there again. His opportune appearance at this moment, sitting in a more sheltered corner than ever, facing a blank white wall, gave Maud an opportunity of recovering herself.

"Dear Arthur, are you finding it all very classic," she said, "and just a little melancholy? Never mind; we can't take you to the museum, as we threatened to do, because it closes at twelve, so you need only just walk up as far as the Parthenon, because I want to look at something, and then we'll all go down. Really, you are a very bad chaperon ; you sit in a corner opposite a blank wall. Mr. Carlingford has been saying the most unconventional things."

" I have been mentioning the objects and purposes of art," remarked Tom.

"Ah, how nice!" murmured Arthur; "all about Doric columns and so on, I suppose. Do tell me some day. Maud, we shall be dreadfully late for lunch."

"Yes, dear, I know we shall," said Maud.

" Well, then, wouldn't it really be as well to leave the Parthenon alone, just for the present? You can see the Parthenon any day."

"Well, you can have lunch any day," said Maud; " and you do have it every day."

Arthur Wrexham made a resigned little sound, partaking of the nature of a sigh, and followed them.

They were lunching with Tom at his hotel, and when they went out on to the balcony afterwards to drink the thick sweet Turkish coffee, they found Manvers sitting in the sun, feeding on his own thoughts. The thoughts chiefly ran on the subject of the possibility of representing lace—real thin lace, and not great fluffy bunches of it—in terra-cotta, and it really seemed as if it might be done. *La dame qui s'amuse* must have lace, all round her parasol and down the front of her dress.

He looked doubtfully at his cigar, after shaking hands with Maud. The class *qui m'ennuie* were not so tolerant. Maud caught the glance.

"Not on my account, please," said she. "I don't mind it in the least."

"Well, on my account, then," said Tom. " He smokes curly Italian weeds, Miss Wrexham. They smell of goat's cheese."

"My dear fellow," said Manvers, "you are in the Havannah stage with all your tastes."

"Isn't that rather a good stage to be in?" asked Miss Wrexham.

"Quite delightful for yourself, but it makes you a little intolerant of other people. Tom dislikes my statuettes as much as he dislikes my cigars."

"I dislike them very much more," said Tom fervently.

"There, you see—you may judge how much he loathes them."

"Bring one out," said Tom, "and see if Miss Wrexham doesn't agree with me."

"I don't carry my own statuettes about with me," said Manvers; "one's own works are very bad company. When you have begun on your life-size Apollo, you will know why."

"Apollo shall dine with me every night."

"My dear fellow, how you will bore each other!" said Manvers.

Maud Wrexham began to laugh.

"You mustn't pea-shoot each other in public," she said. "When doctors disagree, they must do so out of hearing of their patient."

"Are you a patient?" asked Manvers.

"Yes, under treatment. I have been on the Acropolis all the morning, with my brother and Mr. Carlingford. You're not a patient, are you, Arthur?"

"It struck me I was very patient," said he.

Maud reflected a moment.

"No, it's not at all a good joke, dear; it's not either good enough or bad enough to be good."

"Extremes meet, you know," explained Tom.

"That's why you and Mr. Manvers come and stay at the same hotel, I suppose," said she.

"We don't often meet," remarked Manvers. "Tom goes to the Acropolis, and I sit on the balcony."

"Then why did you come to Athens?" asked Maud; "surely there are better balconies elsewhere."

"He's really becoming a convert," said Tom; "he's not so black as he paints himself."

"My dear Tom, I never paint myself, it is you who paint me; and to do you justice, you paint me as black as you can."

Poor Arthur Wrexham looked appealingly at the company.

"I think I shall go for a little stroll," he said. "When are you likely to be ready, Maud?"

Maud finished her coffee.

"I'm coming now," she said. "Don't forget to-morrow, Mr. Carlingford—you call for us at nine."

"They're going up Pentelicus," said Arthur plaintively; "I'm going too."

Tom looked at him severely.

"Yes, it's the one you told me was Hymettus," he said. "It's time you went. You won't confuse them again."

"I didn't confuse them before," said Arthur. "You can't confuse two things, unless you know them both, and then mix them up. I didn't know either."

"Well, you'll know one after to-morrow," said Maud encouragingly, "and then you can get at the other by an exhaustive process."

CHAPTER VII.

MEANWHILE the "sheltered life" had gone on as usual at Mr. Markham's. The delight in Ted's success had moved away into its appointed background, in front of which the slow, happy days passed on as uneventfully as ever. But about November a change took place. The Lord Chancellor appeared to have been suddenly struck by Mr. Markham's admirable editions of school classics, or perhaps the fame of the neat covers of the books May stitched for the parish library had reached him, and he offered him the living of Applethorpe, which had just become vacant. Mr. Markham was unwilling to leave his old parish, and May even more so, but the offer was not one to be refused. Applethorpe was a large country parish, and, what was a distinct advantage, a richer one than Chesterford ; old Mr. Carlingford, in particular, though careful to avoid in his own person direct means of grace, being always ready to supply funds whereby it might be administered to others.

Ted was delighted with the change ; his roots had been transplanted so often in school and university life that they never struck very deeply in the soil of Chesterford. The close neighbourhood of Tom's

house weighed heavily in favour of Applethorpe, and
the accessibility of Lord Ramsden's library, which
contained many dust-ridden old volumes, among which
he had visions, as every book-lover has, of finding un-
discovered treasures in the way of twelfth-century
missals, was not without its effect. May alone did
not like it. It seemed to her that she was going
out into new and more elaborate places, which might
prove perplexingly different from the green fields and
country lanes she knew so well. Things were going
to be on a bigger scale ; they would keep one curate,
perhaps two ; London itself loomed on the horizon,
and when her father had gone to see the place, he
came back saying that it looked a pretty country
but there had been a London fog, which had drifted
down from town.

However, she quite acquiesced in her father's
decision, and before Christmas they had moved.

Their house stood at one end of the long straggling
village, a typical rectory of the older class, with a
tennis lawn in front and a stable-yard behind, a hall
paved with red tiles, and far too much ivy and vir-
ginia creeper on the walls. Ted arrived soon after
from Cambridge, with a large square box full of
books, which could only just get through the front
door.

He and May had gone a long exploring walk in
the country one afternoon, and were returning home
along the clean frozen road through the village. They
had been talking about the place.

" It's so big, Ted," May had said, " it almost
frightens me, as I told you once a big place would

do. It is so hard to get hold of a lot of people like this."

"Well, there will be a curate, won't there?" said Ted. "Of course it's too large for father alone."

"Yes, I know there will ; but you don't understand. I must get hold of them myself. I must do all I did at Chesterford, and more."

Ted looked at her kindly.

"Yes, I know how you feel about it. It's the personal relation you want, isn't it ? "

"No, I don't care about their personal relation to me. They might all hate me if they liked. But the quickest way to get at people's hearts for any purpose is to make them like one."

"Don't be worried, May," said he. "You will soon get to know them all, unless I'm very much mistaken."

"Ah, but just think of the state things are in ! I went to see an old woman yesterday. She couldn't understand at first why I came. I told her I was the new vicar's daughter, and she asked me what I wanted. The late vicar used never to visit anybody, she said."

"Yes, it will be hard work."

"I wish you could come here after you were ordained," said May, "as father's curate."

"I must stop at Cambridge," said Ted. "You wouldn't wish me to give that up ? "

"No, I suppose not," said May ; "and yet, I don't know. I think parish work is the highest in the world."

"There is plenty of that to do in Cambridge," said

Ted, "for that matter ; but I am not the man to do it. I can't do it as you can—and father," he added.

"Ah, but what is good work in other lines compared to any work in that?" said May, earnestly—"especially for a man who means to be a clergyman."

"Yes, but other things can't be neglected. You have no business to leave alone what you think you can do, for anything else. One's talents, whatever they are, are given one to use."

"But is there not 'that good part'?" asked May.

Ted walked on in silence a little way.

"I did not know you thought of it like that," he said at length. "Do you admit no call but that of saving souls directly by your means?"

"I didn't know I felt it myself, till we came here," said May ; "until I saw this place so absolutely uncared for. Look at the rich people, too. Old Mr. Carlingford is very liberal, because he is very rich ; but he never comes to church."

"Ah, that reminds me," said Ted. "Tom is coming home soon, in about a fortnight, he said."

May paused on the doorstep.

"I suppose he will come here, won't he ? I didn't know he was coming back so early."

And she turned rather quickly, and went into the house.

The new curate soon came, and fulfilled to the utmost all the admirable accounts of himself which had led to his engagement. He was strong and vigorous, and exerted all his vigour and strength in the work to which he had been called. He was even bold enough to pay a visit to Mr. Carlingford single-handed, and the latter gentleman conversed to him very fluently and agreeably for half an hour on the coal-strike, and the lamentable weakness of the English fleet in the Mediterranean, offered to draw a cheque then and there to supply coal for villagers who were unable to have fires in this very nipping weather, and courteously declined to interest himself any further.

He was walking back through the village, and met May there, who had been visiting.

"I have just been to see Mr. Carlingford," he said.

May looked up quickly.

"I didn't know——" she began. "Oh! old Mr. Carlingford. Yes. Did you get anything out of him?"

"I got a cheque," said Mr. Douglas.

May laughed.

"Yes, that's not so difficult, though it's something to be thankful for. These poor creatures are half frozen."

"Mr. Carlingford really is very generous. But is there no hope of getting hold of him really? He might do much more than he does."

"I wonder. Tom Carlingford is coming home this week. He might do something with his father. I'll ask my brother about it. By the way, we are dining there to-night. Are you going?"

"No, I've got my cheque," said the young man. "That's enough for one day. Besides, I have a boys' meeting at Chipford Mills. I must leave you here I have to go up to Breigton cottages first."

May turned and shook hands with him.

"It's absurd for me to thank you for all you are doing," she said. "You do all sorts of things which my father couldn't possibly do, and which we have no right to expect."

"Surely that is a curate's business," he said, laughing, and taking off his hat.

Mr. Markham was suffering from a slight cold, and he had not been out that day. He was sitting over the fire in the drawing-room, reading a comedy of Aristophanes, when May came in.

"How cold you look!" he said. "I ordered tea as you were a little late."

"Yes; I couldn't come before, father," she said, "and even now I have only got through half the things I wanted to do."

"Never mind, dear; but you should make an effort to be punctual; and charity begins at home, eh, May?"

May turned from the fire, where she had been warming her hands, and poured out a cup of tea. Her father, seeing he got no answer, continued somewhat reproachfully—

"My cold is rather worse this evening, and I can't think what you did with that medicine. I couldn't find it anywhere."

"I put it on the table in your study."

"No, dear. I think not. I looked for it there."

May went out of the room and brought back the bottle.

"Yes, it was there. You had put some of your papers on to it."

"Thanks very much.   I hope you took care not to disturb the papers."

"No, I disturbed nothing. Will you have some now?"

"No, I've just had my tea. I was wanting it before tea. I always take it before meals, you know."

May sat down in a chair and stirred her tea.

"Mr. Carlingford has given Mr. Douglas a cheque to get coals for the people. It's fearfully cold, and, poor things, many of them can't afford coals."

"A good fellow, Douglas," murmured Mr. Markham, as he smiled appreciatively at Aristophanes.

"I was wondering if we couldn't let them have some wood," said May. "There are stacks of it in the yard."

Mr. Markham put his finger in his place.

"Yes, I will see about it.   Who want it?"

"Oh, half a dozen of the cottages down here, and more at the mills."

"Well, dear, hadn't you better make a little list? It would save me some trouble. Dear me, the fire wants mending.   And then, if you would let me have it in about an hour, I could just finish this play."

"We dine at Mr. Carlingford's to-night," said May.

"Yes, dear, I know.   Ah, δίκαιος λόγος.   How admirable that is!"

Mr. Carlingford felt that he was doing his duty beautifully that evening. He had given a cheque to the curate in the afternoon, and he was having his vicar to dinner in the evening. His definition of duty was vague and comprehensive. It meant doing those things which he either did not wish to do or felt no desire to do. He had no desire to give Mr. Douglas a cheque, and he did not wish to have his vicar to dinner. The latter was therefore more clearly his duty than the former, since the essential character of such acts varied in exact ratio to their unpleasantness. An evening, he reflected, as he dressed for dinner, should be spent alone in a warm room, after a light meal, and be conveyed to the senses through the medium of several glasses of good port. Clergymen were often teetotalers, and it gave him a positive sense of discomfort to see people drinking water. Water was meant to wash in.

To him, in this state of mind, Mr. Markham was a pleasant surprise. He showed no inclination to talk about mutton broth and district visiting, he seemed to be well up in current topics of interest, and he was no teetotaler. In fact, he made some rather knowing remarks on the subject of cellars, and the depreciated nature of corks nowadays. And May really was an admirable girl. "Why didn't that fool Tom fall in love with her, instead of heathen goddesses?" was his mental comment as she came in.

"I heard from my prodigal son to-day," he said, as they were sitting at dinner; "he has decided to continue his prodigality for another month. The fatted calf may get fatter still. Poor boy! he is quite mad, and he means to fill the house with statues. Statues always give me the shivers. They really lower the temperature of the room. It is impossible to see too little of them."

"They'll have to go in the kitchen," said Mr. Markham.

"An excellent suggestion, my dear Mr. Markham, but think of the soup! However, Tom is so dreadfully energetic, he always makes me feel hot. The statues shall be wheeled about with him, and that will preserve the equability of the temperature."

"He wrote to my brother saying he was coming back at once," said May.

"He does not deserve that you should remember that," said Mr. Carlingford, urbanely. "But I shall be so glad to see him that I will tell him."

"Oh, you needn't do that," said May, laughing.

Mr. Carlingford looked up at her a moment, and smiled to himself. That slight flush on May's face might only have been the effect of coming out of the cold night air into warm rooms, but the other explanation pleased him more.

"You and Tom will have great talks about Greek sculpture and Greek literature, Mr. Markham," said Mr. Carlingford, still adapting himself. "I hear you are a wonderful scholar."

"I have so little time for anything but my parish duties," said Mr. Markham, "that I never get the chance of working at classics. We are very busy here, eh, May?"

"Well, it's an ill wind that blows no one any good," said Mr. Carlingford, "and the parish is the gainer."

The two gentlemen sat on in the dining-room afterwards, while May spent a lonely but pleasant quarter of an hour in the drawing-room. She was tired, for she had been out all day, and a low chair in front of the fire suited her mood exactly. She never read much, and the books on the table, chiefly by French authors of whom she had never heard, did not excite her interest. So she fed on her own thoughts, and made quiet uneventful plans for the future. When one is young, difficulties produce a quickening of the hand and pulse, not a tendency to give up, to be content with what is done. The powers of the mind and soul, like the muscles of the body, grow only through their active employment, and the harder the work the fitter they become. It is only when the capability of growth ceases that exertion is labour. Her thoughts ran on the events of the day, on the material as well as the spiritual needs of those clustered cottagers, on the want, the suffering. . . . There was one girl who lived alone in a tiny room in one of the poorer cottages with her week-old baby. It was the common story ; she was weak and ill, and unable to work. Yet to such as her the promise had been made. The baby too ; surely the words " How much more shall He feed you " did not mean the workhouse ? She must consult her father about them. She had already started a Sunday afternoon class for children. Poor mites, they did not need theology yet ; it was better to teach them to be clean, to show them pictures that would amuse them, to let them spend a happy hour in a warm bright room, with playthings and wooden bricks to build with.

And for herself, what? She neither wanted nor contemplated any change. The work that lay before her was so inevitably hers, that any possible change would be to neglect the whole purpose of her life.

She was her father's daughter, and he was a parish priest. What other call could there be for her which could be clearer than that? She rose from her chair and walked once or twice up and down the room, and stopped at length before a long mirror set in the wall. There was a lamp on either side standing on the top of two chiffoniers, and her image was reflected in bright light. She gazed a few seconds at herself without thinking what she was doing, and then drew in her breath with a sudden start, for she saw in the mirror a reflection, not of what she was used to think herself, but the reflection of a woman, and she was that woman. The whole thing flashed on to and off her brain in a moment, but it had been there.

Meanwhile Mr. Carlingford and his vicar were having a comfortable glass of port over the fire. The vicar liked everything to be good of its sort; his terriers were all in the kennel stud-book, his Walter Scott was an *édition de luxe*, and he had a beautiful Romney in his dining-room. And all Mr. Carlingford offered him was first-rate; the dinner had been excellent, the fire was of that superlative mixture, cedar logs and coal, and the port was certainly above criticism. He regretted profoundly that his slight cold had taken the edge off his sense of taste.

Mr. Carlingford expressed singular but original ideas on the subject of money.

"I had the pleasure of giving your curate, a delightful young fellow I should say," he began, "a small cheque this afternoon. So many clergymen, Mr. Markham, if you will excuse a criticism on your fellow-workers, are distinguished only for their superficial grasp of subtleties; but Mr. Douglas is distinguished for his wonderfully keen grasp of the obvious. I asked him for how much I should draw the cheque, and he said at once the sum he wished to receive. I hope you will always ask me when you want anything."

"You are very generous."

Mr. Carlingford finished his glass, and put it down on the chimney-piece.

"Money may be the root of all evil," he said, "but it is in itself a very necessary evil. It is one of those little snares without which we should be always tripping up. But it is a very troublesome thing. Tom, I know, detests money; perhaps that is why he spends it so quickly. However, there is always a chance of something smashing and his being left penniless, so he needn't abandon all hope of being happy yet. He is a great friend of your son, is he not ?"

"Yes, Ted saw a great deal of him at Cambridge, though he was a year or two the senior."

"I was so glad to see he had got his Fellowship. I suppose he will remain at Cambridge."

"Yes, he means to. He is fond of the place, and it is a pleasant life."

"And that, after all, is the best investment you can make of your time," remarked Mr. Carlingford.

"Not financially, I am afraid."

"My dear Mr. Markham, you are confusing the end and the means. The harmless necessary cash can at the best only secure you a pleasant life, and if the pleasant life comes to you without, it becomes not necessary, but superfluous."

"Well, there is no fear of cash ever being superfluous to Ted."

"Cash is always superfluous, except when you cannot get credit," said his host. "If there were no cash in the world we should all live in our several stations on our credit with each other, and how much simpler that would be!"

"I am afraid there would be complications ahead."

"There are always complications ahead," said Mr. Carlingford, "but in the fulness of time they fall behind. Meanwhile one rubs along somehow. Shall we move into the next room?"

It is to be feared that if Tom, in the new life that had opened for him at Athens, could have seen how Ted was spending his life at Cambridge, he would have been far from satisfied with him. It requires strong vitality or real originality to avoid the paralyzing effect which routine brings with it, and though Ted was original enough to give birth to some theories concerning patristic literature which were received in the most favourable manner by past masters of his craft, his horizons were imperceptibly narrowing around him. It is the peculiar property of such changes that they are imperceptible; to be alive to them would be to guard against them, for no thinking man acquiesces in limitations which he can see. He spent long mornings of steady work, he took gentle exercise in the afternoon, and played whist for an hour or two after hall; and any routine, when one is surrounded by men who are engaged in similar routines, is deadly. He let old acquaintances drop, he did not care to initiate new ones, and he lived with a few men who were in the same predicament as himself, and was perfectly happy. He worked not for fame's sake, but for the sake of the work, and though his method of working is undoubtedly the more highly altruistic, yet it has to be paid for in other ways. A little personal ambition is a very human and therefore a very suitable thing for men, for it keeps one alive to the fact that one is one man among other men, not one machine for producing knowledge among other machines. A machine may very likely do the work better; a perfect machine would do it perfectly, but it will not become a man by so doing, though a man, as the higher of the two, may quite easily degenerate into a machine.

Ted's talk with May about parish work led to his taking a district in Barnwell, and doing work there. But, as he told her, he had no power of doing that sort of thing—he had none of the missionary spirit, nor any desire now to enter into the personal relation with his fellows, which distinguished, though in opposite ways, both his sister and Tom. The sight of dirt and squalor was productive in him, in the first instance, not of a desire to make it clean, but to go away. He realized to the full how deplorable a state of uncleanliness, physical or moral, was, and he would have been very uncomfortable to think that there were not well-endowed institutions the object of which was to rectify it.

Before Tom had gone away in November, he

completed a couple of statuettes, which he had made during the summer, had them cast in bronze by the *cire perdue* process, and sent them to a winter exhibition. He had only just received the news that they had been accepted before he went away, and had heard nothing of them since. But one day in the winter Ted had been turning over a current number of the *Spectator*, and found them mentioned in a notice of the exhibition with that high praise which is both rare and convincing, and felt a strong but unsympathetic pleasure, for, judging from his own point of view, he would have felt none himself that a casual critic thought them good. A few nights afterwards, by one of those coincidences which would be so strange if they were not so common, he met at dinner with the master of another college, the sculptor Wallingthorpe, who talked chiefly about himself, but a little about his art. He was a picturesque man, and his picturesqueness added a strong flavour to his conversation.

"I seldom or never go to exhibitions," he said. "A beautiful subject badly treated warps one. One has to be convalescent after it. One's artistic sense has been bruised, and it has to recover from the blow: the injured tissues have to heal."

Ted mentioned the name of the exhibition where Tom's studies had appeared, and asked if he had been there.

"Yes, I did go there—no wine, thanks; I never take wine, by the way. It is a stimulant, and I don't require stimulating, I require soothing. I am glad you mentioned that exhibition; there were two studies there of extreme, unusual merit. They produced in me that feeling that I could have done the thing myself, that I wished I had. That is the final excellence from one's own point of view. They realized to me the vision I might have had."

"Whom were they by?" asked Ted.

"By quite a young man, I believe; certainly by quite a new one. Carlingford was the name."

"Ah! I know him well," said Ted.

They were sitting over the wine after dinner, and Wallingthorpe, who did not care to talk to Ted exclusively any longer, but wanted a larger audience, bent forward and shook him warmly by the hand. This was done in a dramatic and fervid manner, and naturally drew the attention of the rest of the table.

Wallingthorpe turned round to explain himself.

"I was congratulating Mr. Markham on knowing a man of genius," he said.

The natural inference was that these felicitations were offered to Ted on the happy event of his having become acquainted with Wallingthorpe, but that gentleman was self-denying enough to dispel the idea.

"I was speaking of two very remarkable little works in the Ashdon Gallery, by a young man called Carlingford, with whom Mr. Markham tells me he is intimate. They are very faulty in many ways, but faults matter nothing when there is the divine essential burning behind them. Mr. Carlingford is an uncut diamond. There are superficial flaws in the stone, which will be polished away. He has only got to work and to live."

"Carlingford," said some one; "he was up at King's till quite lately, was he not?"

Mr. Marshall blinked intelligently behind his spectacles.

"Yes, but we had no idea we were harbouring a genius. In fact, no one even suspected he had real talent of any kind. But he was not stupid."

"It is possible, even probable, that he had no talent," exclaimed Wallingthorpe. "Genius and talent have nothing in common. You might as well expect to find a bird that had hands because it has wings. Genius flies, talent—the metaphor breaks down—walks on its hands and feet. But what made you think he had no talent?"

"His work was always very careless, and showed no very distinct promise."

Wallingthorpe beat the air with prophetic hands.

"His Greek prose! His Latin verses! His οὐ and his μὴ! That is very likely. Did it not occur to any one that you might as well have set a wild Indian to hem handkerchiefs?"

"You see we all have to hem handkerchiefs here," said his host urbanely; "that is the reason why young men come to Cambridge."

"And you wonder when your thorns bear grapes and your thistles figs!" said Wallingthorpe. "Yet those are to blame who did not know that the thistle was a fig-tree."

Dr. Madeford laughed good-naturedly.

"But we are all delighted when we find it bearing figs," he said, "although, of course, we don't allow that we thought it a thistle. We have a higher idea of what we study."

Wallingthorpe became pacific.

"Consider me rebuked," he said, "but think of the pity of it. Four or five years ago that boy ought to have been alternately turned loose in Rome and shut up with a model and a mountain of clay. By now those defects would have vanished. They would never have been in his nature. Their possibility would have been taken out of him before they had birth."

"Then you have really a high opinion of his work?" asked Markham.

"My dear young man, I have the highest. He has genius, and he has love of his work. Show me the man of whom I can say that, and I hail him as a brother."

Wallingthorpe's egotism was too deep to call conceit; it was a conviction that was the mainspring of his nature, the driving-power of his work. It should not matter to the outside world what the driving-power is, if the result is admirable, and Wallingthorpe's results certainly were admirable.

But further conversation would seem bathos after this, and the party passed into the drawing-room.

Wallingthorpe had a word or two more with Ted as he was leaving.

"What is Carlingford doing now?" he asked.

"He's in Athens, working there."

"A dangerous experiment. Is he much impressed by classical art?"

"Very much indeed; he believes in nothing else, he says."

The sculptor frowned.

"That means he will try to stand on tip-toe for a

month or two instead of flying. However, he will get tired of that. He will soon learn that the only real art is realism."

" He says that a sculptor out there called Manvers is always impressing that on him."

" Manvers ? Well, no one ever accused Manvers of not being a realist. That is about the only crime he has never been suspected of. Manvers is extremely talented, but he has not a touch of genius. However, for diabolical cleverness in his work he can't be touched. On the other hand, any tendency in Carlingford to idealism might be encouraged by Manvers indirectly. He would find it impossible, if he had leanings that way, not to have his bias strengthened by anything so rampantly realistic as Manvers' work."

"Tom Carlingford is coming back to England in a few weeks."

" I'm glad of that. The future is in his own hands."

CHAPTER VIII.

MANVERS' good intention of taking a holiday had presumably gone to pave the worst of roads, for before a fortnight was up he was working hard at the new statuette. The solid ingot of inspiration which had been tossed in his path was only slightly responsible for this; the burden of it lay with Maud Wrexham.

For Maud Wrexham was to him a new type of womanhood, common enough in England, but a type which does not foregather with young artists in Paris; and Manvers was beginning to think of the Paris days with a sort of disgusted wonder. To be received into the society of a well-bred English girl, to see her day after day, to be admitted by her into a frank, boyish sort of intimacy, was a proceeding he would have looked upon, a month or two ago, as a very doubtful privilege. He thought of our English marriageable maidenhood as a kind of incarnation of lawn tennis and district visiting, with a background of leaden domesticity, and when Maud began, somehow, to usurp an unreasonably large share of his spare thoughts, he was at first a little amused at himself, and, after a time, pulled up short and began to review the position.

He had seen almost at once who it was who usurped her thoughts, though he felt sure that a casual observer, one whose own mind was fancy free, would not have noticed it. She was intensely conscious of Tom's presence, and to Manvers she betrayed herself by a hundred tiny signs. When they were alone, she, as was most natural, for they were a trio of friends, often talked of Tom, and when he was there she evidently listened to all he said, and was intensely conscious of him, though she might be talking to some one else. As a rule, she behaved quite naturally; but once or twice she had exhibited towards him a studied unconsciousness, which to Manvers was a shade more convincing than her consciousness. He had a weakness for weaknesses, and the dramatic side of it all, her self-betrayal to him and Tom's unconsciousness, would have given him a good deal of satisfaction, had he known that he was without a stake in the matter. But as the days went on, he became aware that it mattered a good deal to him, and the satisfaction he got out of the drama was a very poor wage for his own share in it.

Besides, he distinctly did not wish to fall in love. "Love may or may not blind," he said to himself, "but it plays the deuce with your eye, if you are a sculptor." And so, by way of keeping his eye single, he set to work, with patient eagerness, on *La dame qui s'amuse.* The title itself brought a savour with it of Paris days, and Paris days could hardly help being antidotal to the feelings with which Maud Wrexham inspired him.

There was yet one more factor which made him

plunge into his work, and that was the thought of Tom. Tom just now was sublimely unconscious of anything so sublunary as falling in love with mortals, for he had lost his heart to antique goddesses, who again presented a fine contrast to Miss Wrexham. Manvers, as a rule, left morals to moralists, among whose numbers he had never enlisted himself; but a certain idea of loyalty, of letting Tom have fair play when he came to take his innings, made him avoid the idea of setting up personal relations with Miss Wrexham. Whether he would have taken the chivalrous line, if any one but Tom had been concerned, is doubtful, but Tom somehow exacted loyalty. His extraordinary boyishness made Manvers feel that it would be an act of unpardonable meanness to take any advantage of him. Besides, in a sense, the fortress to which he himself would have liked to lay siege was, he felt sure, ready to capitulate to another, but it struck him that it was likely to repel an attack from any other quarter but that with much vigour. To sit still and do nothing was more than flesh and blood could stand; it was hard enough to work, and the only thing to do was to work hard.

Tom's tendencies towards idealism were, as Wallingthorpe had suspected, encouraged rather than discouraged by Manvers. "If that," he thought and often said, "is realism, God forbid that I should be a realist."

He said this to himself very emphatically one morning when he came to see Manvers after breakfast. The latter was already at work, and Tom gazed at "La dame" for some moments without speaking. Manvers' handling of the subject was masterly, and the result appeared to Tom quite detestable.

"I quite appreciate how clever it is," Tom said to Manvers, who was testing his powers of "doing" lace in terra-cotta with great success, "and I wonder that you don't appreciate how abominable it is."

Manvers was at a somewhat ticklish point, and he did not answer, but only smiled. Nature had supplied him with a rather Mephistophelean cast of features, and he had aided her design by the cultivation of a small pointed beard. At this moment Tom could fancy that he was some incarnation of that abstraction, dissecting a newly damned soul with eagerness and delicacy, in the search for some unusual depravity. After a moment he laid the tool down.

"I appreciate it fully from a spiritual, or moral, or Greek, or purist point of view, he said. But I am not in the habit of taking those points of view, and in consequence I am—well, rather pleased with it."

"I think it's a desecration," said Tom. "Why you are not struck with lightning when you call it art, seems to me inexplicable!"

Manvers laughed outright.

"My dear Tom, I never called it art—I never even called it Art with a big A. That is not the way to get on. You must leave other people to do that. If you were an art critic, which I hope, for my sake, you some time may be, you would be immensely useful to me. One has only got to get an Art critic (with a big A) to stand by one's work, and pay him so much to shout out, 'This is the Abomination,' and one's fortune is made. I am thinking of paying some one a handsome salary to blackguard me in the Press. Criticism, as the critic understands it, would soon cease, you see, if every one agreed, and so the fact that one critic says it is abomination, implies necessarily that another critic will come and stand on the other side and bawl out, 'This is Sublime' (with a big S). Artists and critics are under a great debt to one another. Critics get as much as sixpence a line, I believe, for what they say about artists, and artists would never get a penny if it wasn't for critics, whereas, at present, some of us get very considerable sums. What was I saying? Oh yes, one critic damns you and the other critic blesses you. Then, you see, every one runs up to find out what the noise is, and they all begin quarrelling about it. And the pools are filled with water," he concluded piously.

Tom did not answer, and Manvers went on with slow precision, giving each word its full value.

"Of course it is chiefly due to the capital letters. Whether the criticism is favourable or not matters nothing as long as it is emphatic. In this delightful age of sky signs, the critics must be large and flaring to attract any notice. Therefore they shout and use capital letters. They write on the full organ with all the stops out, except the Vox Angelica. And the artist blesses them. Like Balaam, their curses are turned into blessings for him, so he blesses them back. A most Christian proceeding."

"But, honestly," asked Tom, "does the contemplation

of that give you any artistic pleasure? Do you try to do for your age what Phidias and Praxiteles did for theirs?"

"Certainly I do. I try to represent to people what their age is. I have no doubt that ancient Greeks were excessively nude and statuesque. We are not statuesque or nude. Apollo pursuing Daphne through the Vale of Tempe, through thickets where the nightingales sing! What does Apollo do now? He arranges to meet Daphne at Aix-les-Bains, where they have mud-baths, and drink rotten-egg water. She wears an accordion-pleated skirt, and he a check suit. In their more rural moments they sit in the hotel-garden. It really seems to me that this little Abomination here is fairly up to date."

"Oh, it's up to date enough!" said Tom. "But is that the best of what is characteristic of our age?"

"That doesn't concern me," said Manvers blandly; "worst will do as well. What I want is anything unmistakably up to date. Your gods and goddesses, of course, are more beautiful from an ideal point of view. By the way, that reminds me, I want to look at some of those early figures; the drapery is very suggestive. I am going to do a statuette of a nun who has once been—well, not a nun, and I want archaic folds; but if I produced them now, they would be nothing more than uninteresting survivals. And to produce an uninteresting survival seems to me a most deplorable waste of time."

"Why don't you make a statuette of a sewing-machine?" asked Tom savagely.

"Oh, do you think sewing-machines are really

characteristic of the age ?" said Manvers. "I don't personally think they are, any more than Homocea is. Sewing-machines are only skin-deep. I wonder when you will be converted again—become an apostate, as you would say now. You really had great talent. Those statuettes of yours at the Ashdon Gallery are attracting a great deal of attention."

"I wish I had thrown them into the fire before I sent them there!"

"Well, when you come round again, you will be glad you didn't," said Manvers consolingly.

Tom took a turn or two up and down the room.

"You don't understand me a bit," he said suddenly. "Because I think that the Parthenon frieze is more beautiful than women with high-heeled shoes, you think I'm an idealist. I am a realist, just as much as you are, only I want to produce what I think is most beautiful. A beautiful woman has much in common with Greek art—and you want to produce what men, who are brutes, will say is most lifelike. You work for brutes, or what I call brutes, and I don't."

"But if I have come to the conclusion that what you call brutish appeals to more men than what you call beautiful, surely I am right to work for them ? Of course most artists say they work for the few, but I, like them, confess that I wish the few to be as numerous as possible."

"The greatest evil for the greatest number, I suppose you mean," burst in Tom. "I call it pandering to vicious tastes."

Manvers paused, then laid down the tool he was working with.

"You are overstepping the bounds of courtesy," he said quietly. "You assume that my nature is vicious. That you have no right to do."

Tom frowned despairingly.

"I know. It is quite true. I hate the men who always tell you that they say what they think, but I am one of them."

Manvers laughed.

"I don't mind your thinking me vicious," he said. "I dare say I am vicious from your point of view, but you shouldn't tell me so. It savours of Billingsgate, and it is quite clear without your telling me of it. You insult my intelligence when you say so."

"In that I am sorry," said Tom. "I never meant to do that. I wish you would leave your—well, your Muse alone, and come out."

Manvers looked out of the window.

"I suppose I shall have to come," he said. "But you are so violent, you never will consent to take carriage exercise. Luckily you can't ask me to play outdoor games here, as there are no outdoor games to play. Dominoes is the only outdoor game I can play—I have done so outside French cafés. I'm afraid I can't say it's too cold."

"I should insult your morality if you did," said Tom.

"Well, that's not so bad as insulting my intelligence."

"And that is exactly where we differ," said the other.

Arthur Wrexham was giving a small party the next evening, of a very *recherché* order, the dinner being served frothily in paper frills, shells, or on silver

skewers, and the candles shaded in so cunning a
manner that it was barely possible to see what the
food was. He lived in a somewhat sumptuous set of
rooms on the upper square of the town, and for a
week or more, as the sirocco had been blowing, had
been in a state of apparently irretrievable collapse.

A little balcony opening out of his dining-room
overlooked the square, and as the night was very hot,
the glass-door on to it was left open, and the noises
of the town came up to the guests as they sat at
dinner, like a low accompaniment to their own voices.
It had been one of those days when the divine climate
of Athens gives way to all the moods of an angry
woman. The morning had dawned bright and hot,
but before ten o'clock sirocco had sprung up, and
whoso walks in the face of sirocco is bathed through
and through in a fine white dust, most gritty. The
sirocco had brought the clouds from seawards, and
about one o'clock the rain came down, and laid
the dust. Then the sun shone violently till nearly
five, and the air was like to a sticky warm bath.
Later on it had clouded over again, and Tom remarked in a pause in the conversation that it had
begun to lighten.

It was quite a small party, the two younger sisters
of the American *chargé d'affaires* balancing Tom and
Manvers, Arthur and his sister making up the six.
The two Miss Vanderbilts both talked as much as
possible, sighed for " Parrus," and referred to the
Acropolis as " those lonely old ruins," but agreed that
Athens was " cunning."

" Well, I'm right down afraid of an electric storm,"

remarked Miss Vanderbilt, to whom Tom's remark about the lightning had been addressed, "and as for Bee, she won't be comfortable until she's said her prayers and is safe in the coal-store."

"The doctor at Parrus told me I'd a nervous temperament," remarked Bee, "and we all knew that before, but he made Popper pay up for saying so."

"'Speech is silver,'" remarked Manvers.

"Well, his speech was gold," said Miss Vanderbilt.

"Don't you dread electric storms, Miss Wrexham?"

Maud was sitting at the head of the table fanning herself. She had borne up against sirocco, but the sticky bath stage had finished her, and she felt, as Bee would have expressed it, as if they'd omitted to starch her when she was sent from the wash.

"No, I love them," said Maud. "I wish it would begin at once. It may make the air less stifling."

"Well, I'd sooner be stifled than lightning-struck," said Bee, "it's so sudden. Popper"—she referred to her father—"Popper says that an average electric storm discharges enough electric fluid to light Chicago for ten days. I think the table is just too elegant, Mr. Wrexham : where do you get your flowers from ? "

Things improved a little as dinner went on, and after fish Maud felt better.

"What a dreadful materialist one is, after all," she said. "Before dinner I was feeling that life was a failure in general, and I was a failure in particular, and now that I've had some soup and fish and half a glass of champagne, not only do I feel better bodily, but mentally and morally."

"Why, I think that's just beautifully put," said

Miss Vanderbilt. "When I feel homesick and lonesome, Bee says, ' It's all stomach.'"

"It's quite true," said Manvers. "I've only felt homesick once this year, and that was when Tom and I went to Ægina. It was fearfully hot, and all the lunch they had given us was hard-boiled eggs and cold greasy mutton. At that moment my whole soul, like Ruth's, was 'sick for home,' and the little cafés with oleanders in tubs, and awnings. I say my soul, but I suspect it was what Miss Vanderbilt tells us."

"Have I said anything wrong?" asked Miss Vanderbilt, looking round inquiringly. "I was only telling you what Bee said."

Tom laughed.

"It's easy enough to assure one's self that one is only an animal," he said. "I wish any one would prove to us that we are something more. When Manvers says his soul was sick, he is quite right to correct himself, and suspect that he meant the other thing."

"My dear fellow, the soul epidemic has ceased," said Manvers, "though I believe certain cliques try to keep it up. When you have looked at one of your gods or goddesses for an hour, you think you have been enjoying it with your soul, but you haven't really. At the end of the hour you feel tired, and after eating a mutton chop you can look at it again. The mutton chop feeds that part of you which has been spending tissue on the gods and goddesses. Well, we know what the mutton chop feeds."

"I won't assure you that you have a soul," said Tom, "but I assure you that I have."

"It's a most comfortable belief," murmured Manvers. "I don't grudge it you—I envy you. I wish you would do the same for me."

The storm was getting closer, and every now and then the pillars on the balcony were thrown into vivid blackness against the violet background of the sky. The balcony was deep and covered with the projecting eaves of the third story, and after dinner they all sat out on it. The air was absolutely still, and apparently all the population of Athens were in the square, making the most of the evening air before the storm broke.

Tom was sitting on the balustrade of the balcony, and Maud in a low chair near him. She leant forward suddenly.

"Do you remember hearing the hum of London one night, and saying it was the finest thing in the world?"

"Yes, very well. It was at the Ramsdens' dance. I shall hear it again soon."

"Ah, you are going almost immediately, I suppose, now?"

As she spoke, the sky to the south became for a moment a sheet of blue fire, with an angry scribble running through the middle of it, and Miss Vanderbilt ejaculated in shrill dismay.

Tom turned as Maud spoke, and the lightning illuminated her face vividly.

The glimpse he had of her was absolutely momentary, for just so long as that dazzling streamer flickered across the sky. But in the darkness and pause that followed he still saw her face before him, phantom-like, as when we shut our eyes suddenly in a strong light we still preserve on the retina the image of what we were looking at.

The phantom face slid slowly into the surrounding darkness, but it was not till the answering peal had burst with a sound as of hundreds of marbles being poured on to a wooden floor overhead that Tom answered the question which her voice had translated, but her eyes had asked.

"Well, I hardly know," he said. "When are you thinking of going home?"

In that moment, when the thunder was crackling overhead, a flood of shame and anger had come over Maud. Of her voice she had perfect command, as she knew, but that the lightning should have come at that moment and showed Tom her face was not calculable. But the absolute normalness of his tone reassured her.

"I shall go back in about a fortnight," she said.

"Why, that's just about when I am going," he said cheerfully. "I hope we shall travel together."

And with the unhesitatingness of well-bred delicacy he got off the balustrade and began to talk to Miss Vanderbilt.

Tom was far too much of a gentleman to let his mind consciously dwell on what he had seen during that flash of lightning. He regarded it like a remark accidentally overheard, of which he had no right to profit. In this case the wish was also absent, for though he liked Maud Wrexham immensely, he was already in the first stage of his love of idealism, which at present allowed no divided allegiance. Had Maud been an idealist herself, she

might have appeared to him merely as the incarnation of the spirit of idealism, in which case he would
have fallen down and worshipped. Tom had experienced a great shock the day before, when she
had expressed admiration for Manvers' *Dame qui
s'amuse.*

They were on the Acropolis together when Tom
mentioned it, and asked if she had seen it.

"Yes, he showed it me this morning. I think it's
extraordinarily good."

"But you don't like it?" asked Tom.

"Is it so terrible if I do? I don't like it as I like
this"—and she looked round largely at the Propylæa
—"but it gives me great pleasure to look at it. It's
so fearfully clever."

"No man can serve two masters," he said. "If
you like this, as you tell me you do, you loathe the
other necessarily."

"Oh, but you're just a little too fond of dogma-
tising," said Maud. "What you lay down as a
necessity may be only a limitation in your own
nature. How do you know I can't appreciate both?
As a matter of fact I do."

"Well, if you admire *La dame* you can't possibly
think of this—this which we see here—as supreme
and triumphant," said Tom.

"I'm not sure that I do. I think perhaps that I
have a touch of the scepticism you had—oh, ever so
long ago; six weeks, isn't it?—when you expected
to find that the grand style was obsolete. How we
shall quarrel when we manage the world, as we said
we proposed to do."

"It's quite certain that we shall never manage together, if there is this difference between us. I shall be wanting to celebrate Olympic games while you are laying out boulevards."

"Well, there's room for both," said Maud.

"No, no," said Tom, "there is never enough room for the best, far less for the worst."

"You are so splendidly illogical, Mr. Carlingford," she said suddenly ; "you see, you assume one is the best, and one the worst, and then build upon it. It is all very well to do that for one's self, but one becomes unconvincing if one does it for other people."

"It was better than if I had said at once that we differed fundamentally."

Maud turned away.

"Yes, perhaps. But what is the use of saying unpleasant things at all ? "

"Unpleasant ? " asked Tom, wrinkling his forehead. "Why, I differ from all my best friends diametrically on every conceivable topic."

That classification of her with his best friends was exactly the attitude of his nature towards her, and what he saw during that flash of lightning was naturally extremely surprising, for, as he reflected to himself, despair should not look from one's eyes when one hears that one's best friends are going away. But, as he was bound in honour to do, he dismissed it as far as possible from his mind, and listened to Miss Vanderbilt's scientific discourse about lightning.

"I should really feel much more comfortable if you would turn that big reflector round," she was saying to Arthur Wrexham. "They say it attracts the thunderbolts, and I'm sure we don't want to lay ourselves out to attract thunderbolts."

Arthur Wrexham remonstrated gently.

"Oh, it really has no effect whatever on it," he said. "In fact, glass is an insulator."

This entirely vague statement was found to be consoling, and Miss Vanderbilt continued—

"I should be ashamed to be as silly as Bee about it," she said. "Bee took off all her rings the last electric storm we had, and of course she couldn't recollect where she put them, and you should have seen the colour of her frock when she came out of the coal-store. Oh, gracious! why, that flash went off quite by my hand here."

Manvers was looking meditatively out into the night.

"The chances of being struck are so infinitesimal, Miss Vanderbilt, that I think it must have had a shot at you that time and missed. So by the law of probabilities it will not even aim at you again for a year or two. It really is a great consolation to know that one wouldn't hear the thunder if one was struck."

"Why, if you could hear the thunder, it would be all over," said Miss Bee, with a brilliant inspiration.

"So after each flash we must wait anxiously for the thunder," said Tom, "and then we shall know we've not been struck."

"I guess there's no great difficulty in finding out if you've been struck," said Bee. "Popper saw a man struck once, and he went all yellow. Tell me if

I am going all yellow, Mr. Manvers. I shan't try to conceal it."

" No amount of dissimulation would conceal the fact that one had gone all yellow," said Manvers.

The worst of the storm was soon over, but the clouds took possession of Hymettus, and continued growling and rumbling there. The two Americans took advantage of the lull to make their way home. "For nothing," Miss Vanderbilt protested, with shrill vehemence, " will make me get into a buggy during an electric storm ; " and Tom and Manvers followed their example, and walked back to their hotel.

Manvers had seen that look on Miss Wrexham's face at the moment of the flash of lightning, and he determined, wisely or unwisely, to mention it to Tom.

They were the only occupants of the smoking-room, and after getting his cigar under way, he asked the other lazily—

" By the way, what were you saying to Miss Wrexham that made her look like an image of despair? I caught sight of her face for a moment during a flash of lightning, and it looked extra-ordinary."

" Yes, I noticed it too," said Tom carelessly, " and wondered what was the matter. She had been rather upset by sirocco, she said."

" My dear fellow, girls don't look like petrified masks of despair because sirocco has been blowing for a couple of hours in the morning."

" Well, I suppose it must have been something else then," said Tom.

"What a brilliant solution! I am inclined to agree with you."

Manvers remained silent for a few moments, balancing in his mind his disinclination to appear officious or meddling, and his desire to perhaps do Tom a service. As a matter of fact he had heard the question which had accompanied that look on Miss Wrexham's face, and it had confirmed the idea he had long entertained that she was falling in love with Tom, and Tom was not consciously in love with her. His tone of absolute indifference to the subject might be either assumed or natural.

"You see a good deal of her, don't you?" he went on. "She's clever, I think, and she's certainly got a good eye. She made several suggestions about my little figure which were admirable."

"She told me she admired it," said Tom, "and I told her she couldn't admire it if she admired Greek work."

"She wouldn't agree with that. She thinks that she can appreciate both. It must be so nice to have that belief in yourself, to think that you are all sorts of people, instead of one sort of person. But it breaks down in practice——"

Manvers paused a moment, and decided to risk it.

"That look on her face this evening was of a woman who had broken down. I have often wondered, by the way, whether you ever have guessed how fortunate you are."

Tom sat up.

"Did you hear what she said?" he asked.

"Certainly, or I shouldn't have mentioned it."

"Look here," Tom said, "it was quite accidental that either of us ever saw that look. She couldn't have foreseen that a flash of lightning would come at that moment. I have tried to keep myself from thinking of it, but it won't do. I hate conceited fools who are always imagining things of that sort, but as you have spoken of it, it is absurd for me to pretend not to know what you mean. Damn it all! She looked—she looked as if my going away made a difference to her."

Manvers drew a puff of smoke very slowly, and held his breath a moment. Then he began to speak, and it seemed to Tom slightly appropriate that his words should be, as it were, visible. They seemed a concrete embodiment of practical advice.

"I think she is very fond of you," he said.

"What am I to do?" demanded Tom.

"Do?" he said. "I really don't understand you. If you are in love with her, I imagine your course is not so difficult; if not, you may be sure you soon will be."

"I should think it was the most unlikely thing in the world," returned Tom. "If I had thought that, it is hardly likely I should have asked you what to do."

"Pardon me, you never asked me, except under pressure. I made it quite clear that I wanted to be asked; you did not wish to ask me at all. I have my opinion to deliver. Listen. You are very fond of her, whether you know it or not. Just now you are stark mad about heathen gods. You say to yourself, or you would say to yourself if you formulated your thought, that you could only fall in love with a girl in the grand style.   That is quite ridiculous. They may or may not be very good as statues, but they would certainly not answer as wives.   In the natural course of things you will get over that.   Try to do so as quickly as possible.   Look at Miss Wrexham instead of the Parthenon.   You can't marry the Parthenon.   That flash of lightning occurring when it did gave me a stronger belief in the existence of a beneficent Providence than I have ever felt before. It is only a superstitious idea, I know, but when a chance falls so divinely pat as that, you feel inclined to applaud somebody."

Tom did not look at all inspired by these practical suggestions.

"It won't do," he said.   "You take an admirably sensible view of the situation, if it happened to be you, but unfortunately it's I."

"I may be a knave," said Manvers resignedly, "but, thank God, I am not a fool.   I don't suppose you will deny that you are a fool, Tom; and you really should give my advice a great deal of consideration.   It is not every day that a flash of lightning shows you how high an opinion a perfectly charming heiress has of you, and it is, I think, both folly and wickedness not to suppose that it was sent you for some good or clever purpose.   You really can't help feeling that it was a very clever thing to send the lightning just then.   You must have a special Providence who looks after you."

"I hope you don't think you will convince me," said Tom.

“Oh dear, no, but I had to ease my—my conscience by entering a strong protest. I feel better now, thanks.”

“That's right. But to descend to practical details, won't the fact that she suspects I saw what I did make it rather awkward for us to meet?”

“Are you sure she suspects it?”

“No, not sure, or I should go away at once. I may be a fool, but I am not a knave.”

Manvers extended his hand in the air deprecatingly.

“Oh, don't make repartees during a thunderstorm. They so seldom mean anything, in fact the better a repartee is, the less it means; and they give a nervous shock to the repartcee—if I may coin a word. Also he is bound in mere politeness to cudgel his brains to see if they do mean something. When you have an opportunity you must say she looked so awfully tired last night, and that you noticed her face once in a blaze of lightning, and you were quite frightened; she looked so out of sorts, or done up, or run down, or something. It's very simple. But is there no chance——”

“No, not a vestige,” said Tom. “Besides, I don't believe that you really advise what you say.”

“Tom, you've never heard me give advice before, and you must attach the proper weight to it as a rare product.”

“Why, you are always giving me advice about turning realist.”

“No, you're wrong there; I only prophesy that you will. That I often prophesy, I don't deny. There is nothing so amusing to one's self, or so unconvincing to other people. It is the most innocent of amusements. Besides, you can always compare yourself to Cassandra—she was classical—when people don't believe you."

"Yes, that must be a great comfort," said Tom slowly, who was thinking about Miss Wrexham.

Manvers got up.

"You are falling into a reverie. You ought to know that reveries are an unpardonable breach of manners. I shall go to my statuette. That is the best of being up to date in your art ; you never need be without companions."

"Come down, O maid, from yonder mountain height," quoted Tom, half mock-heroically.

"My dear boy, it won't do," said Manvers. "She won't come down for that. You have to fetch her down, and she is very like the rest of us really. She soon assimilates. Besides, luckily, maids on mountain heights are rare. They find it doesn't pay."

Tom left the room, and Manvers went to the window. The rain had come on again, and was falling hot and heavy through the night. Manvers dropped a steadfast oath into the storm, and then, instead of going to his statuette, went to bed, and lay awake till the darkness grew grey.

"The world is damnably awry," was the burden of his thoughts. "I suppose it is to teach us not to set our affections on things below. They might have chosen a less diabolical method of teaching us, Providence is really very vulgar sometimes."

Maud woke next morning in the rationalizing mood, and the event of the thunderstorm, which had made her disposed to be uneasy the night before, fell back into its proper place in the scheme of things. The absence of the sirocco no doubt contributed to this calmer attitude, for, as a philosopher found out very long ago, it is possible to reach the soul through the subtle gateways of the body, and a thin light Athenian north wind is one of the subtlest physicians of the mind, and can find out the most tortuous and intricate passages through the house of our body. This acting on a naturally rational mind had produced its legitimate effect. Probably Tom had not noticed it ; in any case, if he had, there were much less metaphysical reasons which would lend themselves to a much more obvious inference. She was tired, the lightning had dazzled her, Miss Vanderbilt was on her nerves ; all these things were so likely, and the real reason so unlikely. Consequently, when she left the house after breakfast, to go up to the Acropolis and finish a sketch, with the almost certain probability of seeing Tom there, she felt that their intercourse would be as easy as usual.

The view she had chosen was of the little Niké temple seen through two headless columns of the Propylæa, with a glimpse behind of the sea and the hills of Argolis, and she painted on for half an hour or so without thinking of anything but what she was doing. But by degrees her glances at the far hills became longer, and the acts of painting shorter, her eyes saw less and less of what she was looking at, though they rested more intently on the scene, and at last she put down her palette and leant against the white marble wall behind her.

What was the matter with her? Why had she this unfathomable feeling for a man who was perhaps less unfathomable than any one she had ever seen? A frank English face, a keen boyish vitality, an almost comical self-sufficiency, demanding as its only food the contemplation of Greek sculpture—it all seemed fathomable enough. She half wished he would go back to England at once, yet even with that view in front of her, for the sake of which she nominally climbed up to the Acropolis, she felt that another factor was wanting, a nought, she told herself, which had the inexplicable trick of turning her units into tens. In any case she would go back to England not with him, but by herself. He was spoiling everything for her. Then came the reaction. "How ridiculous it will be! I asked him when he was going back, and hoped we might go together, and now I am deciding not to go with him. He is a most pleasant companion, and what is he to me"—the next thought came like an echo—"or I to him?"

Her thoughts had taken the bits in their mouths, and were running away, and so, metaphorically speaking, she jumped off the runaway vehicle and came into serious collision with *terra firma ;* literally, she took up her palette and went on with her painting.

To Tom, also, his visits to the Acropolis distinctly gained something by the constant expectation of meeting Maud there. She had run him to ground the other day when she had made him confess that he cared for nothing but his art, and though the conclusion had been forced from his mouth, he knew it was not quite true. What he cared for was life and its best possibilities in the way of beauty, and his enthusiasm, he knew, saw and tended to state everything too violently. He found Maud sympathetic, eager and charming as a companion, and no other thought had entered his head about her, until the incident of the thunderstorm, which had been unexpected and very bewildering. And in his deep perplexity as to what he had better do, he took the eminently straightforward and most promising course of doing nothing at all, of behaving normally. He had, as it were, taken a tentative mental sounding of his feelings towards her for his own satisfaction, but he found that the bottom was soon reached. In any case the depths were not unplumbable, which would have been the only reason for doing anything. He was in love with life, with all of life that was best, and the idea of falling in love with any particular little bit of it would have seemed to him as incredible as writing sonnets, in the style of the eighteenth-century poets, to women's finger-nails; and these always appeared to him most profitless performances. To fall in love must always seem slightly ridiculous until one falls in love.

Then it came about that not long after Maud had begun painting again, Tom walked up the steps as usual, and sat with his hands clasped round one knee, on the steps at Maud's feet, and talked as usual, and absorbed the beauty of the scene.

"It's the only way," he said on this particular morning, "to hope to get hold of the spirit of Greek art. You can never arrive at the spirit of a thing through its details—the details shape themselves if you know the spirit. You see artists in the Louvre copying Raphael all their lives, but they never really remind you of him. If they were to go to Umbrian villages and live the life he lived among the people, and to feast—I don't mean literally—on the ox-eyed faces of peasant women and then come back, they might be able to copy him with some success, or still better, if they had genius, produce original pictures which were like Raphael's. They go the wrong way about it."

Maud was painting intently, and did not answer for a moment.

"Yes, I think you are right," she said. "It's no use copying merely. A mere copy only, at its best approximates to a coloured photograph."

"It's so utterly the wrong way to go about it," said Tom. "To arrive at the right results, you have to follow the right method from the beginning. For instance, when I go back to England, and am shut up in a dingy studio under a grey sky, and my work looks hideous and dead, I shall bring back the inspiration not by thinking only of Hermes, but of the time I have spent here on these steps, looking out over the Propylæa to Salamis."

He leant back on the step where he was sitting, and looked up at Maud for a moment. She put down the brush she held and was looking at him, as if she was waiting eagerly to hear something more. But Tom apparently was unconscious of her look, and she took up her brush again.

Tom tilted his hat a little more over his eyes, and took out his cigarette-case.

"It's becoming real to me at last," he said. "I think I am beginning to know what it all means."

"You'll have to show us," said Maud. "A man who is a sculptor, and who knows what this means, is certainly bound to produce statues which are really like Greek statues."

Tom sat up.

"I don't care how conceited it sounds," he said excitedly, "but I am going to try to do no less. It is astonishing how little I care what happens. That is my aim, and if I don't realize it, it will be the fault of something I can't control."

"But what is there which a man who is earnest cannot control?" she asked.

"There is only one question in the world which is even harder to answer," said Tom, "and that is, what is there in the world which he can control? What is to happen to me if some morning I wake up to find that I think Manvers' statuettes ideal, and Greek art *passé?* How do I know it will not happen to me? Who will assure me of it?"

"Oh well, how do you know that you won't wake up some morning, and find that your nose has disappeared during the night, and a hand grown in its place?" asked Maud. "The one is as unnatural to your mind as the other is to the body."

"But all sorts of unnatural things happen to your mind," said Tom. "That I should have suddenly felt that nothing but Greek art was worth anything was just as unnatural. It is just as unnatural that, at a given moment, a man falls in love——"

He stopped quite suddenly and involuntarily, but Maud's voice broke in.

"Not at all," she said. "You see, it happens to most men; it is the rule rather than the exception, whereas the disappearance of one's nose would be unique, I should think."

Her voice was so perfectly natural, so absolutely unaffected, that Tom made a short mental note, to the effect that Manvers was the greatest idiot in the world except one, which was a more consoling thought than he would have imagined possible. His determination to be quite normal had become entirely superfluous—a billetless bullet.

"Yes, but because it happens constantly, it makes it none the less extraordinary," he said.

"Certainly not; but you can no longer call it unnatural."

"I call everything unnatural that seems to me unintelligible," remarked Tom, with crisp assurance.

Maud began to laugh.

"What a great many unnatural things there must be," she said, "according to your view. Why, the sun rising in the morning is unnatural. But it would be much more unnatural if it did not."

"If I go on, I shall soon begin to talk nonsense," said Tom, concessively, "and that would be a pity."

"Well, let's get back on to safe ground," said Maud. "Come and tell me what to do with that column. It isn't right."

Tom picked up his stick, and shoved his hat back on his head.

"I don't understand you," he said, after looking at the picture for a moment. "I believe you know what the spirit of all this is—at least, your picture, which is admirable, looks as if you did—and yet you like Manvers' statuettes. I think you are unnatural."

"Do you remember a talk we had, when we were staying with you, about being broad?"

"Yes, perfectly. Why?"

"Because I think you are being narrow. I dare say this is the best, but that doesn't prevent other things from being good."

Maud bent over her painting again, because she wanted to say more, and it is always easier to criticize if one is not biassed by the sight of the person whom one is criticizing.

"You seem to think you can see all round a truth. If the truth is big enough to be worth anything, it is probable that you can only see a little bit of it."

"Why—why—— " began Tom.

"Yes, I know. I am thinking of what you yourself said the other day about religion, when you told me what passed between you and Mr. Markham after the revivalist meeting. I am quoting your own words. They seem to me very true!"

"But how is it possible in this instance?" said Tom, striking the marble pavement with his stick. "If one of the two is good, the other is bad. They are utterly opposed."

Maud turned round on him suddenly.

"Ah, I thought you would say that," she said. "It

would be as reasonable for you to say that because there is sunshine here now, there is sunshine all over the world. Yet in Australia it is about midnight. Light is utterly opposed to darkness. Yet this is one world. You don't allow of there being more of it than you can see."

Tom shifted his position.

"Go on," he said. "I am not so limited that I do not wish to be told so."

"You showed just the same smallness when you talked to me about Cambridge," she said. "You thought that you were broad, because you thought that it was narrow. Did it never occur to you that you thought it was narrow simply because you were not broad enough to take it in ? The one explanation is as simple as the other."

"I'm quite convinced I'm broader than Markham," said Tom, frankly. "He thinks about nothing but snuffy old scholiasts."

"And you think about nothing but Greek art ; you have said so yourself. Is it quite certain that you are broader than he ? "

Tom stood for a moment thinking.

"Do you think I'm narrow ? " he asked at length.

"That is beside the point," she said. "If I did not, it might only show that I was narrow in the same way as you."

"No, that can't be," said Tom, plunging at the only opening he could see. "You must remember you like Manvers' statuettes."

"Well, from that standpoint I do think you narrow,"

she said. " It seems to me very odd that you shouldn't see how good they are."

" Do you mean how clever they are ? "

" It is the same thing, as far as this question goes. You don't recognize their cleverness even, since you dislike them so."

Tom drew a sigh of relief.

" Oh well, then, you are wrong about it. I fully recognize how clever they are."

" Then you don't admire cleverness, which is a great deficiency."

" On the contrary, I do admire cleverness; but Manvers' seems to me perverted cleverness. I admire ingenuity as an abstract quality, though I don't care for those diabolical little puzzles which every one used to play with last year."

Maud shut up her paint-box, and rose.

" It's no use arguing," she said. " An argument never comes to anything if you disagree; no argument ever converted any one."

" But I'm quite willing to be converted," said Tom.

" Well, to tell you the truth, I'm not at all sure that I want to convert you. I like you better as you are. Who is it who speaks of the ' genial impulses of love and hate' ? Your hatred for Mr. Manvers' things is so intensely genial, so natural to you."

They walked down the steps together, and stood for a moment looking over the broad plain, with its fields of corn already sprouting, stretching up towards the grey mass of Parnes.

" This place suits me," said Maud. " I shall be sorry to go."

"Have you settled when you are going?" asked Tom.

"Not precisely ; why?"

"Because I shall come with you, if you will allow me : I must be going soon."

Maud's face flushed a little, and she turned towards him.

"That will be charming. I shall go in about ten days or a fortnight, as I said last night. You know, now and then, even here with all this winter sun, and the Acropolis there, I want a grey English sky and long green fields."

"So do I ; and cart-horses, and big green trees— even snow and frost, for the sake of the clean frosty smell on cold mornings. Here's Manvers coming under a large white umbrella. I wonder what he wants to come to the Acropolis for."

Manvers came up to them, and paused.

"I am taking a little walk," he explained. "Mrs. Trachington has been paying me a little visit, or rather, I have been paying her a little visit."

"Who is Mrs. Trachington?" asked Maud.

"Mrs. Trachington is a female staying at our hotel," said Manvers, gently wiping his face. "She has praying-meetings. This morning I was walking past her room, when she came out and asked me to look at some picture she had just got. It was a charming landscape by Gialliná, of delicious tone. But after a moment I looked up and caught her eye. There was a prayer in it. It is wicked that a woman with blatant prayer in her eye should possess such a picture. So I ran away. I came up here for safety."

Tom laughed uproariously.

"Manvers is fanciful," he said. "His is a morbidly sensitive nature."

"My dear fellow, you would have done just the same," he said. "I don't think Mrs. Trachington's methods are at all straightforward. They are Jesuitical. Besides, I can't go praying about all over the hotel."

"Well, you'd better come down with us," said Tom.

Manvers looked at Maud a moment.

"No, I'm going to stop here a little. Of old sat Freedom on the heights. I shall be free here."

"But she stepped down, you know," said Tom.

"So shall I by-and-by," said Manvers. "That was after she sat on the heights."

Maud and Tom walked down past the theatre and into the low-lying streets to the east of the Acropolis. The fresh oranges had come in from the country, and they passed strings of heavily laden mules and donkeys, driven by dirty, picturesque boys, barefooted, black-haired, and black-eyed. It was a festal day, and the women had turned out in bright Albanian costumes, and the streets were charged with southern colour, and brilliant with warm winter sun and cloudless sky. Through open spaces between the houses they could see the tawny columns of the Parthenon standing clear-cut and virgin against the blue ; for the moment the earlier and later civilizations seemed harmonious.

Tom and Manvers met later in the day, and Tom retailed his decision of the morning.

"We were both utterly wrong," he said. "It makes me grow hot all over to think of what we said last night. I acted just as a man of that class which I detest so much would act."

"I drew the inferences demanded by common sense," said Manvers, who was not convinced.

"By your common sense!" rejoined Tom. "You can't talk of common sense as a constant quality; it varies according to the man who exercises it. There are certain occasions when one's inferences are based on instinct, which is a much surer thing than common sense. One of these occasions occurred this morning."

"Ah, but your instinct may be wrong, and nobody can convince you of it. It is a much more dangerous thing to trust to. If you base your action on reasons which can be talked out lengthways, you can make certain whether you are right or not."

Tom rose with some irritation.

"My dear fellow, I don't believe you know what I mean by instincts," he said, and strolled away.

Manvers found a certain delicate pleasure in this exhibition of human weakness on the part of Tom, and the reason by which he accounted for it in his own mind was clearly a very likely one. He argued that Tom was not quite so certain that he was right as he had hoped, and such a state of mind, Manvers allowed, was very galling.

Meantime Maud had gone home, lunched with her brother, and announced that she was going home in about a fortnight in company with Tom. Arthur

Wrexham had a vague feeling that this was not quite proper, and indicated it.

"Is that the sort of thing people do now?" he asked. "I really only ask for information."

"I don't understand," said Maud.

"I mean girls travelling alone with young men."

Maud laughed.

"Don't be anxious on my account," she said. "I shall outrage no one's sense of propriety."

Arthur felt he had done his share, and subsided again.

"Of course you know best," he said. "I only suggested it in case it had not occurred to you. So Carlingford is going too, is he? I thought he meant to stop here longer?"

"No, he's going to begin work at once. He says he has got hold of the spirit of the thing. He is so delightfully certain about everything."

"A little dogmatic sometimes, isn't he?" asked Arthur.

"No; dogmatists have always the touch of the prig about them. He has none of that."

Arthur Wrexham put his feet upon a chair.

"I think he is just a little barbarous," he said. "Doesn't he ever make your head ache?"

"No, I can't say that he does," said Maud slowly "I think he is one of the most thoroughly satisfactory people."

"He is so like a sort of mental highwayman sometimes," said her brother. "He makes such sudden inroads on one's intelligence. He catechizes one

about the Propylæa.   That is so trying, especially if
you know nothing about it."

Maud laughed.

"Oh well, if your purse is empty, you need not
fear highwaymen," she said.

A fortnight afterwards they both left for Marseilles
by the same boat.   She sailed on Sunday morning,
and Arthur Wrexham and Manvers came down to
the Piræus to see them off.   Manvers and Tom took
a few turns about the upper deck and talked, while
Arthur sat down in Maud's deck-chair and was
steeped in gentle melancholy.

"So in about a year's time you will see me," said
the former.   "I shall be in London next winter.   At
present I feel like an Old Testament prophet in his
first enthusiasm of prophecy.   I wonder if they ever
had any doubts about the conclusiveness of their
remarks.   I at least have none.   I won't exactly
name the day when you will become a convert, but
I will give you about a year.   Consequently, when
you see me next, our intercourse may be less dis-
cordant."

"I hope it won't," remarked Tom ; "and I don't
believe it will."

"It's always nice to disagree with people, I know,"
said the other ; "it adds a sauce to conversation.
But I don't mind abandoning that.   You really will
do some excellent work when you come round."

"I am going to do an excellent Demeter mourning
for Persephone," said Tom.

Manvers lit another cigarette from the stump of
his old one.

"I did an Apollo, I remember," he said. "I wish you would do an Apollo too. I have mine still; it serves as a sort of milestone. It has finely developed hands and feet, just like all those Greek statues."

"And you prefer neat shoes now," said Tom.

"Why, yes. Whether Apollo has finely developed feet or not, he wears shoes or boots, the neater the better. I hate seeing a man with untidy boots. But even untidy boots are better than none at all. Ah, there's that outrageous bell warning me to leave the boat. Good-bye, Tom. Athens will be very dull without you. I shall cultivate Mrs. Trachington."

"Do, and make a statuette of her. She is a very modern development. Good-bye, old boy."

It was a raw December day when their train slid into Victoria Station, and a cold thick London fog was drifting sluggishly in from the streets. Any desire that Maud may have felt for English grey was amply realized. The pavement under the long glass vault was moist with condensed vapour, and the air was cold in that piercing degree which is the peculiar attribute of an English thaw. The Chathams were in London, and Lady Chatham had "worked in" the landau with such success that she just arrived at the platform when the train drew up. She was immensely friendly to Tom, and remarked how convenient it was that they had arranged to come together.

Tom said good-bye to them at their carriage door. Just as they drove off Maud leant out of the window.

"You've no idea how I have enjoyed the journey," she said. "You are at Applethorpe, aren't you? Come and see us soon."

CHAPTER IX.

THE weather signalized Tom's return to England by
a blizzard from the north, which for twenty-four hours
spread sheet after sheet of snow on the ground, till
one would have thought that the linen-presses of the
elements were empty.   He had caught a slight cold,
and the only possible course was to sit by the fire,
talk to his father, who seemed actually pleased to see
him, and think of the Acropolis.   But during the
second night the soft snow-laden outlines of the hills
and trees suddenly crispened and crystallized, and a
still, windless frost gripped the white earth.   A winter's
sun hung like a burnished copper plate low in the
south, and the sight of the keeper with his round
cheery face, asking if there were any orders, rendered
the house impossible.

"Yes, I'll come out in half an hour," said Tom.
"Get a few beaters, and we'll just walk through the
woods.   And send down to the vicarage to ask
Mr. Markham if he'd care for a tramp.   They don't
have pheasants in Greece, Kimberley: there's a
country for you!"

"Mr. Ted's not at home, sir," said Kimberley.

"I know, but his father is.   He shoots very well.
Send at once, will you?   I want to start."

May had already left the house when the keeper came to bring Tom's message to her father, and Mr. Markham left a note for her saying where he had gone, and that he would not be in for lunch. He was devoted to shooting, but of late years had not been able to indulge his taste; so some parish work which could easily be put off, as well as the chance of a quiet hour at his Aristophanes, fell into their proper places in the scheme of things.

It was about half-past twelve, and Tom was standing alone at the end of a small clump of fir-trees, round which he had stolen with infinite precautions in order to avoid startling the pigeons. He had studied the habits of pigeons in this particular spot with much care for several years, and the keeper always alluded to it as "Master Tom's cover." It stood on a knoll of rising ground, some quarter of a mile away from the house, and by dint of long experience and frequent failure Tom had found that if the pigeons were artfully disturbed by beaters entering towards the centre from opposite sides they always broke cover at two particular points at opposite ends of the knoll, and that one gun stationed at each of these points became a fiery sword, turning, as far as the pigeons were concerned, every way. Tom was standing at one end of the cover, having seen Mr. Markham to his place, and was expecting every moment to hear the tapping of the beaters' sticks and the swan-song of the pigeons' wings. He was on the edge of a little footpath which led across the park from the village, half hidden from it by a thick bramble bush, behind which he had placed himself so that he could see without being seen. But at this most critical of all moments he heard with some impatience the sound of a footstep coming crisply and quickly along the frozen path. The path took a sudden bend almost exactly as it came opposite to him, and simultaneously he heard the faint tapping of the beaters' sticks and saw a figure come round the corner.

For one moment Time stopped, and he stared blankly, wonderingly. Then half to himself, half aloud, he said—

"Oh, all ye gods, she is a goddess!"

The next moment he recognized her, and springing out from his bramble bush he took off his hat to May Markham, and wondered if she remembered him.

The beaters beat, and the pigeons started from the branches, and flew out in the pre-ordained manner, threading their way between the tops of the thick trees, as they and their deceased relations had often done before. Mr. Markham had one of the most delightful five minutes that falls to the lot of sportsmen, and straight over Tom's head as he stood in the path the steely targets tacked and swerved. But Tom heeded not; the swan-song of their clapping wings for once was unheard and unfulfilled, for in his heart there was another song, no last song of birds' wings, but the first maddening music which a man's heart offers to a woman, the song of a youth to a maid, the song of the lover to the beloved, which rises up day by day, and hour by hour, and keeps this old earth young.

May replied that of course she remembered him, and supposed that he had just come back from Greece, and a golden silence descended again. Tom was standing on ground an inch or two lower than the girl, and their faces were on a level : if anything, she appeared the taller of the two, and as his eyes rested on hers they were inclined slightly upwards, so that a thin rim of white showed below his honest brown iris. May was with her back to the low southern sun, but it just caught a few outlying hairs which strayed from beneath her hat, and turned them into spun gold. Her lips were slightly pouted, and through the length of her mouth ran a thin even line showing the white edge of her upper teeth. She had been walking quickly, and her nostrils swelled and receded with each breath, and one could just see the rise and fall of her bosom beneath her blue tightly buttoned jacket.

She met Tom's eager gaze with unembarrassed, unaverted looks. They had been excellent friends when Tom had stayed with them not long ago at Chesterford, and this seemed simply a continuation of their early comradeship, for it was evident that he was quite a boy still. But almost immediately something in his look, or some half-conscious reminiscence of that moment, a fortnight ago, when she had looked at herself in the glass in Mr. Carlingford's drawing-room, caused her to turn her eyes down, and for the first time she noticed that Tom was carrying a gun. The desire for an intelligible reason why he should have been found standing in a bramble bush on a cold winter's morning had not appealed to her before.

"Have you had good sport?" she asked, pointing to the gun.

Tom followed the direction of her finger, and to him also apparently it occurred for the first time that he was out shooting.

"Yes, very fair," said Tom. "By the way, what's happened to the pigeons?"

Almost as he spoke the head keeper emerged from the bracken, proud in the consciousness of a skilfully executed duty. He touched his hat to May, and turned to Tom.

"Wonderful lot of pigeons in this morning, sir," he said. "Didn't hear you shooting, Master Tom."

"No, I didn't see any birds. Did any come out over me?"

"Ten or twelve at least, sir, and the same over Mr. Markham."

"Oh, well, it can't be helped," said Tom, rather confusedly. "We'll go home to lunch now, Kimberley, and come out again after. We're quite close to the house."

"Is my father out with you?" asked May.

"Yes, I suppose you had gone out when I sent down. You can't come through here—the brambles are so bad. Wait a moment, though."

Tom gave his gun to the keeper, and trampled down the mixed bramble and bracken. There was one long spray which kept asserting itself again and again straight across the path, waving about two or three feet from the ground. In a fit of sudden impatience Tom seized it in his hand and bent it back among the other bushes. As a natural and inevitable consequence his hand was covered with large prickles.

"Oh, why did you do that?" asked May; "I'm sure you've hurt yourself."

Tom laughed.

"The will is destiny," he said. "I wish to go this way, and the bramble was in the light. That I got pricked was destiny, but another kind of destiny. We shall meet your father if we go this way."

To the intensest annoyance of Tom they did meet Mr. Markham in a few moments, walking towards them. The rational thing for him would have been to go round by the path instead of taking a short cut, and poor Tom had pricked his fingers for nothing.

"Capital five minutes I had there, Tom," said he. "Why, where are you from, May?"

"I've just come from the Mills, on my way home to lunch," said she.

"Oh, but you'll lunch with us," said Tom confidently. "We are just going home. Look, there is the house quite close, and we are going to lunch at one in order to shoot again for an hour or two afterwards."

"Thanks, I'm afraid I had better go home," said May.

"Oh, but why—why?" asked Tom, forgetting manners and everything else in the contemplation of his visions incarnate.

May turned towards him, smiling.

"Well, I really must go off again in half an hour. It's very kind of you to ask me," she added suddenly.

"That's splendid! We shall be very soon off

again too. Mr. Markham has been walking me off my legs already, and I know he will want to do it again the moment lunch is over."

Mr. Carlingford was standing at the library window as the party came down the grass slope to the house, and a smile gathered on his lips as he watched Tom talking eagerly to May. Then, half to himself, half aloud, he made the following enigmatical quotation: "'As for the gods of the heathen,'" and rang the bell to order another place at lunch.

Thus entered Tom into the garden of man's heritage; the crowning gift of love was added to youth and life, the golden key which unlocks the gate of Paradise was in his hand. His whole previous life had in a moment been flushed with an intenser colour; he was like a man born blind, who, until his eyes were opened, knew not, could not have known, his limitations. It was bewitching, blinding, but altogether lovely, this new world into which he had entered. For him the period of bitter joy and sweetest anguish had begun.

That night he went to his bedroom early, saying he was tired and sleepy with the cold air; then ran upstairs three steps at a time, feeling an unutterable desire to be alone with his love; another presence, he felt, was a desecration. He blew out his candle, and lay down full length on his bed, while the firelight danced and shivered on the walls and the flames flapped in the grate, and spread out his arms as if to take the truth in. How was it possible, he wondered, that a man who had ever been in love could speak of it? Love was something white and sacred, a clear flame burning in a casket of gold, to be hidden from the gaze of men. No, that was not it at all; love was a glorious conquering god, and his captives should stand in the market-place of cities and cry aloud, "See, I can move neither hand nor foot, I am chained in golden chains, my limbs are heavy with the chains of love. Envy me, bless me, weep for joy that I am a captive. Bind me closer yet, crush me beneath the weight of fetters. Lead me about in your triumphant procession ; I am a captive, a prisoner."

He sat up, wondering at himself. It was not possible. How can the daughters of the gods dwell with men ? " Why, everything is possible to me," he answered himself. " I am in love, I am the king of all the earth. Nothing is impossible."

This modest conviction made lying still impossible. He got off his bed, and began walking up and down the room, stopping now and then opposite the fire, which burned brightly and frostily. In the red glow of the coals his brown eyes looked black ; his mouth was a little open, and his breath came quickly, as if he had been running a race. His smooth boyish face, tanned by southern suns, was flushed with excitement. Once in his walk he stopped, stood on tip-toe, and stretched himself till he felt every muscle in his body quiver and tingle.

Sleep was impossible, everything but violent action was impossible, thought was impossible and inevitable. Surely it was morning by this time. His watch reminded him that it was just a quarter to twelve ; he had been in his room only twenty minutes. Perhaps time had stopped, perhaps he was dead, perhaps this was heaven. He would go to the house-top and cry to the four quarters of heaven, and to the listening earth, the story of his love, how he was out shooting pigeons, and standing in a bramble bush, when he saw her for whom the world was made walking towards him. He would run down through the village to the vicarage, and stand and look at the little house in which she slept. What was space? How could she be in a room, and that room be in a house? for she was everywhere. Heaven and earth could not hold her; even the thought of her filled all the world. That afternoon he had seen the tall bare-limbed trees, the level rays of the setting sun, the rose-tinged fields of snow, all lovely because she was lovely, all bursting with the knowledge of her. He should have stood alone when the sun was just setting and questioned them of her. He should have taken the level rays of the sun into his arms, and kissed them because they were beautiful with one infinitesimal fraction of her beauty. He should have torn the secret of her from all Nature.

Mr. Carlingford laid a little trap for Tom next morning, which that young gentleman fell into head-long, much to his father's amusement. It appeared that Mr. Markham had expressed a desire to consult a certain book which Mr. Carlingford knew was in the house, but had been unable to find till this morning. Would Tom, therefore, be so good as to ring the bell, in order that a boy might be sent down with it?

"I'll take it if you like, father," said Tom, with much over-acted nonchalance.

"No; why should you?"

"I—I rather want to see Mr. Markham and ask him if he can come out shooting again to-morrow, and find out when Ted's coming home."

"Well, why not write a note?" said his father, smiling to himself at this lamentably superficial excuse.

"Oh, I've got nothing to do," said Tom, rising, "I may as well go. And Gibson says the pond bears; perhaps Markham will like to skate."

Tom rang at the vicarage bell, and was apparently unable to make it sound, but at the second attempt produced a peal which would have awakened the dead, and asked if the vicar was in.

"Yes, he is in his study. This way, please."

Tom peeped in through a chink of the drawing-room door, with his heart thumping at his ribs, and followed the servant into the study. Mr. Markham was compiling some notes from an annotated text of the "Clouds," but seemed glad to see him, and grateful for the book. A brilliant idea struck the young strategist, and he blurted it out.

"I came also to tell you that the pond bore, if you or—or—any one wanted to skate, and I shall be awfully glad if you would shoot to-morrow again. And oh, Mr. Markham, you know I'm very stupid at Greek, but since I've been to Athens I've simply loved it. I'm reading Aristophanes—at least, I'm going to, and I wonder if I might bring difficulties and so on to you—it would help me so much, if it's not too much bother to you?"

"That's capital of you," said Mr. Markham heartily. "I do like to see young men behave as if they had not done with classics when they leave the University.

My dear boy, of course you may. Come any morning or every morning. I set to work pretty early, and always read classics till eleven in the morning."

"Thank you so much," said Tom ; "but you'll find me fearfully stupid."

"Nonsense, nonsense ! one is only stupid about the things one doesn't care for. I'll tell you what. You must come to breakfast here whenever you want, and then we can set to work together at nine. I know your father doesn't breakfast till late."

"That is awfully good of you," said Tom, "but I shall take you at your word, you know. And, by the way, perhaps Miss Markham would like to know the pond bore. I might tell her, if she's in."

"No, May's out," said her father. "She is always doing something."

"But what can she find to do here ? " asked Tom, divided between his desire to loiter and his wish to run away.

"She's always visiting these poor folks," said Mr. Markham. "She spends half her day among them. Very nipping weather," and he stirred the fire.

"I see," said Tom ; "how awfully good of her ! Well, I must go. I shall skate this afternoon. Really it would be a pity to waste such a lovely bit of ice. Gibson says it's quite splendid."

"Many thanks. I dare say one or both of us will come. It's a pity Ted's not here. He's so fond of it. Good-bye. Mind you take me at my word about the Aristophanes."

Tom lingered and loitered through the village, ordered a bookshelf which he did not want from the carpenter, in case of May being there, and some bad and unnecessary tobacco from the village store, but saw her not. But there were the prospects of the afternoon and the Aristophanes lessons to fall back on.

So through the quiet country weeks their two young lives flowed inevitably towards each other, like two streams which, rising on distant ranges of hills, yet must some day meet in the valley between them. Though their natures sprang from widely distant sources, it was inevitable they would some time join.

But to continue the metaphor, the bed over which Tom's stream flowed was a bright gravelly soil, on which the water danced gaily and light-heartedly down to the valley, pursuing a straight swift course, whereas May had many rocks and sandy places to get over, and, what was worse, she could not understand, and half rebelled against, the course her stream seemed to be taking. The traditions in which she had been brought up had become part of her nature ; for her, she thought, was the sheltered life, busy in little deeds of love, in caring for her own corner of the world, and bringing it nearer to God, and when at first the stream began to flow in this unconjectured direction, she was bewildered, almost frightened. Was there anything in this world so certain as her own duty? Could anything rightly come between her and this other life she had planned and dedicated humbly and gratefully to God ? What call was there so clear as that still small voice which said, " Inasmuch as ye have done it to the least, ye have done it unto me ? " And when she had come to argue about it, even to herself, the end was already inevitable. As soon as a moral question becomes a thing to argue about, it is already without force. No argument will convince a man that it is better being good than bad ; it is a matter, not for dispute, but of knowledge, and the man who disputes about it is bad.

Meantime Tom had turned a large roomy attic into a studio, and worked with all an artist's regularity, which the world is accustomed to call irregularity. He went constantly to London, made great friends with Wallingthorpe, and caused that eminent sculptor many fits of divine despair, but followed his advice about not immediately setting up a mourning Demeter, though for other reasons than his. A mourning Demeter, he announced frankly, should soon be set up, but not at once. He was merely waiting, so he told Wallingthorpe, for that particular spark of divine fire to descend, and till it descended he was willing and eager to gain greater facility with his hand. He also cordially agreed that no studio could exist in England except in London, but said that there were reasons why he could not live in London just now. "Perhaps before the summer is over," he began, and his face flushed all over, and he asked if anything had been heard of Manvers.

Ted was at Cambridge, and during the Lent Term Tom went up there to see him. He arrived at the close of a lovely day in March, and though the lawns and lower roofs of buildings were already in shade, the four tall pinnacles of King's Chapel burned like rosy flames against the tender green of the evening sky.

Markham had not seen Tom since he came to

England, and he looked forward to his visit with something like passionate eagerness, for Tom was to him the connecting link with the outer world of movement and eagerness from which he had voluntarily banished himself, but towards which even now he sometimes looked back with something like regret. Though his nature was one that hugs the shore, and prefers the quiet monotonous safety of the land-locked creeks and soft-sanded beaches to the risks and possibilities of the open seas, he sometimes cast his eyes to the great horizon where the ocean-going steamers passed and repassed, with their strange cargoes and dead and living freight from those dim mysterious countries whose very existence was becoming a fable to him.

And Tom came, with the seal of art and love upon him, but was his old boyish self, and sat on the arm of Ted's armchairs, and inveighed against scholiasts, and wondered if Ted had ever heard of Pheidias. After tea they strolled down together through the gathered dusk, and sat on the bridge, and once more Tom dropped a match in the river, and waited to hear it fizz. But the difference was there, and Ted wondered if Tom would speak of it. Once he seemed on the point of it. The willow which overhangs the river had just begun to break into tender leaf, and the delicate foliage hung round it like a green mist. Tom paused a moment, and grew serious.

"Look at it," he said, "it's like the loveliest thing on earth; it is youth bursting into——" and he broke off suddenly.

Once again later in the evening he grew serious,

and it was so odd for Tom to be serious twice in a day, that Markham wondered.

"How I can have been such a fool when I was here I don't know," he said. "Somebody told me once that I thought Cambridge narrow simply because I wasn't broad enough to appreciate it. Well, I think she was right. Mind, I don't go back on anything I said this afternoon about scholiasts. You are narrow, old boy, so don't misunderstand me."

"Who was it said that?" asked Markham.

"Miss Wrexham, I think. Didn't you meet her at home? She often tells home truths without making them unpleasant. That is not very common."

"Oh, do you think home truths are unpleasant?" asked Markham. "I rather like you telling me I'm narrow."

"My dear Ted, I never said home truths were unpleasant. I only said that she told me home truths without making them unpleasant."

"What's the difference?"

"All the difference in the world. Whether they are unpleasant or not simply depends on the personality of the person who tells you them."

"You mean you think Miss Wrexham is not unpleasant?" asked Markham.

"Certainly, she's not unpleasant. I think she's quite delightful. I suppose you don't appreciate her."

"Well, I hardly know her. I remember what May said of her."

Tom sat up in his chair.

"What did she say of her?"

"She said she thought she wasn't genuine."

"That's not quite true. Miss Wrexham is nearly always what you want her to be, but she doesn't seem to me to forfeit her genuineness. She is the most adaptable person I ever saw. To me she praises the Parthenon, to Manvers *La Dame qui s'amuse.* But to any one who doesn't know her well, that must appear like want of genuineness."

Tom rose and walked up and down the room.

"I am getting terribly *bourgeois* in my tastes, Manvers would tell me. I care for nothing now but loyalty and honesty and genuineness and quiet country life."

Markham stared.

"My dear Tom, you really shouldn't give me such surprises. What has happened to the bustle and stir of the world, and statuettes bowling cricket-balls?"

"I don't know. It was a phase, I suppose. One can't reach one's proper development except through phases. Paul was a Pharisee of the Pharisees; Augustine was a debauchee, a sensualist with the shroud round his feet."

"Paul, Augustine," said Ted, with a smile; "let us continue the list. What about you?"

Tom paused.

"I don't know. I only know I have changed, that something very big has happened to me. Perhaps some time you will know what it is. I'm going to bed, Teddy."

CHAPTER X.

TOM stayed at Cambridge two days, having meant to stay a week, but he found the need of getting home again imperative. He longed to tell Ted all about it, but something prevented him. Ted was as delightful as ever, but Tom felt that the difference between them could not be bridged by a confidence, as you bridge over a ravine first by a wire or a rope, and strengthen it till it will bear men and beasts. His confidence, he felt, would not reach to the other side, but dangle dismally in the air. Before he left, however, he had another talk with him, in which he expressed his feelings about the ravine, though he made no direct attempts to bridge it over.

"These two days have been charming," he said; "you must be dreadfully happy here, Teddy."

Ted looked up suspiciously.

"Is Saul also among the prophets?" he asked. "You nearly startled me out of my wits yesterday by saying that you liked quiet country life, and cows, and now you like Cambridge!"

Tom frowned and looked about for inspiration.

"I spent a week in London a month ago," he said, "and enjoyed it immensely. There were a heap of people I knew, and I went dancing and dining all

night, and all day the noise of the town roared round
me. Then I went home, and as it was a lovely day,
I got out at the park gates and walked. Do you
remember that little hollow just to the left of the
drive, where I shot two woodcock one day? Well,
it is full of birch trees, and the birch trees were
beginning to have a little green cloud of leaves round
them, and all over the ground were clumps of primroses
pushing up among last year's dead leaves. The sun
was setting, and the rays struck the birch trunks
horizontally. I felt as if I could have sat there for
ever and looked at it. As a matter of fact, in five
minutes I was tired of it, and went on walking."

"Is it a parable?" asked Ted.

"Yes; obviously Cambridge is the quiet, little,
green hollow. I remember I used to think it so
terrible that people should live there for ever, and
only busy themselves with what went on in the little
hollow. I was wrong. When I stopped in the little
hollow at home, I thought there could be nothing
more lovely than to live there always."

"In fact, you wanted to—you envied the birds
which did?"

"In the same way as one envies people who grow
beards, when one is shaving in the morning," said
Tom. "I wouldn't ever really grow one myself.
But I envied the birds to whom such a hollow was
native and natural."

Markham laughed.

"Birds and beards—what metaphor are you going
to employ next?"

Tom stood in front of him, smoking meditatively.

"If the green hollow satisfies you, you are right to live there always ; but one cannot be two people. I couldn't live there always. I said just now I was in love with cows and country life. So I am ; but if I knew there was nothing else, I should be absolutely wretched. Of course, every human being is a mass of limitations, saddled with the idea that he can be unlimited, and, personally, I can't limit myself to living always in the green hollow, and any one who can seems to me necessarily more limited than I. A man is judged by his power of desire. To desire much is better than to desire little."

"You are not very convincing," remarked Ted.

"No one has ever convinced anybody of anything, except by triumphant achievement of some sort," said Tom, "and because I call you a bird in a green hollow, I shan't convince you you had better have been a man, or that I am one either. But what I mean is this. We are all human beings, and we ought to live in a human environment. We differ from beasts chiefly because we have high and intelligible emotions. It is our duty to mix with all sorts of people, to know what every one is thinking about, to be ecstatically miserable, to be ecstatically happy, and to fall in love."

"Oh, that part of human life is well looked after," said Markham ; "it is almost universal to fall in love. I suppose, by the way, that you are going off now because your ten minutes—or was it five—in the green hollow is over ?"

Markham spoke rather bitterly. These two days had been very pleasant to him, and Tom's delightful habit of falling back at once into his old relations with every one made him feel that his own circle had narrowed, while Tom's had widened, and his remarks about green hollows had emphasized this.

Tom looked up.

"No, I am not the least tired of it," he said, "and that is partly the reason why I am going. It is always a pity to stop till one is tired of a thing. You see, necessarily I am not so much at home here as you are, and that I should be tired of it some time goes without saying. But I have another reason for going, which perhaps you will know about soon."

"You said that last night," said Markham.

"Only once? I wonder I haven't said it oftener."

He paused a moment, and mentally threw a rope across the ravine, and saw it fail to reach the other side, and dangle helplessly in the air.

"Well, good-bye, old boy; I must be off if I am to catch my train," he said. "I'm going straight home. Messages of all sorts, I suppose? I read Aristophanes most mornings with your father. I am very stupid, but he is very kind."

It was nearly dark when he got home, but the evening was still and warm, and after tea he took a short stroll up to the top of the hill in front of the house, and watched the crimson-splashed west paling to saffron before the approach of night. In front lay a gentle slope of thick-growing, tussocky grass, and beyond, a clump of silver-stemmed birch trees, standing slender and still luminous in the gathering dusk. Through the bushes the little noises of night crept stealthily about, and one by one the stars were lit in the velvet sky, and all things lay hushed under the benediction of night.

But in his mind, as the colours faded out of earth and air, a golden morrow dawned and brightened. He would see her to-morrow; he would come as a man to a woman; he would claim his right to know his fate, be it best or worst. He would not have hastened even if he could those few hours that lay between him and the next day. There had been something in their intercourse of late which made him know, or think he knew, that it would be well with him. The fine instinct of a lover, which formulates nothing, made him absolutely and entirely happy at the present moment. Unconsciously, he enjoyed the pleasures of the Higher Hedonist, who knows that the long-drawn pause before the full melody bursts out is of infinite moment. The anticipation of pain is nearly always keener, especially to imaginative and emotional people, than the pain itself, and the same thing is true, even in a higher degree, of joy. Not that Tom was conscious at the time that he was *pro tempore* a philosopher of the Higher Hedonist school. All he knew was that the thought of May flooded the half hour he sat alone and looked at the paling west, and made it a rosary of passionately happy moments.

Tom, who could never be in time for breakfast at an easy half-past nine at Cambridge, found no difficulty in getting to the vicarage at half-past eight. Breakfast passed as usual, Mr. Markham making vitriolic comments on the tactics of the Liberal party, and May and Tom trying to originate intelligent observations on politics, which they seldom or never succeeded in doing, and after breakfast Mr. Markham and Tom lit pipes and began on their Aristophanes.

The vicar observed that Tom was even less attentive than usual, and, with a certain amount of tact, remembered, at the end of half an hour, that he had some pressing work to do.

Tom shut up his book at once, and hoped he hadn't already taken up too much of the vicar's time. The vicar replied: "Not at all," and nobody knew what to say next.

But a remembrance of his own days of love and youth, the memory of standing in a quiet shaded garden, and offering to a girl his life and love, came across the elder man, and he turned to the window with his hands in his pockets, so as not to look at Tom.

"You needn't go up yet, need you?" he asked. "I am coming your way in half an hour, and we might go up together. May has got an idle morning to-day; make her play croquet with you. There's a capital new set I ordered the other day, which we put up on Saturday."

"Thanks, I'll wait," said Tom bluntly. "I suppose I shall find Miss Markham in the garden?"

"Yes; I saw her go out just now. You'll be ready in half an hour, then?"

May was seated under a tree at the far end of the garden, and Tom strolled across the lawn to her. There was a book in her lap, which she was not reading, and she saw him coming and smiled. For the first time in his life Tom found the difficulty of seeing some one he knew, a long way off, approaching, and beginning to smile at the right moment, non-existent.

He sat down on the grass by her, and for a few moments neither spoke a word. But when a thing is inevitable the most awkward people cannot prevent it. Then he got up and knelt by her. She was sitting in a low chair, and their eyes were on a level, and he looked her gravely in the face.

" I love you more than the whole world," said Tom bravely, "and I have come to ask you whether you care for me at all."

" Yes, Tom," she said, and their lips met in a lover's first kiss.

Tom's marriage with May Markham took place in July. It was celebrated quietly at Applethorpe, but the world and his wife condescended to take considerable interest in it. The season was beginning to wear a little thin, and the marriage of a wealthy and fairly well-connected young man, who had many friends, with an absolutely unknown girl who, the world said, was extraordinarily beautiful, and who, so said his wife, was rather a stick, was a matter of some interest when interests were beginning to get rather few. Moreover, for various reasons, this particular marriage had been talked about to a certain extent, and when a thing is talked about, its reputation is made. It matters very little whether abuse or praise is showered on anything, as long as it is showered with sufficient liberality, and a little story connected with Tom was the subject of both abuse and praise, and when these are mixed in the right proportions, the matter becomes one of almost overwhelming interest. The story, which the intelligent reader may take for what it is worth, but which certainly was not true, was merely that he had been engaged to Miss Maud Wrexham. But the world and his wife care not at all whether a story is true or not : it is sufficient if it amuses or interests them. Fiction, after all, adds a great charm to human life, and if we did away with fiction altogether, we should have to discard pleasant little fictions as well as unpleasant little fictions. Such a prospect would strike terror into the whole human race from George Washington down to Ananias and Sapphira.

For the next three months the newly wedded pair disappeared out of the ken of their fellows, but about the middle of October they came back to Applethorpe, and lived at the Park with old Mr. Carlingford. That amiable old cynic had completely lost his heart to May, who, for a time, extinguished his desire for observing the weaknesses of human nature. But I am bound to add that, as soon as the two went abroad, his habit returned on him.

His remark on their return is worth recording. May was tired with the journey, and went to bed early, and he and Tom sat up over the fire, while Tom descanted on perfect womanhood. The old gentleman listened with amusement and satisfaction, and when he took up his candle to go to bed he turned to his son and said—

" I believe you are more in love with her than ever. What time are family prayers to be ? "

"At nine," said Tom.

Mr. Carlingford was so much pleased at the brilliance of his induction that he appeared punctually next morning, and seemed to take an intelligent interest in a lesson from Joshua.

Tom and May had been out one day hunting in a delightful sloppy week following a frosty Christmas, and after a long run had got home rather tired and stiff, after dark had fallen. Tea was laid in the hall, and as soon as May had finished she went upstairs to change her riding habit, while Tom sat on with his chair drawn close up to the grate, smoked cigarettes, and reflected that really the nicest part of hunting was getting home again. He proposed to have a hot bath before dinner, but the fire was too good to leave just yet.

He had just arrived at these comfortable conclusions when May came down again, with her hat and jacket on.

Tom looked up in surprise.

"Where on earth are you going, dear?" he asked.

"I've just been told that poor old Lambert is dying," said May, "and I must go down to see him. Poor old fellow, he was in danger yesterday, and he was so frightened of death. I ought not to have gone out hunting to-day, Tom; he may be dead."

"But you oughtn't to go out now," said Tom; "you're awfully tired. I suppose all has been done that can be done."

"Tom, I must go!" said she.

"Well, send round to the stables, and tell them to have the brougham out at once."

"No, dear, I can't wait."

Tom got up.

"Well, you shan't go alone. I shall come with you."

"No, why should you?"

"Nonsense, May," said Tom, putting on his hat and coat, and opening the front door. "Good Lord, it's beginning to snow again! I was afraid it would."

They walked on some time in silence, and then Tom, thrusting his hand through May's arm, found she had only got a thin jacket on.

"May, you really shouldn't come out like this," he said. "You will catch your death of cold. You must go back and put something thicker on."

"No, I can't, I can't," said May quickly. "I may be too late as it is."

"May, it's madness. Here, I forgot—take this."

Tom took off his coat and held it out for her.

"No, Tom, it's all right; I don't want anything more."

"I insist on your putting it on," said Tom.

"Please, Tom."

"May, do as you are told," said Tom. "My darling, you shall put it on. I really mean it!"

Tom had his way, and the two walked quickly on again, Tom's long coat almost touching the ground, and the sleeves coming nearly to the tips of her fingers. This time May thrust her hand through Tom's arm.

"You're very good to me," she said. "Ah, here's the house! Come inside; you can't wait in the snow. They will all be in the other room."

A woman, with eyes red with weeping, opened the door to them, and as soon as she saw May, burst out crying again.

"Thank God you've come, miss," she said. "He's been asking for you all the evening, and he's far gone. And how are you, Master Tom? Won't you come by the fire, sir? You're all over snow. It's a poor fire, I'm afraid, but we've had no time to think of aught to-day."

Tom felt utterly bewildered and helpless. He tried to respond to the woman's greeting, but found no words. May in the mean time had slipped off her coat.

"He's in here, I suppose," she said. "I will go in at once."

The two went in together, and Tom sat down by the fire. The door had been left half open, and he could hear words spoken inside.

"Here's Miss May, Jack," said the woman, keeping to the name she had always known her by; "she's come to see you."

There was the sound of a chair being moved along the ground, and after a moment's silence he heard May's voice.

"Dear old friend, I have come just in time to see you before you go. It is not so dreadful, is it? Christ has taken you by the hand; He is just going to cure you of all your pain and suffering, and what is even better, of all your sin. He has been through all you are going through. We are very weak, but infinitely strong in His strength. Yes, you know that, do you not?"

There came some reply from the dying man which he could not catch, and the harsh, unpleasant voice of the doctor broke in.

"He's going fast," he said.

Tom heard the chair pushed away, and May's voice began again.

"It is nearly all over. You are very tired, are you not, and want to rest. Let us say the best prayer of all over together—'Our Father——'"

The door from the outside opened, and Mr. Markham came in. He looked puzzled and surprised to see Tom there. Tom rose to meet him.

"Hush!" he whispered. "May is in there with Lambert. He is on the point of death. He has been asking for her all the evening, they say."

Mr. Markham began taking off his coat, and stood for a moment before the fire.

"I shall wait a minute or two till May comes out," he said.

At a sudden impulse, however, Tom rose, quietly closed the door into the sick room, and sat down again by the fire. All the sordid shabbiness of the place contrasted too painfully with the supreme scene which was going on within, and he wished to separate the two. On the table stood a teapot, and a teacup without a saucer, into which was thrust a half-eaten crust of bread. A dull, spiritless fire, half-choked in grey ash, smouldered in the grate, and the kettle, with its lid off, stood in the fender, half-overturned, in a puddle of water. A wooden china-faced clock, painted with a scroll of pink and blue flowers, stood on the mantelpiece between two white crockery dogs, and marked the moments with a harsh insistence. There was a slipper, worn down at the heel, lying on the shabby worsted rug, which lay crooked by the fender, and another, presumedly its fellow, half under the table. A hungry, mournful-looking cat sat blinking at them from under the table with anxious, perturbed eyes, while inside that door May knelt by the bed of a dying cottager, and in some mysterious way knew how to reach the dim-lit soul of the old man, and to make it easy for him to die. There was a reality about it which Tom felt the revivalist meeting had lacked.

The clock on the mantelpiece had scarcely beaten out five loud minutes when the door opened again and May came out.

"Ah! you have come," she said in a low voice to her father; "it is just too late. He died quite peacefully and happily."

"I was here this afternoon," he replied, "and I just went back to the vicarage, and came on again."

May turned to Tom.

"Tom, dear, you'd better go home. I must wait here a little. These poor people want me."

"Mayn't I wait for you?" said Tom.

"No, dear. I shall be tidying up and putting things straight. You'd better go home. But I wish you'd send the carriage back for me in about an hour. I'm rather tired, and then you can take your coat."

Tom got up and put on his coat.

"Is there anything I can do, May?" asked her father.

"You might just come in and speak to Mrs. Lambert. Yes, do that ; she would like it."

The two went back into the sick room, and Tom out into the night. Something in what had taken place impressed him profoundly. What was that power which the old man felt, which was able to ease his last lonely moments? How could words be of any avail, when that last horrible, ghastly parting of soul and body came? Tom, like all healthy, vigorous people, felt an intense physical loathing at the thought of death. It was terrible and unnatural that this beautiful machine should in a moment become a dead thing, something to be buried away out of sight. How could words make death seem death no longer, but the beginning of life? For the swindling greengrocer and his increased balance, which to him appeared to be the direct effect of grace, but to Tom to have had a much more sublunary and intelligible connection with his taking the pledge, there was an explanation which he could appreciate, but this was altogether different. The test was a real test ; certain words had for a man round whom the inevitable loneliness of death lay like a cold, blinding mist, a comfort which made him face it with calmness, and to May, as to him, they must have been the expression of something very real. For the first time in his life he had seen, in an aspect that could not be mistaken, the consolation of religious beliefs. The most severe test conceivable had been applied, and a belief in a Power stronger than death had proved itself stronger than death. And Tom, in whom unfamiliarity with such phenomena had bred, not contempt, but absolute want of interest, was much puzzled. Somehow the tragic, simple scene which he had just been through was more convincing than a hundred volumes full of the triumphant sufferings of martyrs.

Tom suddenly felt rather vexed and hurt in his mind. Why did this mean so much to May and to others, and so little to him? If the power of that Life and Death was all-embracing, why had it not touched him? Why had the belief in which he had been brought up passed from him so utterly, being remembered now only as he remembered nursery rhymes and childish stories?

May came back an hour later, just in time to dress for dinner, and in spite of the love and trust which existed between them, neither of them spoke of that which troubled them. May was longing to say to him, "Tom, how is it that this means nothing to you? It was for you He lived and died," but a very natural reticence prevented her. She saw that Tom was rather upset about something, and this was not the time for it. Such a subject must come spontaneously, inevitably, and meanwhile she was content to bide her time, trusting in the Power which never yet failed. But they both felt at that moment that something had come between them.

Just as they were going down to dinner Tom said to her—

"I am glad you went, May; you made it easier for the poor old fellow. How real it all is to you!"

"Yes, Tom," she said, "it is the realest thing in the world."

Unluckily, at that moment Tom's candle fell out of the candle-stick he was carrying, spattering his trousers with wax, and making it absolutely imperative to speak of the annoying ways of wax candles, and the possible opportunity passed, and it became harder to take advantage of the next.

Old Mr. Carlingford was not very well. He was suffering from a slight attack of gout, and the man who behaves cheerfully and equably under such an infliction has yet to be found. Consequently at dinner he spent his irritation by being less amiably cynical than usual, and he discussed questions of ethics in a somewhat unpleasant manner.

"Good and bad is a very poor division to make of the human race," he said. "How is one to know in ninety cases out of a hundred if a man is good or not? He doesn't wear a certificate round his neck. You might as well divide the race, for any practical purpose, into those who have got strawberry marks on their left arm and those who have not. Fools and wise is the only proper classification."

"But they don't wear certificates round their necks," said Tom.

"No, Tom, and people don't wear certificates round their necks to say whether they've got noses or not. The fact is so patent."

"Only to the wise," said Tom.

"Exactly so, and the fools don't matter. Whereas about good and bad, the better a man is the more easily is he deceived, because it is impossible to know much of this wicked world and remain good. 'Keep yourself unspotted from the world!' Yes, you can do that if you seal yourself hermetically up in a convent or monastery, in which case it is hard to see why you have been born at all. To live like that casts a stigma on the intelligence of the Creator."

Tom unthinkingly laughed, for the conviction which his father threw into this last remark amused him, but looking up he saw May flush deeply and bend her eyes over her plate. Dessert was on the table, and she ate her orange quickly, and rose to leave.

Tom saw the trouble in her face, but did not see how to remedy it. He and his father drew their chairs up to the fire, and the latter, abstaining for hygienic reasons from port, "took it out" in cynicism.

"I don't mind saying these things to you, Tom," he said, "because I don't think you are a fool. Do you remember when you told me you were going to be a sculptor, how I warned you against folly? A dislike of folly is the one thing I have successfully cultivated, and I should like put on my tombstone: ' He hated a fool.' Especially I hate those fools who talk about their consciences. Conscience is simply ecclesiastical argot for digestion. No man with a good digestion has a bad conscience. The health of the conscience varies with the health of the digestion."

"But people with bad digestions have good consciences sometimes," said Tom.

"Yes, because their health is so inferior that they cease thinking about their bodies, and as they have to think about something, they think about an imaginary existence which they call their souls."

"Is that all your creed?" asked Tom. "I believe in my digestion."

"No, it's not my creed at all. It is a self-evident proposition; nobody makes creeds of self-evident propositions, or we should all say twice two are four every morning. My creed is, I believe in nothing, but I am amused at everything except the gout."

Tom laughed and helped himself to some more port.

"I wish you had the gout, Tom," went on the old gentleman; "it is perfectly loathsome to see you drinking port when I can't. I never am quite sure whether I would sooner have port and gout or neither, but I believe that if one goes on drinking port when one has gout one dies. That would annoy me immensely. Any one can die."

"Yes, it's very easy," said Tom. "I suppose that's why every one does it."

"It's sheer laziness in most cases," said his father; "people die when they cease to be interested in things. Unless, of course, they catch small-pox or cholera, but gentlemen don't do such things."

"Poor old Lambert is dead," said Tom, after a pause; "he died this evening. May was with him."

"That wife of yours is an angel," remarked Mr. Carlingford. "I really begin to believe in angels, at least in one angel, when I think of her. If I was Providence I should be immensely proud of myself for having invented her. I suppose she helped him through it?"

"Yes, she did help him," said Tom eagerly; "he had been asking for her all the afternoon, and she prayed with him, and he died quietly instead of being afraid."

"What did she say to him?"

"Ah, don't ask me, father," said Tom, rising. "It was all very strange to me, because it was so real to them both."

"But what was real to them?" asked his father. "Don't you suppose that the mere presence of May was what soothed the old man?—it would soothe me, I know. I hope May will be with me when I die. But I shan't want soothing—I shan't die until I no longer want to live. I am sure of that, and it is a most comforting thought, and as soon as I no longer want to live I am quite content that the powers of hell should do their worst, as that hymn we had on Easter Sunday says."

"No, it wasn't her mere presence," said Tom; "it was that she reminded him of what they both believed."

"Well, if he believed it, why did he need to be reminded of it?" demanded his father. "It is so odd that Christians send for clergymen on their death-beds, especially as those particular Christians who do so seem to me to look upon God Himself as a sort of immeasurable clergyman. It ought to be the one time they do not want them. No, you may depend on it, it was simply her presence. Have you finished drinking liquid gout? If so, we'll go."

When May went to bed Mr. Carlingford kissed her very affectionately.

"My dear, I wonder whether you are as nice to Tom as you are to me," he said. "I don't believe you can be, or else I should be jealous of him. Good-night, dear ; you've had a tiring day."

The two were moving up to London the next week, whither old Mr. Carlingford absolutely and entirely declined to accompany them. "London is only tolerable," he said, "when it is quite full of fools. I dare say there are plenty, even in January, but I can't go to the New Cut to look for them. The New Cut smells of cabbages and Salvation armies."

"You'd much better come with us, father," said Tom. "You know you will feel awfully lonely without us."

"I would sooner be lonely than live in that barrack in Grosvenor Square in January," said he ; " besides, the house will be full of models and clay. I believe we are all clay, and I don't want to associate with models."

"There will soon be clay models too," added Tom. " I'm going to work hard."

His father looked meditatively out of the window. The carriage had come round, and they were putting in the luggage.

"If all men had to work and all women had to weep, every self-respecting man would cut his throat this moment, and every self-respecting woman would drown herself in her tears. What charming things family parties would be, you know! Perhaps it's right for you to work, though I don't see why you should ; but don't let May weep. Ah, here she is ! Well, good-bye. I suppose one or both of you will be coming down here soon."

May's inclination had been to stop down in the

country longer, but Tom represented that he really had to begin to work at once, and that no one in the world—not even himself—could work in the country. The Golden Age was going to return—the earth was again to be peopled with gods and goddesses ; a shining procession was to begin to walk out of his studio. The grand style was possible. While the Hermes stood still and smiled at the baby on his arm nothing was impossible. Art ruled the world. He thought of the old paradox that nature copied art, and found that it contained its grain of truth. Until Turner painted golden liquid sunsets, they did not exist, or at any rate no one saw them, whereas now any one who had seen a first-rate Turner could find one on any clear summer's evening in the country ; and until he saw the Hermes he did not know there were such people, but as a matter of fact he met half a dozen of them now in every street in London. They were there all the time, but one had to be taught how to see them. And he finished up with " Ars longa."

This last argument appealed to May. Tom was ready to begin working ; it was criminal to delay. The herald of the Golden Age, the Iris who was to bring it down from heaven, was a statue of Demeter mourning for her lost child. Tom had already made a small clay sketch of it, and he could wait no longer. Besides, there was Wallingthorpe to be confuted. That eminent artist had used all his powers of eloquence in abuse, persuasion, and lament over Tom, who had heard him unmoved, and merely asked him as a personal favour to wait until he saw what could be done. Wallingthorpe talked about civilization and advance, and the torchlight procession of artists who ran and handed on the flaring brand from the one to the other until it reached the goal. The torch was in Tom's hands, and instead of running on with it towards the goal, he was deliberately running backwards and laying it at the feet of Praxiteles. It was a Vandalism.

Tom roared with laughter over that brilliant tirade, and vowed he would make a heroic group, in which he himself was kneeling before Praxiteles and handing him the torch of Art, while Wallingthorpe in a frock coat and tall hat was trying to snatch it away. It was a fine subject. Many thanks for the suggestion.

So May yielded, and paid farewell visits among all the old parishioners, and one snowy afternoon in January, as has been stated, they drove away from Applethorpe up to London, and Tom started his work as an artist seriously and with set purpose.

CHAPTER XI.

PARLIAMENT met early that year, and when Tom and May migrated to London the two Houses were already sitting. London was consequently fairly full, and the Wrexhams, among others, were installed there. Lord Chatham was one of those quietly effective men whose opinion is held to be safe and reliable, chiefly because they support everything of the old order, and oppose, not vehemently, but steadily, everything of the new. Lady Chatham and Maud were with him, and the excellent arrangements which her lady-ship was in the habit of making were very frequently thrown completely out of gear by the fog. In fact, she had serious thoughts now and then of permanently allowing twenty minutes extra per mile for the carriage, and fifteen for pedestrians.

Maud was very well pleased to be in London again. Measures of considerable material import were being debated, and she liked to feel the heart of the country beating. She had never been more interested in life generally, and the Chathams' house was becoming famous in a manner for the large number of clever people whom she collected round her. She had a certain gift of making people talk, without letting them know they were being made. The autumn she would have confessed was dull, but the reason why she found it so she would not have confessed, even to herself. She had attended Tom's wedding, and had behaved delightfully, but when it was over she found herself, as it were, facing a blank wall. Blank walls are not inspiriting things to contemplate, and after a few weeks of contemplation she arrived at the sensible conclusion that she would face it no longer, and she had spent the autumn in demolishing it stone by stone. And now by dint of real exertion, which was almost heroic in its untiringness, she could conscientiously say there was not one stone left on another, and in consequence the advent of May and Tom was an event which she regarded with pure pleasure. In other words, she considered she had "got over it." Tom, she felt sure, was completely unconscious of what had been going on, and they could meet again with perfect frankness and unreserve. She had met May once or twice before the marriage, and thought of her as a sort of exceedingly beautiful cow.

Maud was just writing a note to accept Mrs. Carlingford's invitation to dinner. There were only to be four of them, the fourth being Manvers, who had come to England for a week or two, and whom May thought Maud had met at Athens. May had got a slight cold and was going to wear a tea-gown, and would Maud do the same? She called her "Dear Miss Wrexham," and remained "hers truly."

Manvers had been to see Tom already that day immediately on his arrival in London, and Tom had scouted the idea of his going to a hotel, and insisted on his staying with them. Manvers made sundry efforts to talk to May and make himself agreeable to her, but he did not think he had succeeded very well. Like Maud, he thought of her as a sort of cow, and he did not appreciate her style of beauty. But Tom was as nice as ever, and still quite mad, which was, he confessed, disappointing, but it would certainly pass off.

The three had gone together to see Tom's studio and the herald of the Golden Age in clay. The pose he had chosen was admirably simple and wonderfully successful. The goddess stood with one foot trailing behind, the heel off the ground, resting on her foremost foot; the arms hung limply by her sides, and her head was drooped in sorrow for her lost child. The face was the face of his wife, subtly idealized, but preserving the look of portraiture. Tom had been working very hard at it, and in the clay it was sufficiently finished to allow one to see what it would be like. He worked in his old desultory manner, with fits of complete idleness and spells of almost superhuman exertion, with the difference that the fits of complete idleness were now the exception, not the rule.

The studio was an enormous room at the top of the house, with an admirable north light. It had been furnished by Tom without the least regard to expense or coherency. Things of all ages and styles were jumbled up together, but everything was good of its kind. It was the sort of room which, if you did not happen to think it perfectly hideous, you would think entirely charming. The furniture itself was Louis Quinze, for Tom's taste told him that there was no furniture but French; the walls were hung with Algerian and Cairene embroideries; in one corner of the room stood a cast of the Hermes, in another a bronze Japanese dragon. Two wide shelves ran round three sides of the room, and on these were massed together, with fine artistic catholicity, spoils from half the world. There were Tanagra statuettes from Greece, blue hawk-headed porcelain gods from Egypt, earthenware from Cabylia, a great copper Russian samovar, "laborious orient ivory" from India, plates from Rhodes, and embroidery from Arachova, a bronze helmet fished out of the river at Olympia, a great tortoiseshell box from Capri, a bronze Narcissus from Naples, blue-bead mummy nets, hideous German silver pipes, and amber and arrows from the Soudan. The platform where the model stood was covered with a great tiger skin, with grinning jaws and snarling teeth, and in the middle of the room stood the clay sketch of the mourning goddess. The incongruity of the whole touched completeness when May, Tom, and Manvers stood there side by side and looked at it.

Manvers's first impulse was to laugh. His appreciation of contrasts was strong, and the contrasts here were really picturesque. What was this poor *passée* goddess doing in this atmosphere of complete modernity? She was as much out of place as a Quaker at a music-hall. But he was far too much of an artist not to admire and wonder at the extraordinary power of the thing. Tom seemed to have learned *technique* not by experience, but by instinct. He was an artist by nature, not by practice; like

Walter, he sang because he must. To Manvers this was puzzling, because he held firmly to the creed that an artist makes beautiful things because he chooses to, not because his artistic nature compels him. They stood silent for some moments, and then Manvers spoke.

"Yes," he said slowly. "It seems to me almost perfectly Greek."

Though the prophet has no honour in his own country, it is at least gratifying for him to find it in another. Tom had been almost painfully anxious that he should say that, but now it was said he had an unreasoning fear that Manvers had not meant it.

"Do you mean that?" he cried. "Are you sure you are not saying it to please me?"

"My dear Tom, I am saying it neither to please you nor myself. I don't like Greek things, you know."

May turned on him gravely.

"Surely it is admirable?" she asked.

"It is admirable surely," replied Manvers, "but it is my nature not to admire it. You should hear Tom heap abuse on my little things. His tongue was an unruly member whenever he looked at *La Dame qui s'amuse*,—by the way, she is finished, Tom. It would have pleased him in what he calls his unregenerate days, and I his Paradisiacal days, before the fall."

"We've got a little statuette of his downstairs which I'll show you," said May. "It is of a boy shooting. He never quite finished it."

"That beast of a thing which was in my room at Applethorpe?" said Tom. "I shall smash it."

"No, dear, you won't: you gave it me. I shall go and get it."

"No, it shan't come up here," said Tom. "We'll all go down. This Temple is no place for Manvers."

But Manvers was interested, and he stayed some minutes more, advising, suggesting, and praising. It was as impossible for him not to admire the prodigious skill of the work, as it was not to dislike the spirit of it. The whole thing he regarded as a most lamentable waste of time and skill which might have been most profitably employed.

But before the statuette of the boy shooting his praise was of a very different order. It was thoroughly modern, and though not ugly, was undeniably pretty. The figure represented a lad in volunteer uniform, lying on the ground, shooting, or rather aiming, with a rifle. The head was bent over to the back-sight of the gun, the mouth slightly open, one eye shut, and one leg lightly crossing the other just above the ankle. The thing was marvellously fresh and unstudied. May claimed it as her possession, and showed it with just pride. Tom really had succeeded, as he had vowed he would, in making trousers beautiful.

May left the two friends together, and went off to pay some calls, and in her absence Manvers talked more freely. He had felt something of a traitor in her grey eyes when he had said that the Demeter was not in his line.

"It's the best thing you've ever done, Tom," he said, handing the statuette respectfully. "It really is abominably good, from the top of the forage cap down to the bootlace tag, and that bottom of the trouser rucking up slightly over the other boot is an inspiration. You really are an unfortunate devil to be saddled with the grand style. As for that horror in the studio—you call my things horrors, so why shouldn't I call yours?—the sooner you pitch it out of the window the better. Not that I don't think it good—I think it is admirable—and as I said, almost perfectly Greek, but it simply won't do. If you are to do anything nowadays you must be intelligible—that is to say, modern. You must not produce exercises, however good, in an art that is past. You are like those estimable people—I think they are archdeacons as a rule—who are always writing Latin translations in elegiac verses of 'Hymns Ancient and Modern' in the pages of the *Guardian.* Nobody cares for interesting survivals. Why should they? People will not cudgel their brains to see what things mean. You have to label them!"

"Yes, you have to label a thing like *La Dame qui s'amuse,*" said Tom, "or else no one would know whether it was meant for a woman of fashion or a *cocotte.*"

"No, I don't mean that," said Manvers. "I don't care what they call it, but you must make them understand the spirit of the thing. The spirit of Demeter is out of date. But that boy shooting is intelligible. Any one can see how good it is, and yet somehow it is not vulgar. To be vulgar is to be popular. You haven't seen my ballet girl dancing. It is incomparably vulgar. I think it is the vulgarest thing I ever saw, and I'm not boasting when I say all Paris raves about it."

"All Paris!" broke in Tom; "all the cities of the plain!"

"Not at all: all the most civilized people of the most civilized town in the world. You really had better smash the Demeter. What will you do with her? They will probably take her at the Academy —in fact, I should think they certainly would, and in the autumn they will send her back to you, or rather you will have to go with a drayman's cart and fetch her. She'll be very heavy. If you were an academician, and got a very good piece of Carrara for her, Pears might buy her, 'after using our soap,' you know."

Tom grew more and more impatient, and could contain himself no longer.

"Don't talk blasphemy here!" he shouted. "The only object of art, according to you, is to make fifty silly women look at the abortions you produce for five minutes while they are racking their brainless heads for a new piece of scandal. You are welcome to them. And if no one else cares for my Demeter, May does, and the rest of the world may go to the deuce for all we care. You are a rank heretic, and when you die you will go to a place entirely peopled with the types you love, while I shall sit at wine with gods and goddesses."

"What will happen to your other people? The boy shooting, for instance?"

"If he shows so much as the muzzle of his ugly gun, I shall kick him downstairs to join you and your fellows."

"Many thanks. I have your promise. He will be

a charming addition, and I shall be delighted to see him."

Tom burst out laughing.

"Do you know I'm delighted to see you, heretic or no heretic. We won't talk shop any more. Miss Wrexham is coming to dinner to-night. You remember her, don't you?"

"Very well. She flattered me about my statuette. I never forget any one who flatters me."

"You flattered yourself, you mean. She was fonder of the Parthenon."

"I am not jealous of the Parthenon," said Manvers; "she may flirt with the whole Acropolis if she likes. But you'll have to let me go at ten. Wallingthorpe has a gathering. He is very refreshing."

"He is a social Narcissus," said Tom. "It is so silly to be Narcissus."

"Not if other people agree with you."

"But nobody admires Wallingthorpe as much as he admires himself."

"No; but he never ceases to hope that they soon will. Hope springs eternal, you know. He is very sanguine. Whether they will or not has nothing to do with the question; the only point is whether he sincerely believes they will, and he certainly does that."

"His motto is, 'The proper study of mankind is me.'"

"That's not grammar," said Manvers.

"Possibly not; but the sublimity of the theme is sufficient excuse."

Manvers took out a cigarette-case, and then paused.

"Is it allowed here?" he asked.

"Oh, it doesn't matter if we open the windows afterwards," said Tom; "but May doesn't like smoke all over the house."

Manvers shut his cigarette case up with a click.

"My dear Tom, if one fails in the small decencies of life, one is lost. Take care of the pence, and the pounds will take care of themselves."

"That's a silly proverb," said Tom; "it is tithing the mint and anise and cummin."

"No; that's just what it is not doing. It is keeping them intact, and not tithing them."

Tom laughed.

"I don't think that means anything," he said. "But let's go to the smoking-room; we'll have tea sent there. No, you shan't come to the studio; I don't wish to force my uninteresting survivals on you. I'm quite delighted to see you again. And this evening it will be the dear old Athens party over again, only we shan't have Arthur Wrexham to peck at!"

Maud Wrexham, as her custom was, came rather late, and began making excuses before she was well inside the room.

"It really wasn't my fault this time," she said; "all the conceivable accidents happened, and where the carriage in which I was to have come is now, I can't say. Mother made a beautiful plan—it seemed to work all right on paper—that the brougham was to drop three of us in different parts of London at the same moment. But the laws of time and space intervened. Ah! how do you do, Mr. Manvers?

It's charming to see you again, and there was a block at the corner, and I had to go back for my gloves."

Tom laughed.

"You must have started wonderfully early," he said, "because you are only ten minutes late. May I take you in?"

Maud, Tom, and Manvers had much to say to each other, and May a good deal to listen to. They all rather tended to talk at once. Every now and then one of the others would drop out of the conversation and pick her up, but naturally enough Tom did not talk much to her; Manvers made several well-meaning efforts, but was unable to sustain the conversation long, as he was listening to what the other two were saying, and talking himself, and Maud sat on the opposite side of the table, and the candles and flowers made communication difficult. It must be confessed that May found the dinner a little wearisome, for in her somewhat isolated life she had not had any opportunities of acquiring that most useful accomplishment of talking nonsense, or of talking naturally and fluently about nothing particular.

Manvers was maintaining a new and startling theory that the only readable descriptions of any place on the face of the earth were written by people who had never set eyes on the place in question, and supported his theory by his own experiences at Athens.

"I knew," he said, "as we all know, that there was an Acropolis with buildings of white marble on it, and when you looked out from it you gazed over the grey olive groves, and the plain of Attica, and the violet crown of mountains, and the sea, and Salamis. Before I went to Athens, I could have described it in beautiful language, and talked of the delicate air, and the rose gardens. But now I've been there it is all spoiled for me."

"There aren't any rose gardens," objected Maud, "and there is usually sirocco."

"Exactly so. It is folly to be wise. The rose gardens are part of the spirit of Greece, just as much as the plane-trees by the Ilyssus and the *soi-disant* delicate air."

"And there are no plane-trees," said Maud.

Tom laughed.

"So much the worse for the Ilyssus. If there are not, there ought to be."

"Yes ; but when some one who has been to Athens reads your description," said Maud, "he will know that it doesn't resemble Athens at all."

"But one doesn't write descriptions for people who have been there, nor do people who have been there read them," said Manvers. "Books of travel are written for people who have never been abroad, and who will never go. Don't you think so, Mrs. Carlingford ? "

May crumbled her bread attentively.

"I'm afraid I don't quite understand," she said ; "but go on. Won't you tell us more ? "

Manvers frowned. If one never takes one's self seriously, it is terribly disconcerting to find that other people do.

"What I mean is that the literal accuracy of a description does not matter at all," he said. "When Turner painted a picture, he arranged Nature as suited him. He raised the level of the sea two hundred feet, and made a valley where there was a hill. He made the crooked straight, and the rough places plain."

"So you would have Greek maidens and Greek youths walking about the streets in your description of Athens?" asked Maud.

"Yes, if I thought they should be there, but I don't. They must have been so uncivilized. Fancy dressing in a yard and a half of bath-towelling."

"Then all you do is to reconstruct Athens as it seems to you it ought to be?"

"Yes; that is just what I mean," said Manvers. "Unfortunately, I have been there now, and I know that there are square, white hotels, and dirty streets, and ugly little boot-blacks, and horrible smells. All that warps the original and typical conception. I have an idea of what Athens ought to be, and if I write about it at all, it would be my duty to memorialize that."

"All the same," said Tom, "your conception of what it ought to be may not tally with that of any one else; and if such a person goes there, he will see that your conception is not only false, but, according to his ideas, not characteristic."

"But if there is some one—and who shall assure me there is not?—who never has been, and never will go, whose conception tallies with mine, think of his infinite delight! It would more than counterbalance the cold accuracies of all those people who say I am a liar. He will say, 'Here am I who never set eyes on Athens and never will, and behold, it is exactly as I hoped and thought it would be.'"

Tom laughed uproariously.

"I believe you are right," he said. "I shall write a description of America."

"Do, do," said Manvers. "Describe New York, with 716 avenues, and telephones and telegraph wires making a fine network of the sky, and elevated road-ways—whatever they are—every hundred yards, with Pullman cars, containing gentlemen playing lacrosse, running on them every hundred seconds at a hundred miles an hour. Describe the molasses-stores, and Vanderbilt driving Maud V. down Broadway, scattering gold to the Irish constabulary; describe the omnibuses in the street, and the omniboats on the river, with their cargo of hams, which but ten minutes before were pigs. And describe the back-woods, with the solitary redskin burying his tomahawk under a primeval banana tree against the sunset sky. America is a magnificent subject. Half England will say that it is exactly what they thought it was, and that there is no longer any need of going there. After all, the great point of books of travel is to save one going anywhere."

May's feeling of being out of all this was strong upon her. Manvers, she felt sure, was talking sheer nonsense, but how was it that Tom and Maud evidently felt amused by it all? As he was speaking, she found herself going rapidly over in her own mind what he had said—of course he did not mean it, but to her that was an argument in its disfavour. She had finished dessert, and glanced across at Maud. But Maud did not catch her eye, and was sitting with her elbows on the table, and evidently no thought of going into the next room had entered her head.

A man came in with coffee and cigarettes, and handed them round. Maud raised her hand to the box, but looked suddenly across to May, and dropped her hand again.

Tom caught and intercepted her look.

"May doesn't mind — do you, May?" he said. "Miss Wrexham wants a cigarette. It was I who taught her to smoke out in Athens."

"Yes, it's quite true," said Maud.

"Oh, please smoke if you want to," said May. "I don't mind the smell in the least. Tom wanted to teach me, but he gave it up. But why shouldn't we go into the studio or the library? It is more comfortable."

"Oh, let's stop here," said Tom, "it's just like Athens. We all used to sit with our elbows on the table after dinner, and drink coffee, while Manvers talked to us."

But Maud interposed. Her passion for being nice to everybody had suffered no cooling. She saw, too, that May was rather put out at the possible transgression of that wonderful English custom of women leaving the men at the dinner-table not to drink wine. She pushed her chair back and got up.

"Oh, I think the library would be much nicer," she said. "Those big chairs you have got there are made for talking in. And it's so nice and dark in there. Every one is more amusing in the dark."

Tom and Manvers rose too, and they all went into the library. Maud looked round the room until she had found what she called "her chair," and sank down into it with a little contented sigh.

"That's so nice," she said; "and now let's go on exactly where we left off."

The room was lighted by a couple of heavily shaded lamps on the table, which cast a small brilliant circle of light on to the near surrounding objects, and left the rest of the room in darkness. Maud was sitting opposite the fire; Manvers and Tom on a low settee on each side of it, and May at some little distance off.

"Really life is becoming beautifully simple and easy," said Manvers. "One can get almost anything one wants if one pays for it. And usually one has to pay so little. Look at Niagara in London! I am told by people who have been to the real one, that it is exactly like. You can see Niagara for a shilling, and allowing eighteenpence for a cab, you have seen one of the greatest marvels of Nature, purified by art, for the ridiculously small sum of two-and-six."

"How purified by art?" asked Maud.

"Well, there are no mosquitoes, and no beggars, and no American tourists. And if only they would bottle up the noise of Niagara in a phonograph and have it sent to London, the thing would be quite perfect—a complete triumph of Art over Nature."

"It's all very well to talk about an equal distribution of wealth," said Tom, "but an unequal distribution is the only possible working arrangement. If every one had enough, or was equally rich, you couldn't get anything unpleasant done for you."

"It's too terrible to think of," said Manvers. "You would have to brush your own boots, and cook your own dinner, and make your own bed. It is only because we hope to receive rewards, perishable or imperishable, that we ever do anything at all. Nirvana will be all very well when we don't wear boots, or sleep in beds. If a man is poor enough he will do anything for a sovereign. It's so nice that the pauper class should be so numerous."

"But there's plenty of room for improvement yet," said Maud. "One can't give a man a sovereign to go to the dentist for one, or have one's hair cut. Those are the really unpleasant things."

Manvers stared pensively at the fire.

"Of course one's body is a most rough and ill-made machine," he said. "An oculist told me the other day that the lens of the eye was a very imperfect instrument, and that they could make much better lenses nowadays. Our bodies are the only natural things there are left, and we see in them how very inferior Nature is."

May sat silent. The whole tone of the conversation, especially Manvers' last speech, grated on her. She longed to get up and say what she thought, but somehow she felt awkward and uncultivated. Manvers' glib tongue and easy sentences seemed to her like the buzzing of a mosquito in the dark—a little thing, no doubt, but sufficient to make one very uncomfortable. Was life with its hopes, fears, aims, its possibilities and limitations, just food for an epigram or a paradox spoken between two cigarettes and a cup of coffee? Were the poor, the drudges, the unhappy of this world, no more to any of these three than a peg on which to hang an idle joke about the conveniences of modern life? If Manvers did not mean what he said, it was terrible enough, but if he did, it was more terrible still. And why did not Tom say something and stop this unseemly jesting? The feeling she had had at dinner that they were talking about things she did not understand or care for, had given place to a keener and more poignant indignation that they were talking of things of which they knew nothing, but which she loved and cared for with all her soul. Were the poor poor, simply in order to administer to the pleasures of the rich? Was there no mighty all-merciful plan working behind and through misery and poverty, and wealth and happiness?

At last she could bear it no longer, and she got up out of her chair and walked slowly up to the fireplace. Manvers instantly rose and drew a chair up for her.

"I was afraid you would find it cold over there," he said.

"Thanks! Please don't get up," said May.

She stood warming her hands for a moment, and then turned to him.

"I think it is terrible to talk like that," she said ; "turning the frightful suffering and poverty we see around us into a mere jest. Of course you did not mean what you said, but it is no subject for jesting."

Manvers was vexed and angry. To take things seriously appeared to him an almost unpardonable breach of social etiquette: it really was not decent.

"I assure you I meant all I said," he replied; "though of course you are quite right about the terrible misery and poverty round us. I don't deny the tragic side of it for a moment. But I am an optimist; I prefer to look on the brighter side of things, and instead of dwelling on the tragedy and horror of poverty, I like to dwell on its more cheerful aspect, namely, the immense conveniences which it affords to people who are not poor. In that I am bound to say I find a certain consolation."

The room was dark, and Maud did not see how grave May's face was. She listened to what Manvers said, and laughed. Then for a moment there was a dead silence until May spoke again.

"Then do you really think that three-quarters of the world is poor in order that one-quarter may be able to make them do distasteful work for them?"

"Oh, I don't go as far as that," said Manvers. "I don't attempt to account for poverty or misery. I only notice a perfectly obvious effect of the unequal distribution of wealth, namely, that the rich can get almost all unpleasant things done for them by proxy, in exchange for varying quantities of gold and silver."

"You can never have seen the real misery of poverty if you can talk about it like that," said May.

Manvers lit another cigarette.

"Ah, there you are wrong," he said. "I have known it myself, real grinding poverty, when you don't know how or where you will get your next meal. I don't ever speak of it, because, as I said, I prefer the cheerful side of life. It was unpleasant, I confess, but I did not make a martyr of myself—I don't like martyrs—so why should I look on others in the same state as martyrs?"

Tom had left the room some moments before, and came back during this last speech. He knew what Manvers' early history had been, but was surprised to hear him mention it. He regarded it, he knew, as sensitive people regard some slight deformity.

May looked up at Manvers.

"I am sorry," she said; "of course I didn't know. But I feel very deeply about these things."

"Then you will spare a little pity for my early years too," he said, laughing. "That is charming of you. Good heavens, it's after ten, Tom; I must go at once, and if you will lend me a latchkey, I needn't wake anybody up."

Maud got up.

"And I've got to go down to the House," she said. "My father is making a statistical speech, and there will be a division. It is so tiresome his speaking to-night. I should have liked to sit in that armchair for ever. Good-night, Mrs. Carlingford. Do you know, I can't call you Mrs. Carlingford any longer. Good-night, May. Do come and see me again soon."

Tom went to see Maud off, and came back to the library. May was sitting in one of the big chairs with her hands idle on her lap.   Tom threw himself down on the sofa near her and stared at the ceiling.

"London suits me," he said, "and to-night I had London and Athens and you altogether.   What had you and Manvers been talking about when I came in ?   You looked so grave."

"Oh, nothing.   He told me that he had known what fearful poverty was like."

"Poor chap, yes.   He doesn't often speak of it.   I'm awfully fond of him.   He is nearly always amusing."

"Yes, he seems clever," said May.

Tom was silent a moment.

"Really I am a lucky devil," he said.   "I have everything I want.   I have you first of all, and all life interests me and amuses me.   And I've just paid my annual visit to the dentist."

"Shall we go to Applethorpe for the Sunday ?" asked May.

"Oh, I think not," said Tom, "at least, unless you want to.   I think Applethorpe would seem a little dull, don't you ?"

"Well, there are not so many things to do there as here, certainly," said May, "and I suppose Mr. Manvers will be with us still."

"I hope he will stop for a fortnight or more.   It's absurd his going to a hotel if we are in London."

"Oh, of course," said May, "but I want to go to Applethorpe soon.   We didn't go last Saturday or the Saturday before."

Tom gave no answer for a moment.

"I'll do exactly as you like," he said ; "we'll go on Saturday if you wish."

"Let's go," said May. "Mr. Manvers can come with us or go to the Chathams'. I know they want him to stay there a day or two."

"Why not get Maud Wrexham as well, then?" said Tom. "If they would both come it would be delightful."

May paused a moment. This was not exactly what she meant by a Sunday at Applethorpe.

"I expect they have people with them," she said.

Tom was a little perplexed, but assumed that for some reason May did not want Maud Wrexham to come.

"Well, there's no need to ask her unless you like," he said, rising.

"I never said I didn't want her."

"No, dear, but I thought from your manner that perhaps you didn't."

May made a grab at the skirts of her retreating serenity.

"No, it would be delightful if she would come," she said with an effort. "I'll write a note to her to-night."

CHAPTER XII.

EASTER was late, and when Tom and May left London to spend a week or two with old Mr. Carlingford at Applethorpe, spring had already burst out into freshest and greenest leaf. As they drove along the avenue from the Lodge gate, May thought she had never seen anything so beautiful. The ground sloped sharply from the road up on either side, and the russet of the last year's dead bracken was mingled with the milky green of the fresh new shoots. Here and there an ash-tree with its black buds, or a lime on which the little fans of green leaves were beginning to burst from their red sheath, stood firmly among the young yearly plants, an experienced guarantee to the steadfast kindness of the varying seasons. Now and then a white-scutted rabbit bundled across the road, or a squirrel whisked up to some safer eminence, and scolded violently from among the branches. As they passed the lake, a moorhen half swam, half flew to seek the shelter of the rhododendron bushes, leaving a widening ripple behind it, and a sudden gust of wind arose, shaking half a dozen catkins from the listless birch-trees. The whole air was redolent of spring and country, and promise of fresh life.

Tom was driving, and May sat beside him. She

had not been very well for a week or two, and as the wind struck her, he thought she shivered slightly.

"You're not cold, are you, darling?" he said.

"No, Tom, only very happy."

He laughed.

"Well, so am I; but I don't shiver. Put that cloak round you."

"Do you remember giving me your coat one night, Tom?" she asked.

"Yes; you were so obstinate, too. You refused to put it on for a long time."

They drove on in silence for a little way.

"Are you glad to get down here?" asked Tom.

"Yes, very. I've got so many people I know here. You see, Tom, I'm not very clever, and I do like little quiet everyday things to do. And I see more of you here. You're always so busy in London. Ted's here, too. He got here two days ago."

"Why doesn't he come as your father's curate?" asked Tom.

"Well, he has all his Cambridge work to do. He can't very well give up that. And yet I don't know."

"I think he's right," said Tom. "He is doing splendid work, I believe. It doesn't interest me, personally, but I do believe it ought to be done."

"Ted told me you always used to howl at him so for working at scholiasts or syntax or something."

"I know I used. But after all if the world is ever going to reach perfection, you have to work up all lines perfectly. And he says that scribes are terrible fellows for scamping their work and making stupid mistakes; they must be shown up."

"But there are bigger things in the world than scribes and scholiasts, Tom," said May, half-timidly.

"Yes, dear; but what is a man to do? He cannot work passionately at things he does not feel passionately."

"But there is one thing which it is every one's duty to feel passionately. And when a man goes into the church, it seems to me a sort of visible sign that he does feel it passionately."

"But there are other things in the world," said Tom. "What is beauty made for, or love, or anything lovely? Surely they are worth giving one's life for? If there was only meant to be one thing in the world which it is right for men to strive after—I mean the personal direct relation with God—why are all these wonderful and beautiful things given us? Not just to look at and wonder and go by?"

"No. To help us to realize the personal and direct relation with God. We should look on them as signs of His love for us. Do you remember the first present you gave me, that little diamond ring? It was awfully pretty, but I loved it because you gave it me."

Tom was silent.

"It's no use talking of it, darling, even with you," he said at last. "It is your passion, and I have another passion. Neither of us can really conceive that there is another standpoint besides our own. We acquiesce in there being others, but unless one experiences a thing, one cannot feel it."

"I am not afraid, Tom," said she. "He will teach us all in the way it is best for us to be taught. If

we are willing to receive, He will give us the knowledge of Himself, when it is good that we receive it."

"And there we are at one," said Tom. "That I
believe with my whole soul."

They reached home just as evening was falling,
but the night came on warm and cloudless. Tom
helped May very tenderly out of the carriage, and
after tea they walked a little up and down the gravel
path above the long terrace. The beds were already
odorous with spring blossoms, and white-winged
moths hovered noiselessly over the flowers, and
glided silently away again like ghosts into the surrounding dusk.

The mist was rising a little from the low-lying
fields towards the village, across which two country
lads were walking home, one with an empty milk-pail
in his hand, the other with a spade over his shoulder,
whistling loudly. And in the dusk husband and wife
spoke together of the dear event that was coming, and
in that human love and longing their souls met and
mingled. May thought no more of the barrier which
still stood between them even in their almost perfect
love and confidence. She, in her clear unquestioning
faith, was apt to lose sight too much of the use and
value of beauty and love and life, which are as directly
gifts from God as faith, and to wonder, with something like anguish, when she thought how completely
they had possession of her husband, what the end
would be. But now that the fulness and perfection
of a woman's life was promised her, she, too, for a
little felt the sweetness and strength of living. She
was a woman, and the crown of womanhood was

coming to her; the divine miracle was near its fulfilment. She was alone in the hush of evening, beneath the opening stars, with her husband, and things human and divine seemed so mingled together, that neither failed of their completeness.

The next few days passed very peaceably. May, who had been rather languid and out of spirits in London, soon regained her serene health. She and Tom strolled together in the woods or drove out for an hour or two every day. Ted and his father were with them a good deal, and Tom, who had rather overworked himself in the last few weeks, found a new pleasure in hanging about doing nothing. May insisted on his going long rides or walks, in which she herself could not join, and after spending the morning quietly in the woods with Tom, or paddling about on the lake exploring the little creeks and islands, she would send Tom and Ted off together in the afternoon for a long tramp or a ride over the Surrey downs.

They had spent one of these afternoons, about a week after they had come to Applethorpe, in this manner, and about four o'clock had descended on to a little red-backed village standing in a hollow of the downs, surrounded by hop-gardens and strawberry fields, and having had tea in the country inn, proceeded homewards. Their way lay through the village street with its neat white cottages, and long strips of garden fronting the road. In one were flowering clumps of primroses, and a border of merry daffodils lay underneath the windows. In another a more ambitious show had been planned, and sundry little wooden labels, stuck about in beds of young fresh green, not yet in flower, promised a crop of annuals. In another a box hedge, cut into fantastic shapes, gave a genteel privacy, and marked it off from its neighbours. The little Norman church stood at the bottom of the street, and just as they passed the gate a group of mourners came away from a grave which the sexton was filling in. Tom waited for them to pass, and stood a moment watching them ascend the street. They went in, he noticed, at the house with the box hedge. A moment afterwards the clergyman, who knew Tom, came out, and as they stopped to speak to him, Tom asked what the funeral had been.

"A poor woman here," he said, "who died in childbed two days ago. Poor thing! she leaves her husband, such a nice young fellow, quite alone. They had only been married nine months."

Tom turned angrily round on the astonished young man.

"How can you say such horrible things?" he said, and walked off, followed by Ted, at five miles an hour.

Ted caught him up in a few moments, and made him abate his pace.

"Poor old boy," he said, "don't get in such a state about it!"

They walked on a few moments in silence.

"It's all too horrible," broke out Tom at length. "How can such things be? Poor darling! And I have been such a brute to her. Our lives are lived apart really. She thinks the passion of my life is no more than a plaything sent to amuse us, and the passion of hers is unintelligible to me. It is no more than a beautiful unconvincing fable."

"But what if the fable is true?" asked Ted.

"It may be true, but how can I tell? All I know is that it isn't convincing to me. It may be so, or it may not. But if it doesn't convince me, what am I to do? I would give the world to be convinced of it."

"She is very happy in your love," said Ted.

"She is the best and sweetest woman on this earth," said Tom. "I love her more and more every day. But I do love my art too. My life would be in-complete—impossible without either."

Ted sighed.

"You are very fortunate. Your circle of complete-ness is widening every day. You are in love with love and life."

"Teddy, do leave that place," said Tom earnestly. "It is changing you. You always were narrow, you know, as I often told you, but you are getting narrower. You only care about dead things. You had better care about the worst of living things than the best of dead."

"So you tell me. But no one can realize any one else's conviction, as you have also told me. You are playing symphonies to the deaf. It may be so, or it may not be so. How can I tell?"

"But you know it is so," said Tom.

"Sometimes I think it must be so. I know, at any rate, that you, for instance, get more keen and active happiness out of life than I do. The best emendation doesn't give me the quality of pleasure which the smell of a spring morning or a hundred other things give you."

"I told you so. You do know it," said Tom. "Why don't you act on it?"

"I can't. There is no other reason. It is no use to say to myself: 'You shall care for a spring morning more than you care for Zenobius.' I don't care passionately for Zenobius, but I don't care at all for a spring morning."

"I agree with you to a certain extent, you know," said Tom—"more, at any rate, than I used to at Cambridge. I think scholiasts ought to be studied. They are a leaf, or a line in the book of ultimate perfection. But you have got them out of focus. They are too close to your eyes, and conceal everything else. Well, here we are at the vicarage. Good-bye, Teddy! I must go home quickly."

Tom passed along the village street, and at the church suddenly the words of the clergyman came back to him with a sickening sense of revulsion. He paused at the door a moment, and then by a sudden impulse went in and knelt down in the nearest seat. He was not aware of conscious thought, only of an overmastering need. "Why am I here," he thought to himself, "I who have no right here?" Then like an overwhelming wave the thought of May came upon him—May, the love of his strong, young life, soon to be in pain, perhaps in danger of death, like the woman in the cottage with the box hedge, with that yet unborn life within her. And the same impulse which had prompted him to come into the church, prompted him to say, "If there is One all-powerful and all-loving, may He be with her now." And like the old pagans in Homer, he felt inclined to vow a hecatomb of oxen if his prayer was granted.

And thus in his terrible fear and need Tom was

brought by his love for May to the feet of the unknown God.

He waited a moment before leaving the church, and looked round. There were the old windows he knew so well : a pink Jonah being fitted neatly into a green whale ; a yellow-haired, long-legged David standing on the chest of a prostrate Goliath, and with immense difficulty lifting the giant's sword ; a perfect Niagara of dew descending on the fleece of Gideon, Joshua laying violent hands on a red sun and a yellow moon, and the walls of Jericho falling over symmetrically in one piece. The east window consisted of three narrow lancets, still faintly visible in the dusk, and the middle of these showed a figure crowned with thorns, with arms outspread, drawing the whole world unto Him. . . .

He went quickly up over the fields from the village where he and May had walked the first night they came, and along the terrace walk. A little wind stirred in the bushes, and blew across him the faint odour of the flowers. In the house the lamps were already lit, and looking up to May's bedroom window he saw through the white blind a light burning there. For one moment his heart stood still with fear, and then, regathering courage, he went into the house.

His father was sitting in the library, with a green reading-lamp by him, and he looked up quickly as Tom entered.

"Where is May ? Where is May ?" he asked.

Mr. Carlingford shut up his book.

"My dear boy, how late you are, and what on earth is the matter with you ? Tom, for God's sake don't be hysterical or faint. It's all right, but it has been very sudden. May's child was born—a son— just about four o'clock. She is asleep now, and doing very well."

Tom stood there, perfectly pale, with his mouth slightly open. Then quite suddenly his hat and stick fell from his hand, and he collapsed into a chair.

Mr. Carlingford rang the bell.

"Tom, if you behave like that, I shall disown you. I never saw such an absurd exhibition. Are you going to cry, or die, or what? Here, bring some brandy quickly," he said to the man who answered the bell.

The brandy revived Tom somewhat, and he stood up, still looking dazed and puzzled.

"I don't know what happened to me, father," he said. "I never behaved like that before. I want to see May and—and my son. Say it again. What has happened exactly?"

"My dear Tom, from the way you behave, I should have thought that such a thing as the birth of a child was a unique phenomenon, whereas it is one of the most common exhibitions of the forces of Nature. It occurs, I am told, many times every minute on this earth. You can't see either of them now."

"The baby, just fancy!"

Tom picked up his hat and stick, and stood looking into the fire. Even Mr. Carlingford was slightly shaken from the web of cynical observation, out of the meshes of which, like a kind of spider, he culled the weaknesses of mankind Tom, with his smooth hairless face, looked so boyish himself, and for a moment the old man's memory went back with a sudden feeling of tenderness to the time when Tom had been a soft helpless atom like that which was lying upstairs now at its mother's breast.

"Tom, old boy, I'm so awfully pleased," he said. "I always had an absurd wish—I don't know why—to see you with a baby sitting on your knee. You are a good boy; you chose the wife I would have had you choose, and she has behaved as a wife should behave."

Tom turned round to his father with a beaming face.

"Then we are all satisfied, father," he said, "and now I'm going upstairs very quietly to see if I can see her—them. Them!"

May was asleep, and he was told to delay any further visit till the morning. If she woke she had better not be disturbed; but she should be told that Tom had come in, and that he had been up to see her.

Next day was Sunday, and Tom awoke very early in that most delicious way of all, slowly, with a vague growing consciousness of utter happiness. The window was open, and he lay a few minutes letting the cool breeze ruffle his hair before he stirred. Then rising and putting on a dressing-gown, he went to make inquiries as to whether May was awake, and whether he might see her. The nurse answered both questions affirmatively, and he went in. She was lying propped up by pillows, and by the bed was a little pink-and-white cot, in which Tom could just see a little crumpled red face.

May welcomed him with a smile, and laid her finger on her lips.

"Hush, Tom, he's asleep," she whispered, "but you may look at him."

Tom availed himself of the permission.

"What a queer little thing it is!" he said.

"Queer! It!" objected May. "It's him, and he's beautiful."

Tom knelt down by the bed.

"My darling, my darling!" he whispered. "I didn't know how happy I could be till I woke this morning. And it's all real and true. I was almost afraid till I saw you that it was a dream or a wish of mine."

He raised himself and bent over her, and their lips met in a long kiss of passion purified by tenderness.

He stood there for a moment, till the son and heir awoke and began to howl, bringing the nurse into the room, who incontinently dismissed Tom.

He went back to his room and drew up the blind, letting a yellow splash of sunlight on to the floor. In the bushes below the window a thrush sang out of the fulness of his heart the wonderful repeated song which he always knew, and which no one else will ever learn. Through the soft air swept the first swallows of the new summer, flying high over the shrubs and trees in the garden. Tom looked out for some minutes, sniffing in the clear morning air, when from the village began the church bell for early communion. A sudden impulse, an irresistible need to thank some one for his happiness, as strong and urgent as his need the night before of commending May to some protection stronger than man, made him dress quickly and walk down to the church.

It was almost empty. Ted and his father were at

the altar, and a few parishioners were kneeling in the body of the church. The Ante-communion Service was nearly over, and Mr. Markham was reading the Prayer for the Church Militant as Tom entered. He went to the pew where he had knelt the night before, and soon the blessed command fell on his ears—

"Draw near with faith, and take this holy sacrament to your comfort."

What did it mean? How could he draw near with faith? What was faith? And the grave, solemn voice from the altar answered him, that faith was to know that God so loved the world, that He gave His only-begotten Son.

Was this, then, the answer to his strange unformulated desire to thank some one for his happiness? Did it all come from this, from the quiet, still church, from the memory of that sacrifice which sanctified love and all that is beautiful?

He had wanted to vow a hecatomb of oxen the night before ; he had longed to be able to promise something to any power which would give him what he had seen in May's room that morning, and instead of that he himself was bidden to the feast, and with the others he went up and knelt at the table of Christ.

Tom waited outside the church for Ted and his father, in order to give them news of May, and then turned homewards again. The desire to seek aid which had prompted him to come to the church the night before had given place to the desire to give thanks. He had come one step nearer to the unknown God ; he approached Him, not as a power, but as a benefactor. The words of the great

thanksgiving had thrilled him through and through.
" We praise Thee, we bless Thee."

That desire of the human creature, constant
through all centuries, to seek for that which is outside itself, and stronger than itself, and passes under-
standing, had come to him. Some hand had knocked,
so he thought, on the door of his soul, and wakened
it from its sleep of indifference. Was it perhaps,
after all, only the result of this sudden change from
his deathly fears of the night before to the embracing
happiness of this morning? He could not tell ; he
scarcely cared to ask himself.

After breakfast he saw May again, and when the
nurse put an end to their interview he went out
under the cedar, filled with the double thought. The
bell for eleven o'clock church was ringing, but Tom
had no intention of going. The sacredness of the
morning demanded solitude. He watched the servants going down to church in their Sunday clothes,
and marked two footmen stealing away towards the
woods, and by degrees the house grew still. Tom
went in and found a Bible with some little difficulty,
and brought it out. He wanted to know more of
that wonderful Life that had died, and had risen
again for ever in men's hearts, and he turned to the
Gospel of the Apostle of Love. There he could
learn all that a man need know, all that he had
missed all his life.

But how to get at it ? How to know that those
words were spoken for him ? All he did know was
that words and sentences which he had often heard
before were meaningless no longer, that something

which was very real and sacred to others had a
sudden interest for him. He had never had doubts
on such subjects ; simply the belief in which he had
been scantily brought up had faded and died a
natural death, as leaves die in autumn when the sap no
longer feeds them. So now the simple Gospel narra-
tive struck him as so probable, so convincingly literal,
that there was no question of sifting or examination
possible. He remembered vaguely, and with some
contempt, a book he had read not long before which
seemed to deny the fundamental truths of Chris-
tianity because the writer could not bring himself to
believe that Balaam's ass really spoke. Even the
literal truth of the Gospel did not seem to matter ;
the conception was divine ; it was the best life that
could have been lived : it was perfection, no less, and
that which is perfect is not man, but God.

Socrates warns us of the inutility of an unexamined
belief, a statement which is not universally true.
For a man who is gifted or saddled—for it is a
dangerous bequest—with a critical nature the remark
is profoundly true. To deliberately refuse to look a
doubt in the face is an act of cowardice, a sacrifice
and a stifling of our intellectual capacities. But there
are many natures, highly developed intellectually,
which are not critical, and to such religion is a matter
of either indifference or conviction. Whether there
ever was a Garden of Eden with a tree in the middle
of it, round which was coiled a serpent, is a question
which has no interest for them. If pressed they may
say that some things are not meant to be taken
literally, and dismiss the subject from their minds.

The critical mind finds some slight but spurious consolation in shrugging its shoulders and labelling them as fools, but its consolations end there, for there is no doubt which is the happier of the two, and that an uncritical mind is synonymous with a foolish one is not the case.

There is a certain experiment known to chemists as the solidification of a supersaturated solution. Some fluid is heated, and while hot there are dissolved in it large quantities of salt or alum. Now, a liquid when hot can hold more substance in solution than when it is cold, and when this surcharged liquid is allowed to cool quietly it actually holds more salt than it is theoretically capable of holding, and as long as it is left still it can do so. But if an atom of the same salt is put into it, the whole mass solidifies. Tom's spiritual fluid had been subjected to a somewhat analogous experience. It had been surcharged with the salts of love and life, and then came the atom as momentous as the straw which breaks the camel's back—the birth of the baby and the safety of May. It was necessary for him to have something to which he could refer, and from which he might derive his happiness; there must be for him a Superior Being. He did not wish to argue about it, to examine reasons for granting the existence of a first cause, or to split hairs over the precise way in which God became incarnate in man. Simply his happiness was too great for him to bear alone; his nature held more happiness than it could hold by itself, and he had to refer it to something outside his nature.

CHAPTER XIII.

Tom went back to London about a fortnight after
the baby's birth, and plunged into his work with
more vigour and earnestness than ever. His new
interest in religious matters was a thing apart from
his work, just as was his love for May, and it did not
get between him and his models, or interpose angular
substances between his hand and eye. His religion
was not fanatical or aggressive : it had come to him
as the explanation of his human love, and inasmuch
as the white heat of that had burned out of his life
all that was sordid or impure, the conduct of his life
was left unchanged. According to moralists, all sin
partakes of the nature of decay, and Tom's nature
was very vital. And as his religion was not fanatical,
it did not fill him with any half self-conscious and
wholly morbid convictions of sin, either in himself or
others, and he pursued his cleanly honest life much
as he had done before.

But as the days went on, and May got steadily
stronger again, a doubt began to look him in the
face. He remembered the Revivalist meeting at
Cambridge, and his own rejection of the idea that
one moment, one flash of seeming revelation could
change any one. He himself had faced an anxiety

blacker than death, had felt a relief purer than heaven. Did not that perhaps account for it all? Was not his own case as intelligible as that of the greengrocer who became a teetotaler? And because he was honest with himself he put himself a straightforward question: "Would he feel another and a fiercer anguish if he again got to believe that Christ was merely the best man who had ever lived and no more?" The question haunted him, but he was unwilling to answer it.

To his surprise Tom found Manvers waiting for him at home one evening when he came back from some party about a week after his arrival in London. The latter was sitting in the smoking-room consuming cigarettes until Tom returned.

"I hear there are three to the *ménage* now," he said. "I am delighted, of course. I should so like to have a baby. There can be nothing more interesting than to see a helpless thing with nothing it can call its own, except the tendencies it inherits from oneself, slowly acquiring intelligence."

"It's a great responsibility," said Tom, throwing himself into a chair and scratching his head with an air of wisdom.

Manvers stared at him incredulously.

"My dear fellow, the man who thinks about responsibilities is no longer a responsible being. It is a sign of mania or extreme old age. The age of responsibility begins at eighty-three or eighty-four, and I once knew a man of eighty-five who was still irresponsible. You are upset and excited. Go to Paris for a week. Paris is strangely regenerative, I always find."

Tom laughed.

"Talking of Paris, why aren't you there?"

"I am staying with the Chathams," said Manvers. "They were in Paris just before Easter, and they asked me to come to London and see them for a week or two, and as I had nothing to do I came. I always have a great success with middle-aged gentlemen. There is something peculiarly seductive about me to the mature male."

"I don't care for mature males much," said Tom.

"Oh! that is a mistake. They make one feel so young. It is so easy to be seductive to them. You have to be very deferential, but imply at the same time that it is a very great compliment, and give them the impression that you yourself have vast stores of experience at your back, but prefer that they should produce theirs."

"Did you come here simply to make yourself seductive to Lord Chatham?"

"No, I can't say that was my object. My coming was only the effect of my having done so. I came to see other people."

"How is Maud? I haven't seen her lately."

"As charming as ever," said Manvers with some finality.

"May is down in the country still," said Tom, after a pause, "with my father and the baby."

"And are you ridiculously happy still?"

"Quite ridiculously. But why still?"

"Oh, I don't know. We are limited, and so are our emotions. I have a natural tendency myself to get tired of the things I like."

"But you said just now that Maud was as charming as ever."

"Obviously then she is an exception."

He rose to go.

"I must be off," he said. "You came in so late,
and I wanted to talk to you—but it's after twelve,
and they will all think it most unseductive of me to
wake the house up at nameless hours. I suppose I
shall see you again soon?"

"Yes, I dare say I shall come to the Chathams' at
tea-time to-morrow. I haven't seen them for an
age."

In the thirty-two years of his life Manvers had been
amused at many people, had liked a rather smaller
proportion, was totally indifferent to most, and had
loved none. It was consequently almost distressing
to him to find that Maud Wrexham was losing none
of her preponderance in his thoughts. He remembered
how at Athens the thought that she was in love with
Tom had galled him, but left him dumb, and he had
been enormously relieved and pleased to hear of Tom's
marriage. He had not much experience of the ways
of girls in the upper classes, but he supposed that in
such well-regulated institutions a man who married
went into a different orbit, and, ceasing to be a
legitimate object of affection to all the world but
one, naturally ceased being an object of affection at
all. He gave himself not undeserved credit for
having behaved really very well. He had made it
quite clear to Tom that in his opinion Maud Wrexham
was approachable, and Tom had rejected the notion
theoretically then, and practically a short time after

by marrying May. He had done all that could be expected or demanded of him by the most Lycurgan codes of friendship and honour. Those claims were satisfied, and Maud was still free. His work had kept him in Paris during the year after Tom's marriage, and he had himself felt that it would be wise to keep away for a time. He suspected that Maud had some private business to transact with her own emotions, and that, while she was doing that, she would not perhaps wish to be interrupted. She might, in fact, declare that she would not be interrupted. Manvers, who was essentially a reasonable being, had considered that a year was time enough for her to clear off her private business, and the year was now over. He disliked waiting very much, but he summoned to his aid that admirable common-sense which had stood him in such good stead at Athens, and had worked harder than ever.

During the past week his intimacy with Maud had advanced a good deal. She evidently found considerable pleasure in his society, and he made himself uniformly entertaining and agreeable. Lady Chatham also, in the intervals of what she called "the whirl of London life," when her genius was not devoted to ordering carriages, and picking up people with mathematical inaccuracy at street corners, found time to talk to him, and make vague arrangements for him. Consequently next morning, after her orders had been sent to the stables, and she needed a little relaxation, when she found him alone in the library, reading papers, she sat down and began to talk.

" My husband tells me you have to leave us on

Saturday," she said. "I suppose you are going back to Paris. What day of the month will that be?"

"Saturday is the 26th, I think," said Manvers.

"No, I am sure you are wrong. Saturday is the 25th. Well then, as you meant to go on the 26th, you can stop here till Sunday. We shall be able to send you to the station."

"It's very good of you," said Manvers, "but I am afraid it is the day of the week that matters, and not the day of the month. I have to be in Paris on Saturday night."

"And what do you do then? You ought to be settling down, you know."

"I am afraid I shan't settle down more than I have done already. I work very hard, you must know. But this holiday has been delightful."

"It must be very widening to live about from country to country as you do," said Lady Chatham appreciatively, "but you ought to give us the benefit of your increasing width!"

Manvers laughed.

"In what way?"

"You might write a book about the comparative tendencies of English and foreign life. Something useful—not like those little scrappy books that describe mimosa trees and amber necklaces and the Soudan, but something that really helped one to understand the difference between one nation and another, the influence of climate—climate has a great deal to do with character. Food too—the meat we eat in a day would last an Italian for a week. That must make a difference. And, as I said, you ought to settle down and marry, and become the centre of a little circle."

"Tom always fills me with the envy for married life," said he ; "he really is ridiculously happy. But as regards the other, I don't think I am made for a centre. I prefer circling myself."

Lady Chatham rose to go.

"Well, it is five minutes to eleven," she said, "and I must be off. You must think over all I have said."

"I will think it over very seriously," he replied.

Lord Chatham was dining at the House that night, and Maud sent a note to Tom asking him to make the fourth with Manvers and her mother. There was no one else coming, and little coats and black ties were the order of the evening.

The night was beautifully warm, and after dinner they all sat on the little terrace outside the drawing-room window.

Tom was in rather a sombre mood. His account of himself was that he had unaccountably stuck in his work and had been unable to get on. Manvers administered consolation.

"That is one of the chiefest pleasures of being an artist," he said : "one has the sort of feeling that one is really a channel through which inspiration flows. Now a solicitor or a clerk can go on copying briefs or making a digest or a *précis* in any mood. He is a mere machine. No doubt his work is more distasteful at one time than it is at another, but it goes on just the same. Nothing comes between him and it except death or very severe toothache, which shows he works without conviction, and is consequently a very feeble sort of animal. It is the same with all mankind except artists and clergymen."

" But what is one to do in the meanwhile ? " asked Tom. " I don't find these intervals, when some one cuts off the inspiration, at all inspiriting."

" Why, do nothing," said Manvers ; "don't think about it. You can't force a mood. The mood forces you."

" I can't acquiesce in that," said Tom. " I am not going to be ordered about by my own temperament."

" Ah, my dear fellow, what are you going to be ordered about by if you are not to be ordered about by your temperament ? The temperament is the only thing that can order one about. In everything else, if one wants a thing enough one gets it."

Maud leaned forward.

" I don't believe that. At least it is not true for all people. Some pass their whole lives in failing to do what they want. But they have a consolation ; for they are exactly the people who for the most part give other people what they want. Personally I hardly ever get what I want, and that is why I have a passion for making other people like me."

At the least hint of anything so superlunary as the mildest metaphysics, Lady Chatham always recorded a protest.

" Maud dear," she said deprecatingly.

But " Maud dear " was interested, and so to judge by his face was Manvers. His dark eyes had lost their look of slight amusement, and he leaned forward eagerly to hear what Maud had to say next.

"It is the old story," she said; "half the world is active, and the other half passive."

"But you exert yourself to be passive."

"Oh, certainly; one is simply nothing if one doesn't exert one's self. My mission, I am sure, is to be material for the active people."

"But you told me once you wanted to take the world into your hand," said Tom, "and make its heart beat fast or slow as you wished."

"I know I did, but I have changed."

"Radically, completely?"

Maud lifted her eyes for a moment and looked at Tom, then dropped them again.

"My desire has not changed, but I now know I can't do it. It's not my line at all."

Tom looked up.

"Do you mean you acquiesce in defeat?" he asked. "Can you contemplate wanting a thing and not getting it?"

"He is monarch of all he surveys," remarked Manvers.

"Of course I am," said Tom, "so is everybody."

"Oh, but we can't all be monarchs of all we survey," said Maud.

"But we can," replied Tom, "simply because we survey so very little. All our horizons are limited. As a matter of fact, of course we are terribly limited, all of us, but we have a beautiful gift of not believing that. We can be monarchs of all we understand, which is what I mean by survey, and that is why people marry. Two people understand each other, and so as they are both monarchs of each other, it is a law of nature that they should then be no longer two, but one."

This remarkable statement was received in silence.

" Then what do you make of people who are failures —real failures ? " said Maud at length.

" God help them ! " replied Tom ; " they have tried to get what they did not understand.   There is nothing so pathetic as that."

" Why did you acquiesce, Miss Wrexham ? " asked Manvers.

Maud hesitated a moment, but assuming with perfect good faith that neither Tom nor Manvers could possibly guess what she meant, replied—

" Because I could not get a thing I wanted, and therefore I assumed that I was not made to get what I wanted."

" That is a hasty generalization," said Tom ; " perhaps you did not understand it."

" Well, I thought I did, and either I am not meant to get what I want, or I am one of those pathetic figures you alluded to."

Tom laughed.

" I don't think of you as a pathetic figure," he said.

" Oh, one can't appear as a pathetic figure in public," she said.   " Don't let us forget that it is a comedy we are all acting."

She spoke bitterly, and Tom was astonished at the hard ring of her voice.   But before the pause became awkward Manvers broke it.

" There is nothing more serious than taking things seriously," he said.   " I never took anything seriously yet."

"What a frightfully risky thing to say!" exclaimed Maud. "It's as dangerous as saying you never had the toothache!"

Tom got up from his chair and perched himself on the edge of the balcony, and at that moment there came into Manvers' mind the evening at Athens, when Tom had sat on the edge of the balcony, and the flash of lightning had illuminated Maud's face. For the first moment he thought it was only one of those strange throbs of double consciousness which we all know so well, but the moment afterwards he recollected the prototype of the scene. And as if to confirm it in his mind, Maud went on—

"My acquiescence came quite suddenly, as suddenly as a flash of lightning."

"When did it come?" asked Tom, innocently.

Manvers waited, in the act of flicking the ash off his cigar, for the reply, and Maud looking up saw he was watching her.

"Lord Byron woke one morning and found himself famous," she said, "but I doubt whether a year afterwards he could have told you whether it was a Monday or a Tuesday."

"But the occasion," persisted Tom: "he could have told one that."

"One occasion doesn't change one," said Maud, fencing; "it is always a whole string of things, half of which one forgets afterwards. It is so untrue to speak of a crisis being the effect of one moment."

Lady Chatham rose.

"How terribly metaphysical you young people are!" she said. "I must go in and write two notes, and then I think I shall go to the House in the carriage which is to fetch Chatham. Maud dear, you look rather tired. Go to bed early."

Lady Chatham said good night and went indoors.

"That is quite true about crises," said Tom, after a pause. "I have had one, two, three in my life, and though they all seemed the results of single moments, they were only the culmination of what had been going on before."

"But the apex of a pyramid remains the highest point. There would be no pyramid without it," objected Manvers.

"But still less would an apex be a pyramid by itself!"

"It's your turn, Tom," said Maud. "I've been talking about myself, and now you shall talk about yourself. Begin at the beginning. What were your crises?"

"The first was when I saw the Hermes at Olympia," began Tom.

"And a most disastrous crisis it was," observed Manvers. "I hope they weren't all as cheerless as that."

"Be quiet, Mr. Manvers," said Maud. "It's his turn."

"Of course that seemed to me the whole crisis," said Tom, "but it wasn't. It was only the apex of the effect Athens had on me."

"Yes, I think that's reasonable," said Maud. "Go on to the next."

"The next was when I was standing in a bramble bush waiting for pigeons to come over, and saw May walking down the path. She looked as if she had just stepped out from among the gods and goddesses on the Parthenon frieze. You see the first crisis was really part of the second."

Maud said nothing, so Manvers took up the part of catechist.

"And the third?"

"Oh, about that I can't talk. But I know now that the whole of my life from the time of the second crisis, since I fell in love with May, was part of the third."

"Oh, but do tell us," said Maud. "I believe you have forgotten what it was."

"It was when I first thought I was a Christian," said Tom simply. "But——" He stopped.

If Tom had said that it was when he first began to hate May, he could not have startled them more. Manvers felt very keenly the indecency of being serious. Maud sat still for a moment. Her knack of turning awkward conversation on to safer lines seemed to have entirely deserted her.

"No wonder you are perfectly happy," she said at length, and stopped. They sat there for a few minutes in silence, and Tom fidgeted.

"It was a crisis no doubt," he went on; "for the time it made a most wonderful difference to me, but somehow it has faded. Why are we all so damnably limited, or rather why are we cursed with that horrible sense of proportion, which makes us realize how limited we are? The happiest moment of my life was that on the morning after the baby had been born, when I went to early celebration. It was the best moment I have ever had, and I was even content. I had been horribly anxious and frightened the day before, and the relief and the joy were so immense that for the moment I was forced, so I thought then, to believe. Unhappily, common-sense is for ever telling me that it was relief and not belief that I experienced. Yet it was a crisis, for I now believe in the possibility of such convictions some day becoming mine, for for a little while they were mine, and what has happened to me temporarily may happen to me permanently. And now," he added, "I have committed what Manvers considers the one unpardonable breach of manners. I have been serious!"

Again there was silence, and neither Maud nor Manvers saw exactly how to break it. But a neighbouring clock striking eleven gave Tom an opportunity.

"It is time for me to go," he said ; "I had no idea how late it was. May comes up to-morrow, I hope."

The other two sat where they were till the wheels of Tom's retreating hansom had merged themselves in the distant muffled roar of the further streets. To Maud it suddenly seemed that malignant hands were building up again in front of her that blank wall she had been at such pains to demolish, and that her work of the autumn was all undone. Tom's presence, mingled with his absolute unconsciousness of its effect, had again reasserted its unreasonable power over her. She felt again as she had begun to feel at Athens, that she was miserable in his presence and incomplete in his absence. But her efforts at self-control had become with her a habit, and though she was dully conscious that her blank wall had rebuilt itself, she did not dash at it with dumb unavailing hands. It had to be picked down again stone by stone from the top to the bottom. The prospect was not a cheering one. She was also more than half conscious that Manvers was standing, as it were, on the other side of the wall, hidden from her by its intervening mass, and she dreaded that he would call to her, and assure her of it. That he was in love with her she could not but know, and she was quite aware that she liked him almost to any extent; but the limitations of the human race forbid us to love two people at once. Nature has provided us with two eyes, two ears, two arms, two legs, two hands, in case some accident happens to one of them, but her wise precaution has not gone so far as to provide us with two people to love simultaneously, in case one of them gets married.

She was sitting in the chair Tom had left, and Manvers, who had been sitting a little way off, moved up and took the chair next her. She had one mad impulse to ask him not to speak, for she saw he meant to. However, if the scene was to come, it was to come, and he had the right, as a man, to know his fate. But though she knew it was to come, she wanted to put it off if only for a minute or two. She rose from her chair again, and leant on the balustrade of the balcony.

" I feel depressed and worried and strung up and run down to-night," she said. " Do you remember that admirably sensible American girl at Athens, who said that all such feelings were stomach ? I expect it is quite true, but I don't see how it helps one. I don't feel sure of myself. Tom very often makes me feel like that. He's so wonderfully sure of himself."

Manvers' hands fidgeted with the arms of his chair, and he lit a cigarette, and threw it away. This sort of experience was new to him.

"And now as we've finished talking about Tom," he said at length, "it is time that we should talk about me."

Maud rushed for the loophole. She might as well have hoped to have stopped an express by stretching a piece of string across the line.

"I should like to talk a little more about him," she said. "I was so surprised at that third crisis."

"Tom is so honest with his crises," said Manvers, "he faces them like a man."

"Well, it's no use running away from a crisis," said Maud; "you might as well run away from a flash of lightning."

"And I too think it is best to face a crisis," said he, "and . . . and . . . my crisis has come."

Maud sat still, waiting for the inevitable.

"It is this," he said suddenly, "that I love you. That I would die for you, or live for you : that I offer you myself to take into your hand."

Maud stood up. The crisis had come, and she knew what she was going to say. It was best to leave no misunderstanding.

"It is impossible," she said, "absolutely impossible. I will not give you any hope. I can't encourage you by telling you to wait. It can never be. Stop, don't speak yet. I am sorry for you, more sorry than I can say; but I am perfectly certain of it."

Manvers stood up too.

"How can you be certain?" he said. "I will take my answer like a gentleman, and not hope to win you by making myself importunate ; but how is there no hope ? "

"It is quite impossible," said Maud again.

For the moment he had forgotten about the existence of Tom and all the world, but as Maud repeated "It is quite impossible," the cruelty of her position and of his stung him intolerably, and forced from him an involuntary protest, as sudden physical pain forces a cry from the most stoical.

"Ah, God help us both !" he said.

Maud turned and looked at him. She was standing with her back to the street, and he was opposite her, so that her face was in darkness, his in light. And in his face she saw pity, love, tenderness and the knowledge of her secret mingled together.

She had one moment of furious indignation with him for even letting her know that he knew all. But he came a step nearer and held out both hands to her.

"Oh, you poor dear! you poor dear!" he said. "Without a thought of any possible gain, I would give my right hand to spare you this. It is much worse for you than for me."

The shadow of convention which had stood between them sank away into nothingness, for convention is born of the head, not of the heart, and when heart meets heart, there is no place for head. Maud took his two outstretched hands and pressed them.

"You are a man," she said, "and that is the highest

praise of all. I have tried very hard to be a woman, but I have not succeeded so well."

"You have succeeded very well," he said. "No one has guessed it."

Pride is not a dominant emotion, and is driven off the field as soon as the greater magnates appear.

"After all," she thought wearily, "what does it matter?" And then because her passion was strong and she was young, she broke down utterly. "My God, what shall I do?" she cried, "and what are you to think of me? I have thrown overboard self-respect, and reticence, and decency. I have nothing left but the hope that he knows nothing of it."

Manvers lied bravely.

"I am sure he has never had an inkling of it," he said. "It has been hard for you."

"And all the time there is the horrible consciousness that one may break down."

"You will not break down. When one has great physical pain, one thinks one cannot endure it a moment longer. But as a matter of fact one can and does. One endures it until it stops."

"But who is to assure me of that? Not you, of all men, who have guessed my secret."

"It was no fault of yours that I guessed it. It was because I fell in love with you myself."

His voice assumed its usual tone of gentler cynicism.

"And love," he added, "which is usually considered blind, is on the contrary extremely clear sighted. Man is a wonderful creature, as one of Tom's Greek poets says, and we are beautifully adapted for bearing things without breaking. There is no last straw for us. We go on hoping that each straw is going to be the last, that we shall break, but we can always bear some more. And there usually are some more."

"Don't say bitter things, Mr. Manvers. One may say bitter things to strangers, but never to friends. There's father's carriage; I must go upstairs. I told mother I should go to bed early. You leave us to-morrow, don't you? I needn't tell you how sorry I am."

"You are very good to me," said poor Manvers.

"I am intensely sorry for you. Spare a little sorrow for me. And you have behaved admirably. Good night."

Manvers heard the front door close, and a few minutes afterwards the voices of Lord and Lady Chatham as they went upstairs. A servant came in to put out the lamps; but, seeing Manvers there, would have retreated. He told the man to leave him a candle, and put the lamps out; he needn't wait up.

The house grew still, and even the noise in the streets sank to a lower murmur in those three hours which precede the summer dawn. It was already after twelve when the Chathams returned, and Manvers sat on in the low chair in the balcony smoking endless cigarettes and reviewing events.

He really was not cut out, he thought, for a man of sentiment. He cursed himself for ever having let himself be led into this horrible situation. He had been so happy to the full capacities of his nature in these last thoughtless successful years. He had lived for the hour in all the branches of his nature; his art was of the hour, his pleasures were of the hour, his aims were of the hour. But now he had acquired a new power—he had found he was capable of loving ; and a new limitation—he was incapable of not doing so. And where did it all lead to ? Tom stood full in his road, with his careless happy face, forbidding him, or rather unconsciously making it impossible for him to pass.

The city turned in its sleep, and a strange nestful of street noises hatched, clacked, and were silent again. The short summer night was drawing to a close. A wavering hint of dawn flickered across the pale faces of the houses opposite, and faded out again, and the deeper blackness of the half hour before the real dawn came on in layers over the sky. Manvers rose and leaned over the balcony looking down into the street.

Why not leave all this behind and go back to Paris as it was ? The hours were still hours, minutes in which to live and enjoy. But it seemed impossible. Some change had come. He was puzzled and bewildered with himself. He had always thought he knew himself as well as he knew his modelling tools, but he had given himself a great surprise. Time would heal everything, would it ? He would go back to Paris and get over it by degrees, and become what he had been before, thanks to Time ! But for that he thought not the better of Time and of himself, but the worse.

And what of Tom ? He would sit here again and again, talking to Maud with intimate freedom, amusing himself, laying down the law about art with a big A, and she would sit opposite him with her uncommunicated incommunicable secret, longing, loving, rejecting. Why had he gone to Athens, why had that series of a hundred trivial events happened, which had forged together this double iron chain, pulling two ways, yielding in neither ?　Damn Tom !

There was no conclusion.　To-morrow he went to Paris.　He was going to a little dinner given by one of the cleverest and most realistic artists of the day, to celebrate the admission of a picture to the Luxembourg.　He had promised himself an amusing evening. Paris was the only place fit to dine in.　Then he had to set to work again.　He congratulated himself that his work sprang from the head, not the heart.　It was summer in Paris by now.　The *cafés* would have their rows of little tables in the street, and their green tubs of oleanders.　There would be the smell of asphalt in the boulevards.　The new advertisements of the year would be out.　Chéret had done two at least, which were quite admirable : one was a Parisienne of the Parisiennes in a long black boa, and balloon sleeves in the new mode ; the other a woman in a yellow dress carrying a red lamp.　How stupid and distasteful it all seemed !

One by one the stars paled, as the first colourless light of dawn crept from the east over the sky.　It was morning already.　There came the sound of heavy wheels, and a string of vans passed eastwards with their loads of flowers and fruit to Covent Garden. They left behind them in the still air a vague perfume of flowers and ripe fruit and vegetables, which floated even up to where he was sitting.　How very short, how infinitely long the night had been !　It was impossible to go to bed ; he would go out.　He went to his room, and put on a grey coat instead of his dining-jacket, and let himself silently out of the house.

It was exactly at that hour when night and morning meet ; cabs and carriages went westwards with women in ball dresses yawning dismally, while eastwards trailed the vans and carts. A woman at the street corner accosted him. Manvers gave her ten shillings, and told her to get home for God's sake. Then he fairly laughed at himself. He was giving himself all sorts of surprises. But he could not bear the thought that one of the sex to which the one woman belonged should stand there.

And in the cool temperate dawn he faced his life and himself temperately. His old life was impossible for reasons which he could not grasp. He had no feeling that it was wrong or immoral ; he approached it from a different side. His taste simply revolted against it. He had said once that he could not possibly feel the least liking for a man who ate cheese with his knife. The two were on the same footing. The old life was out of the question, but where was the new ? And for that he had no answer ready.

He walked eastwards for an hour or so and then turned back, and as he reached the door the pitiless day had broken in a flood of yellow sunshine over the drowsy town.

CHAPTER XIV.

TOM, as he had mentioned on the previous evening, had come to a difficult place in his statue, and he could not get on. He was puzzled to know what the fault was, or where the difficulty was. He saw in his own mind what he wanted to do, but he could not visualize the vision. And when May arrived on the following day she found him inclined to rail at clay, models, drapery and himself. He had seen Manvers off in the morning at Victoria, and that evening he dined alone with May.

"I'm so sorry he's gone," he said to her. "He is so extraordinarily inspiring in a sort of back-handed way. He puts his own point of view so brilliantly, that I realize how diabolical it is, and that spurs me to work for mine. He has the same effect on me as the sight of a drunken man was supposed to have on Spartan boys. Their fathers used to make a slave drunk and then bring him in, and say, ' Look at that. Isn't it horrible ! Take warning !' "

Tom moved over to where May was sitting, and possessed himself of her hand.

"You've grown thin, darling," he said ; "look how your rings slip about. May, I'm so glad you've come. I have been very bad company to myself lately. When

I stick in my work, and you are not here, I don't know what to do. But when I've got you, sticking doesn't seem to depress me."

"I'm afraid I can't prevent your sticking though, Tom."

"I believe there is nothing you can't do for me."

"No, dear," said May, "I'm very sorry, but we must face it. I don't understand about your work at all. I'm not the least artistic. If you are pleased, I am pleased; but when you are not pleased, I can't help you. Mr. Manvers could; for that I am sorry he has gone."

"Don't you like him?" asked Tom.

May was silent a moment.

"Tom, you won't be angry with me, will you," she said at length, "because I am going to say something which I have had on my mind for a long time, and which I think I had better say. It is this. Do you think it is right for you to see much of him, to know him, to be at all intimate with him? Oh, Tom, he is not a good man! I don't know about his life, and you probably do; but I am sure of that. He has no better aim in life than the success of his own wits. He has a bad effect on you. He makes you think lightly of things which are more important than anything else. Oh, I've got such a lot to say to you!"

Tom smiled.

"Say it, darling."

May sat up and played rather nervously with her rings.

"And when you stick in your work, Tom," she went on, "do you think it is well to stimulate yourself in the sort of way you mention? You know you aim at the best, and all that is good comes from one quarter. Do you ever go there for help?"

"You mean, do I pray?"

"Yes, Tom."

Tom got up and walked up and down the room.

"It is like this," he said: "I believe in God, and I believe in good, but I also believe in things like laws of nature, and if God created all things, He created them. He has given me a brain which works in obedience to certain laws, and nothing in the world can alter them. We know a little about the brain, at least by experience we find that certain things stimulate it; it works best when it is keen and eager, and I use those things to make it keen and eager which I have found by experience do so. No, when I stick in my work, I don't pray."

"But that is the essence of good work," said May; "it is that which makes it good—the fact that it is done in a spirit of dedication."

"But, do you then think that a good man, in so far as he is good and dedicates his work to God, necessarily produces good work?" asked Tom.

"I mean that a man who has a gift in any line, uses his gift best and produces more beautiful things if he dedicates it. Why, Tom, look at the difference between your things and Mr. Manvers'. I think he is not a good man, and I think his things are not good for that reason."

Tom sat down again.

"It all depends on what you mean by good and bad work," he said. "I think the object of a beautiful thing is only to be beautiful, and I think his things are bad because they are ugly—at least, they seem to me ugly."

"But the object of all beauty is to bring us nearer God," said May.

"Yet a work of art which arouses religious emotions is not a better work of art than one which does not. Otherwise, a chromo-lithograph of the Sistine Madonna would be a better work of art than that terrible splendid Salome in the Louvre."

"I think Mr. Manvers' things are immoral," said May.

"You don't understand, dear," he said. "His things, so I think, are bad because he has a debased taste. It is his artistic sense that is warped, and it is that which shows in his work, and not his character. Besides, I think you are not fair to him, May."

"Oh, but, Tom," she said, with indignation in her voice, "think of his life, that life among those Paris artists, that horrible vice, and carelessness of living."

Tom smiled.

"Where did you learn about the life of Paris artists?" he asked. "Manvers says they are most inoffensive little people as a rule."

"I read all about it in 'David Grieve,'" said May seriously. "It is horrible."

This time he laughed right out.

"Oh, May, you are a darling!" he said. "Oh dear, how funny! I'm so sorry for laughing; but really it is funny. Have you ever heard Manvers talk about that? He becomes quite virtuous and indignant over it. I don't know much about Paris life myself, I was only there a month or two, but Manvers—he does not strike you as being very like David Grieve in Paris, does he?"

May joined in Tom's laugh, but grew serious again.

"You know I feel about it very deeply," she said; "there is nothing in the world I feel about so much. I think it is our first duty not to condone by word or deed what one knows is bad. To let people see that one will not tolerate it, to fight against it, to—to show that one loathes it."

"Do you mean you want me never to see Manvers again?" asked Tom.

"No, not that," said May, "because you know him well, and he is very fond of you, and I think you do him good. But couldn't you do him more good? Couldn't you talk to him about it, and bear your testimony?"

"No, dear," said Tom, quietly, "I couldn't possibly. It is not my business. I know Manvers as a friend, as an excellent companion, as a most amusing fellow. Why, May, he would think I was mad. Men do not talk to each other about such things."

"But surely it is our business," said May. "Tom, you don't think me tiresome, do you?"

Tom smiled, and took up her hand again.

"My darling, I happen to love you," he said, "and it does not occur to one to think a person one loves tiresome."

May went on with gathering earnestness.

"Surely it is our business," she said. "You believe in God, you believe in Christ, in His infinite love, His infinite care for all. Surely it is your first business to help in His work. I remember what you told me about that early celebration you went to. It completed my happiness : it was that I was waiting for, and I thank God for it day and night. I longed to see you more and talk about it, but you went up to London so soon after, and I have scarcely seen you since."

Tom's eyebrows contracted. It was impossible for him to let May be deceived, but what he had to do was a bitter thing. May's eyes were fixed on his, full of love and trust, but with a question in them, a desire to be confirmed in what she had said.

"May, I am going to hurt you," he said, looking away, " but I cannot help it ; I cannot let you think something about me which is not true. I think I over-rated that—I mean that I thought more of it than it really meant to me. The day before I was in agonies of anxiety and fear for you, and that afternoon Ted and I met the funeral of a mother who had just died in child-bed, and on my way home, as I told you, I went into the church and prayed to an unknown God that you might be safe. I could not bear it alone. And then next morning I could not bear my joy alone. I had—I was obliged to thank some one for it, the some one who had heard my prayer the evening before. And now the whole thing has faded a little. I am less sure. I do not deny that God heard my prayer, and stretched out His hand to save you, but it is less real to me. Supposing you had died, should I have denied absolutely the existence of God ? I hope not. Then why should I affirm it because you lived ? "

Tom's voice had sunk lower and lower, and he

ended in a whisper. But May's hand still lay in his, and she pressed it tenderly.

"Tom, why were you afraid to tell me?" she said. "Ah, my dear, I should be a very weak, poor creature if this separated me at all from you, or made me doubt you. What did you think of me? Of course I am sorry, and yet I am hardly sorry. Am I to dictate to God by what way He shall lead you? He has not led you that way, it was not good. Tom, Tom!"

She bent forward and kissed him, her arm was pressed round his neck, and her head lay on his breast. As once before, on the evening when they reached Applethorpe before the baby's birth, human love and longing had full possession of her; and as she lay there, she felt only that she loved him. And Tom too was content.

But good moments pass as well as bad ones, and the sense that May lived in a different world to him could not but come back again and again to Tom. He could not but feel that there was a passion in her life in which he had no share, and that passion was the strongest she knew. He had tried to grasp it; once he thought he had grasped it, but he was wrong. He was as honest to himself as he was to others, and he admitted that he did not believe in God in the way he believed in May or in Art. The life of Christ was beautiful beyond all other lives, but was it different in kind from the lives of noble unselfish men? Was Christ anything more than the most wonderful, the most unselfish man that the world has ever seen? And from the fact that he could ask himself these questions, Tom knew that he was not convinced. It was just this that was the most essential part of May's life ; her love and tenderness for him and others sprang from that, whereas Tom felt that all that was good in him did not descend from above, but grew up from below.

May was certainly less conscious of this than he. She, so to speak, was waiting for him to come, believing fully he would, while he was struggling towards her, afraid that his efforts were futile. The least he could do, he felt, and the most, was to avoid letting her know that he was so conscious of the gulf between them. He loved her, he thought, more and more as the days went by, and it should be easy to stifle that little ounce of bitter where all else was so sweet. So long as she loved him, he felt that it would be well with him.

Meantime the London season danced and laughed round them ; the clay model of Demeter was finished and was to be put in the pointer's hands at once. May produced a slight stir in a small circle, because she was beautiful, and there is quite an appreciable number of men who prefer that a woman should not talk much, because, as is very justly remarked, if everybody talked much, nobody would have any audience to address. She was always courteous, she always looked admirable, and the general opinion was that Tom had "done himself" uncommonly well.

Moreover—and this was particularly interesting, because it was never spoken above a whisper—Miss Wrexham was not looking at all well, and there really must have been something in what every one was saying last year. Very sad for her, was it not? but a girl has no business to go about looking pale; of course that set every one talking, and a little rouge, you know, would both conceal the pallor and mitigate the blush. Oh yes, it happened many times; only last night, in fact, when we were dining there, Tom Carlingford's name came up and she blushed—several people saw her. And she wasn't at Ascot, nor was he, and that is quite conclusive. And besides, her going to Athens was so very extraordinary. Oh, she had a brother there, had she? We hadn't heard that, and we shall probably forget it again.

Maud, it must be confessed, did not enjoy herself very much that season. In the natural course of things she met Tom often, and the task of unbuilding that most uncompromising blank wall seemed too disheartening. Every time she saw him she felt that things were getting more and more difficult. What made it worse was that May had unthawed to her, and often asked her to come out with her. May out of the fulness of her heart constantly spoke of Tom, and talking about Tom was rather emotional work for poor Maud. That terrible evening before Manvers went away had taken her and thrust her back into all her old hopelessness and blankness. "After all, what good to strive with a life awry?" she asked herself, and then because she was pure and good and sweet, she strove and strove till her strength began to give way. If only Tom would leave London, she thought, or if only she could, things would be more possible.

A little scene which had occurred long before, often came back to her during these weeks. One day at their house in Cornwall, she was walking early before breakfast along a narrow country lane. She could almost smell again that sweet intangible scent of morning, the smell of clean things. Now and then a whiff of dogrose crossed her, and now and then a breeze which had blown through a gorse bush came over her face. At the lodge gate she had spoken to the old keeper's wife, whose son had got into trouble. The poor old lady was rather tearful about it, and said: "Lor, miss, if we were good how happy we should be!" She had repeated the remark once to Manvers, who said he thought the old woman had got hold of the wrong end of the stick, and that she would have spoken more truthfully if she had said, "If we were happy, how good we should be!"

How extraordinarily happy she had been that morning! The whole world had seemed so clean and fresh and wholesome, so delightfully straightforward and uncomplicated. If only she could get back that feeling, just for a moment, she thought she would be rested and ready to begin again. In the old days nothing had seemed hard, nothing out of reach, nothing perplexing. And now her life was spoiled.

One evening early in June she was having tea with May, longing for Tom to come in, dreading that he would come. May had sent for the baby, and he was sitting on his mother's knee regarding his toes, which apparently seemed to him very wonderful inventions and quite original, and his mother was taking a sympathetic interest in his discoveries. Maud, who had been quite fascinating to the infant mind till he found out about his toes, had been thrown over, and as May's attention was riveted on her son, she felt just a little out of it.   Suddenly May looked up.

"Just fancy," she said, "this little mite is our own, Tom's and mine: I never get quite used to that fact. Yes, darling"—she turned her attention to the baby— "how pretty, and that's all yours.   Oh, you angel!"

Maud felt her breath catch in her throat, and on the moment the door opened and Tom came in.

"Baby-cult as usual," he said.   "How are you, Maud?"

Maud could not quite command her voice, but she murmured something.

"That surprising infant usurps far too much of May's time," continued he.   "May will never quite recognize that one baby is rather like another baby."

May bent over the little sparsely be-haired head.

"What an unnatural papa he's got!" she said; "he says you're like other babies.   You know quite well, and so does he, that there never was a baby like you, and never will be!"

Tom's pleasant soul sat laughing in his eyes as he answered her.

"Mothers are said to be biassed in favour of their own young; never you believe that, my boy."

Then he turned to Maud.

"May's manners are cast to the winds when His Smallness is present," he said; "she won't attend to either of us, so we'll attend to each other.   Are you going to the Levesons' to-morrow?   I hear they are going to be very smart, and that it's a case of red carpet.   May, I must smoke a cigarette.   I don't care whether it's the drawing-room or not."

"And fill the room with horrid, horrid smoke," said May to her son.

"I hardly know," said Maud; "I've been overdoing it lately, and I think I shall go into my shell again for a bit. Wouldn't it be nice to have a real shell, and curl yourself up in the middle of a dinner-party if you were bored."

"I shall order one," said Tom, thoughtfully. "You do look rather tired. Where are you going to put your shell? If I were you I should leave London for a week. It would be so original. You would of course let it be known that you were going to read 'Sordello.' 'Sordello' is the fashion now, I think. Of course nobody has read it and that's why they talk about it. No one talks about a thing they really have read."

"That has a slight flavour of Mr. Manvers," remarked May.

"Manvers has such a pungent flavour, that one really can't help catching a little of it, if one sees him at all," said Tom. "But I wasn't consciously Manveresque—I suppose he's in Paris, associating with all the good dead Americans."

May smiled.

"And now mammy's going to take him upstairs," she said, and left the room.

Tom poured himself out a cup of tea.

"Please talk nonsense to me," he said; "I've been seeing Wallingthorpe, and—and of course he's a delightful man, but he is so serious. He takes everybody and everything seriously, including himself. That is so clever of him—and the worst of it is he keeps it up. He is always clever. How tiring he must find it!"

Maud laughed, but the laugh ended abruptly.

"Talk nonsense!" she said; "I have forgotten how. Oh, Tom, the world is a very serious place!"

Tom raised his eyebrows.

"When did you find that out?" he asked.

"I? Oh, ever so long ago!" she said rather wildly "If you take it lightly and pleasantly, it turns round on you somehow, and deals you sudden back-handed blows. I don't know why I am saying all this."

"Hit it back," suggested Tom. "It deals blows back-handed possibly, but it caresses you back-handed too."

Maud put on her gloves, and fitted her fingers carefully.

"I am out of sorts," she said; "the world is grievously awry."

"What's the matter?"

"I am the matter. It's nobody else. But what is one to do?"

Maud knew she was being unwise. She knew perfectly well that she would be sorry for this, but the hope that Tom might understand seemed to her the only thing worth caring for, and at the same time the one thing in all the world which she dreaded. She was afraid, desperately afraid, of saying too much, but she could not help herself. "Why will not he understand?" she thought, "and God forbid that he should." But Tom was in a thoroughly superficial mood. He said to himself that Maud was out of sorts, that she was overtired and worried.

"Man disquieteth himself in vain," he said. "It is best to take living very lightly. We all of us have something we want to do or be, and cannot do or be it. We are wise if we let it alone. There is much I want to do and be, and cannot manage it, and every one is in the same plight. After all, if we aim at being contented, that is enough."

Maud got up.

"Aim at being contented? Aim at being in Heaven! We have to remember that we are on earth."

Tom rose too.

"What is the matter?" he said; "do tell me."

Again Maud felt stifled and choking.

"One is a creature of moods," she said, "and the heavy moods come, as well as the light. Just now I have a heavy mood. By the way, I shall follow your advice. I am rather overdone, and I shall leave London for a time. I shall not say I am reading 'Sordello.' I think I shall say I am reading the Bible—it is the better book. I shall go before the end of the week: at present I am going now. Give my adieux to your wife. She is more charming than ever!"

But at this moment May came in, and Maud gave her adieux in person. Tom was vaguely puzzled.

"It's very sudden," he said. "Are you going really?"

"Certainly," said Maud; "I really am going—I am going away for a whole fortnight. I want tone, and there is no such thing in London."

Tom laughed.

"I am inclined to agree with you," he said.

"Well, good-bye," said Maud ; "good-bye, May— that fascinating child is quite too fascinating."

May sat still a moment after she had gone. "What is the matter with her ?" she asked ; "what have you been saying, Tom ? I never saw her like that."

"Nor have I," said he. " I have said nothing. I have no idea what is the matter with her."

Maud stood on the doorstep, and looked to see if the carriage was in sight, and finding it not there, remembered that her mother had "worked it in," and began to walk home. But she felt hopelessly ill and weak, and told the man to fetch her a hansom. "O God! how tired I am of it all!" she said to herself.

CHAPTER XIV.

IT is probably true that when things are at their worst they begin to mend, but the little complications common to man sometimes exhibit a ghastly ingenuity of contrivance before that most desirable point is reached. As Manvers said, we are wonderful creatures, and beautifully adapted for bearing things. But Nature has been merciful enough to give most of us a weak point, and when the weak point is touched we are privileged to break down.

Maud, whose moral nature was very robust, was not physically strong, and that night she fainted incontinently in the middle of dinner. The doctor came—a doctor whose words were literally words of gold—and said, worry, overstrain, change of air, out of doors, sunshine ; and Maud's determination to leave London was made easy for her.

Lady Ramsden had managed to survive her husband, and was continuing to enjoy unagitated widowhood and her usual ill-health in her house on the Norfolk coast. She had grown a little stouter, a shade duller, and a trifle more monosyllabic, but otherwise time seemed to have let her be. She replied to Lady Chatham's letter that she would be delighted to see Maud, but that her health was indifferent, and that Maud would probably be rather lonely. But if she wanted sea air and sunshine, she could

not do better than come. She would be charmed to
have her, and would she say the day and hour of her
arrival, and whether she was going to bring a maid.

Lady Ramsden's house stood on the edge of the
short-turfed Norfolk Downs, within a hundred yards
of the sea. The sand-cliffs, nibbled off short by the
waves, rose some thirty feet from the beach, and the
grass, fine and smooth, covered them to the edge,
fitting their mounds and hollows so exactly that they
looked as if they had been measured for a green baize
billiard cloth. A mile to the north the red-roofed
little town of Cromer went trooping down to the
shore, with its tall grave tower seeming to confer an
air of safety to the whole, but not checking a terrible
tendency in the town to run to seed, as it were, on all
sides in rows of jerry-built villas. But at this time of
the year the villas were still unoccupied for the most
part, and the town was a fishing village once more.

Maud arrived in the afternoon, and she drew in
long breaths of the fresh sea air with a sense of relief,
of struggle over. She was tired and overdone—tired
of life, of worry, of sensation, and she thought that
here perhaps she could stay still, being cut off from
any thought of agitating impossibilities, of fruitless
self-restraint, and of thrice fruitless desires. There
was an air of complete, contented repose about the
big landscape and the wide flat sea. The tide was
up, and the sea looked full and prosperous. Little
curling ripples washed up over the sand, and now and
then one more energetic than its fellows thrust out
a sharp tongue to the very base of the sandy cliffs and
then drew back again with a louder murmur of content.

Round the house were rambling, uneven lawns, only half broken in, as it were, and retaining something of the freedom of the grass-clad sandhills, and a satisfying medley of flower-beds, full of great hardy plants which cared nothing for the brisk salt air—nasturtiums, great flaring double poppies, the velvet tassels of love-lies-a-bleeding, and thick-leaved stone-crops. Sturdy health seemed the key-note of the place.

At tea she saw Lady Ramsden, who strove to convey to her that she was glad to see her, and that her niece was also staying with her—her coming had been very sudden and upsetting—but that she had gone over to Cromer for a tennis party, and would be back before dinner, and as soon as tea was over Maud went out again and struck for the edge of the sandy cliffs.

Ah! the relief of getting away from London, away from the possibility of seeing Tom, from the possibility of torturing herself, of leading herself into temptation. Surely it was possible here, with this great shining sea on one side, and the firm landscape on the other, to regain her belief in serenity, to recapture an uncomplicated outlook.

She took off her hat, and let the bracing air from the sea blow her hair about. A mile off shore the little fleet of herring-boats were tacking with full, stiff sails down the coast to begin their strange adventure of casting nets into that shifting immensity beneath the deep fathomless sky above the deep fathomless sea. How did morning look to them as it broke in thin red lines on the horizon? How interesting it would be to be able to see the world just for a moment with other eyes, to be rid for one deep-drawn breath of the weight of one's own stale identity! It was in that direction her salvation lay. She meant to cease focussing her eyes on her own microscopic troubles, to gain a wider outlook. How much more attainable such an idea seemed here, where there was some breadth of vision, and a horizon not bounded by house-roofs! London was a mere warren, full of silly gossiping rabbits. You could never see beyond the street corner, nor through the smoke.

The light in the west flamed and paled, and Maud began to retrace her steps. She felt better already. Oh, how right Miss Vanderbilt had been about the seat of the emotions! She would dose herself with sea air, she would bathe herself in sun and sea, she would get back her old serenity, her interest in things, her uncomplicated outlook. How pretty the house looked, standing out against the still ruddy sky, with the lights in its windows! There was some one standing in the porch—a girl. It must be Lady Ramsden's niece. Maud felt quite pleased to have a companion. They would walk and ride and bathe together. Lady Ramsden's niece—on which side, Carlingford or Ramsden?

The door was opened just before Maud got up to it, and the girl was standing by the lamp in the hall, opening a note when she entered. As she looked at her Maud's heart suddenly stood still, and then jumped up into her throat, poised and hammering. There was no need to ask on which side she was Lady Ramsden's niece, for as Maud came in she turned, and for a moment—it came on her like a horrible dream—she almost thought she stood face to face with Tom himself.

The girl looked up with that little raising of the eyebrows which Maud had so often seen in Tom, and greeted her.

“You are surely Miss Wrexham, are you not?” she said, coming forward with boyish frankness. “It is too delightful to meet you. I think you know my cousin Tom? You have had tea? Yes? I wonder where my aunt is.”

Violet Carlingford led the way to the drawing-room, where Lady Ramsden was lying on a sofa by a carefully shaded lamp. Her wheezy asthmatic pug lay snoring at her feet. She looked the incarnation of incompetence.

“So you have met,” she said, “and introduced yourselves.”

Violet laughed.

“I don’t think we introduced ourselves much,” she said. “I said, ‘Aren’t you Miss Wrexham?’ How are you, aunty?”

“Not very well, dear,” she said; “and Flo isn’t very well either. Listen to her breathing.”

Violet smiled, and two dimples came into her face. They were hardly so deep as Tom’s, but in exactly the same place.

“There’s no need to listen,” she said.

“I shall not come to dinner,” went on Lady Ramsden in a thin voice. “You two will dine alone. What time do you like dinner, Maud? We usually have it at eight. Will that suit you? Oh yes; and what is your maid’s name?”

Lady Ramsden got the bell rung for her, and got herself taken out of the room. The pug was hoisted

on to a velvet cushion and was carried before her.
In such manner did the Greeks carry the emblems of
their gods before their images.

As Maud looked at Violet she saw that the likeness
was even more extraordinary, and went deeper than
she had noticed at first. Violet could hardly have
been more than twenty, and her features were still
unsexed. She was tall for a girl, and slightly built,
and her walk and way of sitting, or rather lolling,
as she was lolling now, reminded Maud exactly
of what Tom had been when he came to stay with
them once while he was at Eton, and sat laughing and talking with them all at the end of five
minutes as naturally as if he had known them all his
life. She had Tom's short square-tipped nose, his
clear, open, brown eyes, with long fine eyelashes and
thin straight eyebrows. Her mouth, like his, was
rather full-lipped, and often even when she was not
speaking the white of her teeth showed between the
lips in a straight narrow line. But her manner was
even more fundamentally his. She had Tom's trick
of wrinkling his nose up slightly when he was amused,
of putting his head slightly on one side when he was
listening or considering, and in speaking of just per-
ceptibly slurring his r's, of separating his words one
from the other more like a foreigner with a perfect
command of English than an Englishman.

Violet strolled about the room just as he did,
putting a book or two straight, and making a little
face at the pug's saucer of tea with cream in it which
lay untasted in the corner. Violet disliked that pug ;
he was fat, lazy, wheezy, and selfish, and she gave

Maud a little sketch of his character. Soon she sat down near her and began on more personal topics.

"It is delightful to have you here," she said. "I hope we shall make great friends. I always want to be doing something all day, and if you like playing golf and tennis, and bathing and riding, I'm sure we shall get on."

Maud was leaning back in her chair, feeling somehow unaccountably shy.

"I was quite startled when I came in," she said; "you are so extraordinarily like your cousin."

Violet crossed one leg over the other and clasped her hands behind her head.

"I haven't seen Tom for an age," she said; "but when we were younger we were exactly alike. Tom— it was wicked of him—once dressed up in a skirt and cloak, and hat of mine, and went into my mother's room and asked if she wanted anything in the town as he was going there with the governess. My mother gave him all sorts of feminine commissions and never suspected him till he burst out laughing. His mother and mine were sisters, and our fathers brothers, you know. Has he changed much?"

"He is still exactly like you," said Maud, who was beginning to feel more at her ease.

"Tom's getting quite famous, isn't he?" the girl went on. "That will serve to differentiate us. And he's got a baby. How funny it seems! We always said he would never grow up."

"He hasn't grown up much," said Maud. "He is just like a boy still in many ways."

"It's such a pity one has to get older," remarked

Violet. " I'm sure I shall never enjoy myself so much when I am old, and I shall get stuffy and think about complications and worries. At present I never worry."

Maud smiled.

" I am afraid I must be getting old," she said ; " in fact, I came here in order to forget complications and worries."

Violet sat up with an air of surprise.

" Oh, please don't worry," she said, " or you will spoil it all. And we can have such a charming time if we like."

Maud rose.

" I will do my best to worry no more," she said. " And will you help me ? "

Her voice had a wonderful sweetness and tenderness about it. Violet got up too and stood close to her.

" Why, that's charming of you," she said. " I don't think I could ever help anybody ; but I will promise never to worry, if that is any use, Miss Wrexham."

" The utmost use," said Maud ; " and I am not Miss Wrexham. I have left Miss Wrexham in London. I have done with her. May you never see her : she is a wicked little fool."

" Well, Maud, then," said the girl.

Maud woke next morning slowly and blissfully, conscious of a new interest in life, of a step taken. To be quit of London and all its fuss and worry was the step taken, but the new interest was the more vital of the two.

She and Violet had sat up late the night before talking, and Maud found something exquisitely sweet in being able to look at almost a facsimile of all that had made life bitter to her, to be able to talk and almost hear Tom answering, to be able to see his eyes looking into hers with affection and tenderness. For Maud had told Violet, without of course mentioning the name, the story of her worry and break-down; that she had loved a man and that he had married another, and that the desire of meeting him and the strain of doing so had made London unbearable and had affected her health.

Maud was one of those people who do not often make friends of their own sex, and the relief merely of telling some one about it was great. But when she felt she was almost telling it to Tom, as Violet sat opposite her, the bitterness and struggle she had been enduring so many months seemed quenched at last. Already her perplexities seemed capable of a solution which she could not have anticipated.

And the new interest was Violet. She felt as if Manvers had been wrong when he remarked cynically that Nature did not happen to have given us two people to love in case one got married. She felt as if she had almost cheated Fate, as if a substitute had been provided for her to love. " I shall be with her all day," thought Maud, as she watched her maid moving about the room, " and I must, I will make her fond of me. If I can do that I shall feel as if at last Tom cared."

Indeed this seemed no very hard task. Maud had a great power of attraction when she cared to attract, and she had already won Violet's heart by her confidence of the night before. There is nothing so exquisite as to feel that one is trusted.

The friendship a man may have for a man, or a woman for a woman, is often closer and more intimate than even between husband and wife. However close a man may be to a woman, there still stands between them the barrier of sex, which no one has yet succeeded in annihilating. Members of two different sexes must look at things with different eyes, and the attempt of the woman to become like the man seems only to emphasize the difference. Certainly Violet could do for Maud what no man could possibly do. A girl can say to a girl what no wife could say to her husband, for there are certain things a man can never understand, simply because he is not a woman, nor a woman because she is a woman.

It would have been impossible for Maud to tell the story of her trouble to any one but a girl, and it seemed to her that the very telling of it had taken away half its burden. And the burden removed, her body was able to recuperate itself, for when the body is hurt through the soul it cannot be cured until the soul is convalescent. Living all day in the open air drinking in the fresh saltness of the sea, returning to the first principles of healing, began to have their legitimate effect. And if the air was bracing, Violet was still more bracing. The convalescence of her body and soul kept pace with each other.

They had been playing tennis one morning, and had gone down to bathe afterwards, and the two were sitting on the edge of the beach, Violet with her hat off trying to persuade her hair to behave reasonably. Maud had already dried hers and was absorbed in attempting to hit the pug, who had accompanied them down to the sea, but absolutely refused to wash, with small pebbles and shells.

"I hate that dog," remarked Violet. "I wish you could hit it."

"I wish I could," said Maud. "There! No, it went over it."

"I think I can forgive any one anything," said Violet, "except laziness and want of interest. Not to be interested in things, not to be thoroughly alive, is the only unpardonable sin."

"I've been sinning unpardonably for the last six months. What a fool I have been making of myself!"

Violet wrinkled her nose.

"You poor darling! I didn't refer to you. All the same it was foolish of you."

"But the world is so hard," said Maud.

Violet held up a forefinger warningly.

"Now you know that is one of the things you are not allowed to say. How old are you?"

"Twenty-five."

"For how many years did you say you had been completely happy?"

"Twenty-three and a half."

Violet flicked the warm sea-scented air with the end of her towel.

"Well, then, I should be ashamed, Maud, I should be ashamed, especially when you know you are beginning to be happy again."

"That's your doing."

"We are talking about you, not me"—Violet's voice came out of the middle of the towel—"and you'll please keep to the subject. Just fancy my ever being good for anybody. How funny it seems!"

Maud lay back on her rug tilting her hat over her eyes.

"It's a very nice, warm, kind world just now," she added; "but oh, Violet, will it last? Man is a creature of moods, especially woman!"

"Especially you, you mean. I never had a mood in my life."

"But what would you do supposing something went wrong, supposing something happened to you like what happened to me?"

"I should send for you to come and stay with me at Aunt Julia's," said Violet, "and I should throw pebbles at that loathsome dog, and I should hit it too."

Violet's towel flapped through the air and descended on Flo's head.

Maud laughed as the dog got up, shook herself free of the towel, and then lay down pathetically on the top of it.

"But seriously," she went on, "if you wanted something very badly and couldn't get it, what would you do?"

Violet rescued the towel and resumed her seat.

"I haven't got many wants, you know," she said, "so I can't tell. But I hope I should be reasonable. I hope I should make a real effort to cease to want it. And then, you know, one gets over things; it takes time, no doubt, but everything worth doing takes time."

"Ah, but that's so terrible," said Maud. "It just shows how limited we are. If we were only stronger we should never get used to being without the things we want. It is because we are weak and feeble that we begin to forget. I want to know how we are to be strong and yet to forget."

Violet stared absently at the sea.

"I understand what you mean," she said, "but I think you are wrong. After all we are human ; we can't get over that ; and I think the woman who can't make an effort to forget, who goes on nursing her sorrow, is feebler than the one who can. Of course time helps both. Oh yes, of course I am right. I am very old-fashioned, you know. I don't care about dissecting myself and analyzing my tendencies, and thinking about limitations and aspirations. It seems to me that if you are inexperienced as I am you may kill yourself, as it were, in your analysis, or blind yourself altogether by peering too closely."

"Go on," said Maud, "you are so healthy."

Violet turned to her and lay down close beside her.

"Yes, I want to be healthy anyhow," she said, "and that is the main point. I think the way people dissect their own morbid selves, and put themselves in three-volumed pickle-jars, so to speak, for their friends to look at, is simply indecent. If you have a decayed tooth you don't show it to all your friends and say, 'It is much worse since last week'; you go to the dentist and have it stopped."

"You dear dentist," said Maud, "I'm so glad I came to you !"

"To tell yourself that life is hard and complicated," continued Violet, "is to make it so, because one always believes one's self. To say that it is simple

simplifies it. Of course some people like it complicated, and so I suppose they are right to tell
themselves that it is. But to tell yourself that it is
complicated, and then be sorry for it, is foolishness."

"I hate complications," said Maud. "I hate them
as much as you hate that pug. But supposing you
find simple things dull ; at least, supposing after your
complications you find the simple things which you
liked before bore you ? Complications change one,
you know."

"I don't know," remarked Violet. "Do you mean
that you are bored with this place ? "

"I mean nothing of the sort," said Maud. "I
was only speculating. And the bell for lunch went
ten minutes ago."

"The simplest lunch wouldn't bore me to-day,"
said Violet.

"Nor me."

Violet whistled to the pug and stood for a moment
with her head a little on one side looking at him
disgustedly.

"You are most astonishingly like Tom," said
Maud ; "he looked just like that when he was
examining Mr. Manvers' statuette."

"And how did Mr. Manvers look when he looked
at Tom's statue ? " she asked.

"He looked as the pug looks—rather hurt, but
able to do without Tom's appreciation."

" How utterly different they must be ! "

" All the difference in the world," said Maud. Then
to herself : " One is the man who loves me, the other "
—she pulled herself up—"the man I used to love."

CHAPTER XV.

MAY was driving home one afternoon towards the end of June with a sense of great well-being. The baby was thriving as heartily as the fondest mother could wish, and Tom was as lovable as ever. He had got rather tired of going out to dine or dance, and of late had more frequently spent his evenings alone with May. Two days before he saw her opening a note which obviously was an invitation, and before she had read it he said—

"May, if that is for dinner any time in the next week, I am engaged to dine with you at home."

His guess had been correct, and they were going to spend this evening alone at home. There were always certain pieces of ritual connected with baby cult to be gone through, and though Tom expressed impatience sometimes at the length of the services, he knew that the sight of May bending over their first-born was a very pretty one, and often wished he were a painter as well as a sculptor. Demeter had passed through the hands of the pointers, and Tom was at work again on her, for he meant to finish her himself. Day after day he spent, chisel in hand, working down the whole surface, till he "found" the statue. Various people, remembering the two statuettes which Tom had exhibited eighteen months ago, wanted to know if there were any more to be had, for the two had sold at once for high prices, though Tom had, after his conversion, expressed an unmercenary intention of throwing the cheques into the fire. But when they asked whether he was working at anything, and were shown the Demeter, they became thoughtful and said, "Good morning."

Altogether May was more than satisfied, and she went quickly up the steps and into the house, thinking how terrible it was that she had not set eyes on Tom or the baby since half-past eleven that morning. There was a note for her on the hall table, and she saw with a sudden spasm of anxiety that it was from her husband. She tore it open quickly, and read—

"Father's business has failed. He heard this morning, and he has had a stroke. I have gone down there at once. You had better follow me."

May read the note through twice before she thoroughly grasped its meaning. She waited only one moment to steady herself, and then went quickly upstairs to give orders for a small trunk to be packed for her, and to say good-bye to the baby.

Tom had received the news just after lunch, and was quite unable to remember where May had gone. She had come in to tell him that she would not be in till six, and that she was lunching somewhere, and then going somewhere else, but Tom was finishing a vein on the back of Demeter's drooping hand, and had only said, "Yes, dear, yes," without looking up. May felt one moment of slight pique, and had not repeated her message, saying to herself that if he did not care to know she did not care to tell him.

He had arrived at Applethorpe two hours afterwards, and there learned that there was probably no hope. His father was lying quite unconscious. They thought perhaps he might rally for a few minutes before the end, and so Tom sat and waited. The sun moved slowly round to the west, and it was not till the golden light had begun to be tinged with red that his father moved. He opened his eyes, saw Tom sitting by him, and snapped his fingers in the face of the King of Terrors.

"I'm stone broke, Tom," he said, "and it's lucky for you that you learned to break stones."

And with a jest on his lips he went out without hope or fear into the Valley of the Shadow.

The suddenness of what had happened for a time stunned and obliterated thought in Tom's mind. Though his father was old, no blurring decay had touched him with forewarning hand, and it was in a half-dream that Tom went down from the death chamber into the library. The telegram which announced the failure had fluttered down on to the floor, and the warm garden-scented breeze which streamed in through the open window stirred it every now and then as if it was twitched by some unseen hand. The book his father had been reading was still standing open on the desk of his reading-chair, where he had been sitting when the news came.

Everything was pitilessly unchanged. The servants had come in to draw down the blinds, but

Tom stopped them. What was the use of that unmeaning decorum? Tom had been very fond of his father, but the thought of May and the baby could not but make a picture in his mind. His father, like many very rich men, seldom or never spoke of his money, and Tom wondered vaguely, but with growing anxiety, how complete the smash was. The delights of poverty, of being out at elbows, and working passionately for a living at the work he loved, presented themselves in rather different colours to a man with a wife and infant son, from the glowing difficulties he had painted for himself as an ardent bachelor of twenty-two. What if the worst he feared were true—if they were absolute paupers!

His thoughts went back again to his father lying dead upstairs. Tom remembered so vividly the last time he had seen him, standing with May and the baby in the porch when he went up to London. He had taken an extraordinary interest in the baby, and used to hazard cynical speculations as to its future. He used to allude to it as Mr. Thomas, in order to differentiate it from Tom. "Mr. Thomas's solemnity is overpowering," he said once; "he makes me feel as if I was a small boy talking to a wise old gentleman, or a juvenile offender waiting for an awful judge to pronounce sentence on me. And he makes me realize what is meant by rich silences." Mr. Thomas at the moment broke into his own rich silence by a very creditable howl, and his grandfather added, "And mark how opulently he cries."

Tom met May at the door, and they went together up to the room where his father lay. He did not tell her what the old man's last words had been. They found Mr. Markham waiting for them below when they came down, and the three talked together till it grew late. He stopped to dinner, and afterwards, when May had gone to bed, Tom mentioned the subject of the smash.

Mr. Markham shook his head gravely.

"Do either the London house or Applethorpe belong to you?" he asked.

"No, we rent them both."

"My poor boy! I am sure I am right in telling you to prepare for the worst. I remember from a talk I had with your father once, that the greater part of his money was in this business, and the rest in two Australian banks which broke last year."

Tom stood up and frowned.

"He never told me that. He never spoke about money, you know. I had not an idea of it."

"He probably thought it was unnecessary, for I believe he had the most utter confidence in his partners. I have seen the evening papers, and it appears that there has never been so complete a smash, except perhaps the Argentines."

"Have you got the paper?" asked Tom.

"Not with me. But don't look at the papers about it."

"Why not?"

"Because there are some very unjust things said about your father. Of course we all know quite well that he had nothing to do with the management of the company."

"What an infernal slander!" said Tom, hotly.

'And do you mean you think I have nothing—literally nothing?"

"It is possible it may mean that."

"What is to happen to the bills I haven't paid?" demanded Tom.

"You have a profession," said Mr. Markham. "Ted told me Wallingthorpe's opinion of your work."

"Ah, those horrors!" said Tom, impatiently. "I shall not earn a penny by those."

"But you say you have unpaid bills?"

"Yes, I suppose I have—every one has. Of course they must be paid. The furniture here belongs to us."

"That is your father's. Have you nothing except your income from him?"

"I have £1500 left me by my godmother, and May has £500, has she not? Eighty pounds a year between us—a ridiculously insignificant sum. But I have my profession, as you say. I shall work for my living, work for her and the baby. I long to do that. My God! how I shall work! The Demeter is nearly finished."

"Are you doing it for an order?" asked Mr. Markham, tentatively.

"No. Why?"

"My dear Tom, you must be practical. It is a luxury for rich people only to work six months or a year at a thing if it has no market. I know nothing about art, but there is a practical point of view, which now you must take into consideration. Your work is not only the thing you love, but the thing which has to keep you in bread and cheese."

"Well, we shall see," said Tom. "Perhaps we are counting our cobras before they are hatched. Anyhow, I have now—what I always longed for—the opportunity to work for May."

The two stopped at Applethorpe for a fortnight, and before that time was over they knew exactly how they stood. The smash was complete. A series of disasters had fallen, and Mr. Carlingford's fortune of not less than a quarter of a million had gone. Upwards of £100,000 of this had been in two Australian banks, in which he held both deposit and shares. These two banks had failed; he was unable to withdraw his deposit, and there were heavy calls to be met on his shares. He had known this for some months, but the money he derived from his £150,000 in the business would have enabled him to meet these, for he lived considerably below his income. But for five years or so the business had been managed in a very different manner from that in which it had been carried on under Mr. Carlingford. The elder partner had about this time embarked on several investments, which, though not exactly risky, were not the kind of venture fit for a steady-going house. These had turned out well; he had lost his head a little when he saw a six months' profit safely harvested in two, and he had been led on—by the prospect of making a fortune by a few successful *coups*—into speculations which were on the far side of risky. Luck had been against him, and he had attempted to get back his losses by even more adventurous means, and it appeared that for two years Mr. Carlingford's income had been paid, not out of profits, but out of capital. Then came the *coup de grâce*. The younger partner had got into the hands of money-lenders, had sunk deeper and deeper, and when he found that his own signature was considered valueless, had signed a note of hand in the name of the house. The father, trying to shield his son, had speculated wildly in certain South American securities, and these had failed. Inasmuch as Mr. Carlingford was still a partner, he was liable for the debts of the house, and it was feared that even a complete sale of his furniture and stables would hardly cover his liabilities, even after other stocks and shares which he held had been disposed of.

To Tom himself nothing remained but the £1500 left him by his godmother, which could not be touched by his father's creditors. Against that he had to set his own outstanding bills, about which he felt unpleasantly vague. The anxiety he secretly felt he would scarcely confess even to himself. He had a full belief in his own powers, and it would have been a faithless thing to doubt them at the very moment when the test was to be applied. He talked the matter out fully and frankly with May, and if he had any private anxiety, at any rate she had not.

"We shall be awfully poor, dear," he said. " I don't know what there will be over when our bills are paid, but it won't be much. Of course we won't touch your £500; but we must live on the capital of the other until I have finished something to sell. I wish to goodness I had paid all my bills before. But they must be paid now at once. I want to start fresh.'

"Where shall we live?" asked May.

"Wallingthorpe wrote to me yesterday, and told me of a flat somewhere up in Bloomsbury, which could be had cheap. It's up a lot of stairs, but it has a big room which has a good light for a studio."

"We had better go at once, hadn't we?"

"Well, yes. They will be clearing everything out of here in a day or two, and, of course, we can't go back to Grosvenor Square."

May smiled.

"I think it will be rather amusing," she said, "living in a poky little house. I suppose it's healthy, isn't it?"

"Very, I believe. Manvers said it was rather nice being extraordinarily poor. I wonder if you will like it. I know I shan't mind."

"Tom, I mind nothing with you. You know that, don't you?"

Tom wrinkled up his nose—a trick he had.

"Well, I didn't anticipate that you would apply for a separation."

"Do you know what father suggested? He wanted me to propose to you that I should bring the baby to the vicarage until things were more settled."

"Yes. That sounds an excellent plan. I suppose you jumped at it."

"Tom, you gaby!"

"And what was I to do?"

"You were to make a quantity of little statuettes, and sell them for £80 each. I don't think he believes in the Demeter."

Tom went up to London a day or two later to stay with Wallingthorpe, and superintend the preparations for making the new house habitable, while May and the baby remained at the vicarage. That artist, it must be confessed, was in his heart of hearts not at all displeased at Tom's sudden change of fortune. He would be driven to do that which he could not be led to. Wallingthorpe had not a touch of an artist's proverbial jealousy. If he saw or suspected talents he did his utmost to foster and encourage them, and in Tom he suspected something more. The boy's persistence in working at his heathen goddess really had filled him with genuine pain. He ventured to touch on the subject one night when he and Tom were sitting together after dinner.

"And what will you work at next?" he began. "Your Demeter—that is the lady's name, is it not?—is nearly finished, I believe?"

"Yes, she's ready to be finished. I'm finishing her myself," said Tom. "I don't think you've seen her, have you?"

Wallingthorpe closed his eyes piously.

"I'm sure you'll excuse my saying so, but God forbid! What are you going to do next?"

"Persephone. She is the daughter who is lost, you know, and Demeter is looking for her sorrowing. Well, she'll find her next year, 1 hope."

Wallingthorpe made an eloquent gesture expressing despair.

"You wretched boy, you don't know what you are doing!" he cried. "You have talents, believe me; you perhaps have genius. You are wasting the best years of your life and prostituting your gifts. I must force you to believe it."

Tom laughed.

"You'd better give it up," he said. "I am quite hardened."

"But you'll starve," said Wallingthorpe ; "you've got to think of that. Life-size blocks of Carrara are not to be had for the asking, and on my sacred word of honour no one will buy Demeter or her daughter."

"Well, then, I'll starve," said Tom, cheerfully. "But surely it would be prostituting my gifts if I simply used them to prevent my starving. Eh ? "

Wallingthorpe was silent, and Tom continued—

"But, of course, I shan't starve. Those things 'don't happen,' as Mrs. Humphry Ward says of miracles. Anyhow, before I starve I shall finish the Demeter and her daughter, and then my blood will be on the heads of the British public."

"You miserable boy ! " ejaculated Wallingthorpe again, adjusting the end of his cigar. "You are an apostate, and in the good old days apostates were very justly looked down on by Christians and heretics alike. You have sacrificed to Demeter and Perse-phone, and all the hierarchy of Olympus."

"You may call me apostate on the day I cease to," said Tom, "and that will be not just yet."

CHAPTER XVI.

IT must be acknowledged that Tom's heart had sunk a little when he saw the flat in Bloomsbury. The thought of May, with her queenly Madonna-like beauty, moving through the low rooms or sitting by the small-paned window seemed dreadfully incongruous. But when May came, as she did a few days later, Tom found that the effect was that the rooms were glorified.

It was characteristic of him that before settling into his new narrow house he made a clean sweep of everything which was unnecessary and marketable. He argued that they had better start with a little capital rather than a few bibelots, and that a couple of pieces of Dresden china or a valuable terra-cotta from Tanagra would only look absurdly out of place among the appurtenances of cheap lodgings. He and May had a small tussle over a few pictures which old Mr. Carlingford had given him during his lifetime.

"But they are not good pictures," argued Tom, "and I don't in any case see what we want with them. Besides, it appears that there's a half-year's rent owing for the Grosvenor Square house. No, we must sell everything, May. I only hope there will be something over. I suppose the blue blood of a the Carlingfords ought to be up; but as far as I am concerned it isn't."

"I think you might keep a picture or two," said May.

"My dear May, it's impossible. I can't think what we should do if we had nothing over. But I suppose some one would lend us something."

May frowned; the idea grated on her.

"We can't do that, Tom—that's impossible. Besides, who is there?"

"Perhaps Lady Ramsden might," said Tom. "She certainly would if it occurred to her; but I don't think things occur to her much. But I quite feel with you about borrowing."

The outstanding debts when added together made a total which rather appalled Tom, and it was with some anxiety that he awaited the result of his sales. The upshot was that they were the possessors of £150 capital. Tom drew rather a long face when he thought of the rapidity with which money used to melt in the old days. But Demeter would be finished in a few weeks.

They had settled in during the first week of July, and as they sat together after dinner they talked matters over. To both of them it appeared rather amusing than otherwise to dine off leg of mutton and rice pudding at the top of a house in Bloomsbury. May, with a view to being useful, had had an interview with the cook, and retailed it to Tom.

"We shall have poached eggs for breakfast," she said, "and at lunch the rest of the mutton as hash. I think hash is delicious!"

Tom was looking over some figures.

"£151 4s. 3d. is the exact amount, May," he said.

"Isn't that an awful lot?" said May. "Why, Ted used to live on £200 at Cambridge, I know, and he said it was possible to get on on much less."

Tom grinned.

"I wonder what I used to spend at Cambridge," he said. "I wish I had some of that now."

May sat down by him.

"Tom, I think it will be great fun," she said. "I've always wanted to work for my living; and I can help you, can't I, by seeing the cook and arranging about hash, and mending things."

"I shouldn't mind if it wasn't for you," said Tom.

"Oh, but I enjoy it awfully—I do really! And you know, dear, I shall see more of you. I shan't have to make any calls, and we shan't have to go out to dinner; also I shall mend your socks."

"I'm glad I followed Wallingthorpe's advice about one thing," said Tom, "and learned how to finish a statue myself. If I hadn't learned that I should have had to hire two of those Italian fellows, and that would have been no end of expense. Six weeks from now will see it done, May."

It is difficult to realize, unless one has tried it, how hard it is for a man who has been accustomed to live, if not luxuriously, at least extremely comfortably, to maintain his cheerfulness when he has to make every shilling go as far as it can. Tom, who had been always very extravagant, simply because he had never been obliged to learn the value of money, was suddenly brought face to face with the widely-known fact that wanting a thing is not the same as getting it. Neither he nor May had the least realized what it was to live in an atmosphere of slight discomfort, to have the smell of dinner steal up an hour before dinner-time and invade every corner of the house, to be waited upon by a slatternly girl who breathed very hard and had dirty hands, to sit on horse-hair sofas, to have a cracked mirror over the fireplace, to be obliged to consider the relative prices of beef and mutton, and to banish once and for ever the idea of eating well-cooked food. These details seem small enough, but when all the details of life are slightly disagreeable, however trifling each is in itself, they make up an *ensemble* which is slightly disagreeable too. Before they lost their money both Tom and May would have declared that it could not possibly make any difference to either of them, provided they were together, that the house should smell of dinner, or that as soon as one castor of the table was repaired another broke; but even as water will wear away a stone, these little things wore away the edge of their serenity.

July was broiling hot that year, and day by day the sun baked the studio where Tom worked till it was like an oven. The blinds of the skylight were tattered, and rays of light came hotly down as if through a magnifying glass, making little bright spots on the dingy walls. Tom got rather exasperated one morning, because in adjusting the blind he had torn it further, and a long jagged slit of light fell on his face as he worked. It would have to be mended in the evening, but something must be done at once, and with a brilliant inspiration he got the blacking-pot and painted the offending glass with it. Then the brush slipped from his hand and fell on the top of Demeter's head, and it took Tom ten minutes to get a sponge and clean it. It was certainly more comfortable in

Grosvenor Square; but he tried to persuade himself that these things were details, as indeed they were.

Soon the blacking caked off with the heat of the sun and came filtering down in tiny flakes, and the gash of light fell down into the studio again. Tom lost his temper a little, and climbed up again to paste some paper over it. The paste would not stick at first, and he pressed the thin glass too hard and a small pane broke. It was only a small pane, but it had to be mended. Then the smell of food began.

Consequently when the slatternly servant came in to say that lunch was ready, Tom was not very serene. He said that they must keep the smell of cooking down; it was only because they forgot to shut a door or open a window, and it must not occur again. He put on his coat and went fuming into the dining-room.

"May dear," he said, "the smell of cooking is quite intolerable. I should think on these hot days we could do with cold lunch, couldn't we? It makes one perfectly sick!"

"I told them to get a rabbit for lunch," she said. "You know you told me you were tired of mutton."

"The studio smelt like a menagerie," grumbled Tom.

May was a little hurt in her mind. She had hoped Tom would be pleased at her remembering to get something instead of the mutton, and she was silent. In a moment Tom spoke again.

"And I've broken a pane of glass in the skylight. That blind is torn to rags. You haven't been in this morning."

"I had to take the baby out," said May; "and there was some shopping to be done."

Tom suddenly laid down his knife and fork.

'I draw the line at high rabbit," he said. " I should think this particular one died a natural death some time in June."

" It's very hard to get good meat in this weather," said May; " it won't keep. But mine isn't so very bad."

"Where's the beer?" asked Tom in his lowest audible voice.

May looked vaguely round the table. She was vexed that Tom should behave like this; and yet, after all, it was nothing.

"I think Sally's forgotten it," she said.

Tom sighed resignedly and rang the bell, and sat drumming with his fingers on the table waiting for it to be answered. Nothing happened, and he rang again, this time louder; and soon the shuffling of ill-shod feet was heard on the stairs.

" Beer," said Tom, curtly.

The feet shuffled away again and the two sat in silence. May had given the rabbit up as a bad job, and for the time she felt inclined to treat Tom in the same way. When people were in great trouble she knew exactly what to do, but when they were suffering from merely an absence of beer and a height of rabbit she was completely at a loss. Tom sat in gloomy silence and stared at the darned tablecloth and the plated forks. What an idiot he had been, he thought, to sell everything. It would have been much better to have taken unfurnished lodgings, and have forks which it didn't make you ill to eat off. The entrance of the slovenly servant with a jug put an end for the moment to his regrets. He poured out a glass and drank some.

" Tepid," he said.

It was too ridiculous, and May broke out into a laugh.

"Don't be so cross, Tom," she said. "What does it matter? You haven't said a word to me all lunch time except to blame me for something."

Tom made the necessary effort and laughed too.

"I'm very sorry, dear," he said. "I've been behaving like a pig. As you say, it doesn't matter. But a lot of things which don't matter, one on the top of the other, are trying. First it was the sun, and then the blacking, and then the broken glass, and then the menagerie smell, and then no beer and high rabbit, and then hot beer."

Tom left his seat and took a cigarette. He had resolved to smoke pipes for the future as being cheaper, but it was no use selling the remainder of his cigarettes. Even his clean sweep did not include them.

Pleasant things and disagreeable things alike leave a little taste behind. A pleasant episode may be succeeded by an unpleasant one, or a disagreeable episode by an agreeable one, but the effect of neither wholly perishes. May and Tom alike asked themselves what could matter less than a smell in the studio or a stray slop-pail on the stairs; but an atmosphere, however slightly sordid, of things even so unimportant as a rabbit-smell or a slop-pail, produces its effect on all but those who are genuine Bohemians, and who would rather miss squalor and sordidness. Unfortunately neither May nor Tom had the slightest strain of Bohemian blood in them, and they were not inoculated against the subtle poisons of slop-pails and kitchen smells.

But Demeter progressed and the baby throve, and July went by with hot footsteps. During the day the heat was too scorching to render walking agreeable, and it was almost worse in their sunbaked flat than in the streets. More than once they thought of moving to some cooler house, but shillings were no longer to be treated lightly. The hot spell, they told themselves, could not last long, and it had been business enough to get Demeter up the flights of stairs. Her progress had been regal and dignified, and she had congested the traffic of the house for three-quarters of an hour. So May used often to take the baby into the British Museum, where the gods and goddesses seem to live in a perpetually equable atmosphere; and it was here that Mr. Thomas made his first piece of deductive reasoning. He pointed one day with a little pink fist to the horse's head in the Parthenon pediment and distinctly said, "Gee gee." Tom was delighted, and considered Manvers entirely refuted in his belief that the Elgin marbles were unintelligible : even a baby could understand them. Two days later Mr. Thomas conferred a similar distinction on Tom's own work when, after a prolonged wide-eyed inspection, he said, "Lady."

Tom worked as much as he could without a model, copying exactly his clay sketch ; but for the " lady's " arms one was necessary. And she too helped to melt the £150. She certainly had superb arms, and she stood splendidly. She also added her contribution—a not unimportant one—to the little jars which sometimes occurred between Tom and May.

She was a young woman of unquestionably fine physique, but her tongue was a rather unruly member, and she spoke freely. Tom used to tell her to be quiet and stand, but sometimes she came out with something very breezy and sudden. She once made a particularly breezy remark when May was there. May turned to Tom flushing, and asked him in French to tell her to be quiet. Tom, who had a great sympathy with life in all its forms—the model's remark was not a particularly vicious form—smiled, but told her to be silent. May left the room.

The girl's eyes followed her out of the room, and then without moving she spoke to Tom.

"Well, ayn't she perticler? A lydy friend of mine, she——"

"Never mind about your lady friends. You've moved your arm. A little more forward, plea ·· and the wrist more bent."

May was sitting in the dining-room when Tom came in for lunch, looking angry and flushed.

"Tom, you mustn't have that woman in the house," she said. "She is abominable."

"Who?" asked Tom, who had forgotten the occurence.

"The model, of course."

Tom raised his eyebrows.

"Why?—Oh, I remember. Do you mean that thing she said this morning?"

"Of course I do."

"But, my dear May, it really doesn't matter much, does it? I don't let her talk, and as a model she is one in a thousand. Besides, what did she say? I've forgotten. Nothing very bad, was it?"

May put down her knife and fork.

"Tom, can't you see? It hurts me that she should

be here. It makes me feel ill. It is not right to have a girl like that in the house."

Tom crumbled his bread attentively.

"I think you take rather an exaggerated view of it, dear," he said. "Of course that class of young woman is not very particular in its language; but what has that to do with me?"

"She is wicked," said May.

"Really you seem to me to build a good deal on one remark. Of course I am sorry you heard it. She expected to be allowed to talk as much as she pleased at first; but I stopped that."

"Tom, how can you condone that sort of thing? Oh—— "

"I don't condone it. I don't allow her to talk. Besides, one doesn't select a model for her morals, but for her muscles."

"Do you refuse to dismiss her?"

Tom looked up in surprise.

"You surely can't expect me to send her away, and spend perhaps a week, perhaps more, in getting another? In addition to that, I have engaged her for a week more."

"Pay her the money and let her go," said May.

"My dear May, we can't afford to throw models and money about in that manner. She has most beautiful hands. Wallingthorpe told me he had never seen such a lovely piece of modelling from elbow to finger tips."

"Ah," said May, suddenly, "you don't know—you don't understand. Will you never understand me? Can't you see what it means to me?"

Tom could be very patient and gentle.

"I think you've worked yourself up about it, May," he said. "We won't talk of it just now. Let us talk of it this evening. I must get back to my work. And don't be unreasonable."

"You will not dismiss the model at once?"

"Do you mean now—this afternoon?"

May got up too, and went to the window and threw it open.

"Ah, yes, of course I mean now," she said. "When there is a right and a wrong, how do you dare to put off your choice?"

"May, you ask an impossibility," said he.

May felt she was losing control over herself. She had a headache, the heat was stifling, and her equilibrium was upset.

"You don't care, you don't care!" she said with passion.

"I care very much that you should speak to me like that," said Tom. "I will promise to think it over. This afternoon I shall go on working with the same model."

He turned and left the room, his hands thrust deep down in his pockets, puzzled and vexed. He was really unable to understand his wife. She seemed to him wholly unreasonable. The girl was one of the ordinary class. Wallingthorpe had often employed her, and he, as Tom knew, was rather particular and fanciful in his choice. He had once told Tom, in his florid manner, that it made him unable to work if he knew that a woman, whom he was using to help out his idea of what a thing should be, did not live up to the splendid possibilities which—which—just so.

His model had made an improper remark—a

remark, by the way, which would have passed with a laugh if made by a man among men—and he was seriously expected to dismiss her, to pay her for an extra week, and lose his time in hunting for another, who could not possibly be as good. Tom had begun to get in a fever to have Demeter finished. He felt it was to be his challenge. If Demeter was not good —was not of the best—he had been wrong, he had done what Wallingthorpe had told him he was doing, trying to fly, and only succeeding in standing on tiptoe. The sort of scene he had been through with May, threw him out of gear—it dimmed his eye and unnerved his hand. Why could she not be more tolerant, less apt to judge? Of course, Tom confessed, she was right in principle. If he could get two identical models, one of whom was breezy and the other not, he would choose the unbreezy one. But what had a model's character to do with her muscles? Besides, May was building an absurd superstructure on a very slight foundation. It was ridiculous ; and he set to work.

Meantime, May, in the other room, was scarcely more content. Her fastidiousness had been touched ; she had winced at what the girl said, as if under physical pain. Tom did not know, he did not care to know, she told herself bitterly, how much she disliked the thought of his having the girl in the house. The face of the Demeter was May's face, and that the arms should be the arms of such a woman seemed to her positively insulting. This she had not told Tom ; she felt it too keenly, and it was a grievance the force of which he could not appreciate if he did not appreciate the other. She felt hot, tired, ill-used, misunderstood, and the worst of it all was that she was afraid she had been a little unreasonable. She was, she had a suspicion, a little unreasonable still, and she felt convinced that she would continue to be a little unreasonable. Then she veered round and told herself that she was perfectly right, and that Tom was hard and unfeeling, and then, between the heat and the headache and the worry, she had a dismal little cry all to herself.

Tears are a secretion, but they are sometimes a solution ; they seem occasionally to carry off the cause of the irritation ; and the upshot was that the prevailing feeling in May's mind when she had finished was that she was sorry to have vexed Tom. He really had behaved with great patience to her ; he didn't wholly understand her, that is true, but he was a dear, good boy, and she had been a little exasperating.

Fate, in fact, seemed just to have woke up to the existence of Tom. For twenty-five years she really appeared to have forgotten about him, and let him go on in his own pleasant way exactly as he chose. But some malignant spirit had reminded her of his existence, and she was just reminding him that he was not his own master. She made him another little visit the same afternoon, while he was working, in the shape of a tradesman's boy with a bill.

Tom tore open the envelope and was confronted by a request to pay thirty pounds for a block of Carrara marble which he had bought for a relief he was working at. It had been ordered before the smash came, and he had supposed that it had been paid with the other bills. He dismissed the boy, and wrote a note to the agent who had managed his affairs, asking whether a bill of thirty pounds, for a block of Carrara, had not been paid. He had given orders that every bill should be paid. He clung desperately to the hope that a mistake had occurred, and that the bill had been sent in twice. And then for the first time he felt that emotion, which is stronger than all others—fear, blank fear. Thirty pounds was a solid fraction of their capital. And what would happen next?

He could not pay it. Surely they would wait. Tom thought, with a regretful sigh, of the patient tradesmen who had so often waited till he could bother himself to draw a cheque. But somehow, by a strange unreasonableness, now that he was in want of money, he was almost eager to pay his debts, whereas, when he never thought about money at all, he never felt the slightest inclination to do so. But Fate was playing with him and frightening him. He had a horrible dread of these surprises, and he felt that the inner knowledge of this sum owing would be poison. Besides, it would be necessary to keep it from May, and the thought of concealing things from May was untenable.

The answer came back from the agent; no, the bill had not been sent in before. Tom went on working with mechanical accuracy, thinking of that horrible thirty pounds. After all, why pay it at once? Of course there would be no kind of difficulty with the tradesman. He remembered ordering the block with Wallingthorpe. The price was a large one, and he had not dealt at the shop before, and the man had hesitated, wondering if his master would wish him to send it before it had been paid for. But when Tom gave the Grosvenor Square address he was perfectly satisfied.

What he wanted was to gain time. Thirty pounds represented so many days' work, and why cut that off? Demeter must be finished ; he must show the world what he meant. The artist's need of expressing himself cried aloud in him. To finish Demeter, and do, if only once, the best he could, was necessary. Necessary? It was the only necessary thing in the world for him except—except May and the baby.

Tom put down his chisel.

"You can go," he said to the model. "It is close on four."

The girl stretched herself. She had posed for nearly an hour, and she was a little stiff, and for the moment Tom forgot about bills and everything else, looking at the splendid line of her form from shoulder to ankle beneath the clinging drapery.

"At ten to-morrow?" she asked.

With a flash the whole scene with May came back over him. He walked to the window, putting on his coat, and stood there a moment. She repeated her question.

"Unless you hear to the contrary," said Tom. "It's all right. You will be paid all the same. Put your address down here. I will send if I don't want you."

She retired behind the screen to change her clothes, and Tom still stood where he was. Just as she was passing out he stopped her.

"I don't want to be inquisitive," he said, "but tell me this: you are straight, aren't you?"

The girl flushed.

"Strite! Who says I'm not strite? Your wife, I'll be bound."

"Never mind my wife," said Tom. "Just tell me, will you? I shall believe you, of course."

But the lower classes, when they happen to be respectable, are just as proud of it as the upper classes—perhaps more proud. The girl was thoroughly angry.

"I'll thank you to tell her not to say things agin me what are not true, and never likely to be, s'elp me Gawd. An' what does she know about me? You're too good for her, Mr. Carlingford, with her narsty back-biting ways. I knew she was up to some mischief this morning. Strite? I'm as strite as she is, an' striter, too, for I don't talk ill of folks behind their backs. An' good night to you, sir!"

She flounced out of the room and left Tom to make the best of what she had said.

"Well, that's all right, at any rate," he thought to himself. "I shall tell May."

He filled a pipe and sat in the window, his elbows on the sash. Forty feet below lay the hot street, down which the sun shone pitilessly; but soon it sank below the house-roofs, and a merciful little breeze sprang up from the west. Tom leant out to enjoy it more and let it ruffle his hair. He was tired and weary, but his brain went back to the same old incessant question, "What next? what next?"

Supposing Demeter was a success—not in his sense of the word, but in the financial sense, well and good. If not, what? Three weeks more. There was money for three weeks more, including the wages of the model; and if this bill was not paid, for six. If all went well Demeter would be finished in a month. What next? what next? There were May and the baby, there was the nurse, there was himself. He left himself out of the reckoning. But the others had to be reckoned for. He must get money somehow. But if Demeter brought him none, where was it to come from ? He thought of the horrible little statuette which May kept on the mantelpiece, and he went to look at it. It was not finished, but it would not take long to finish it. Would it come to that ? Was that the shrunken reality to which all his dreams of art were going to awake ? For he felt conclusively within himself that he could not do both. If he abandoned his great aim for a moment he abandoned it for ever. There was no going back. He could not earn his living with things like that, and with the other hand, so to speak, do sacrifice to his mistress. The house of Rimmon or the temple of the Lord—one or the other, but not possibly both.

When his day's work was over he and May usually went out for an hour or two before dinner, and before many minutes were up she came to look for him. She wanted to say she was sorry, but she very much wished that Tom would help her out with it. But as they drank tea before going out, Tom was silent, thinking of other things.

But at last he looked up.

" Another week with the model," he said, "and then I can get on alone for a time. Oh, by the way, May, I think you judged her harshly to-day ; in fact, I am sure you did."

"Yes, Tom. I am sorry," said May. "I've been wanting to tell you."

"Poor old girl, you look rather done up with the heat ! There's nothing wrong, is there, May ?"

" No. It's only the heat and—and being sorry."

" I wish we could get away," said Tom ; "but I can't move till this thing is off my hands. But why don't you go down to Applethorpe for a week ? "

" Not without you. But you'll come away when it's finished ? "

Tom walked up and down the room.

" May, I'm frightened," he said, " horribly frightened, and it's a bad feeling. A bill came in this afternoon, which of course I thought had been paid with the rest."

" A bill? How much for ? "

" Thirty pounds ? "

" Oh, Tom ! "

" It frightened me. I'm losing nerve. I don't see that we can pay it now. There is no reason why it shouldn't stand over. If no one will buy Demeter the time will come, and come soon, when we must get money somehow, and I think I shall let it stand over till she's finished. I hope to goodness I shan't be dunned for it. I used not to mind being dunned when I was at Cambridge, and had plenty of money ; but it's no fun now. They county-courted me once—I've got the summons still. I think if I was county-courted now I should die of it."

" But what are we to do ? "

" I only want to finish Demeter. There will be money enough for that, if the bill stands over."

" And when Demeter is finished ? " asked May.

" When she is finished I shall have done my best. And if others do not think my best good—— "

Tom left the sentence unfinished.

CHAPTER XVII.

MAUD spent a month with Lady Ramsden—four epoch-making weeks. The note of change which had been struck in her when she met Violet had expanded into a harmonious chord. Just as healthy physical surroundings produce physical health, so intimacy with healthy-minded people produces a corresponding well-being in the soul. And thus recuperated, she was able to make the effort she had been unable to make before, and when she returned to London at the end of July she congratulated herself on the change that she alone knew of, as much as her friends congratulated her on the change they could all see.

Parliament was not to rise before the 10th of August, and the Chathams were to remain in London till then. During that fortnight Maud saw Tom constantly, often going to see him and May in Bloomsbury, and Tom, with or without May, more than once coming to see her.

The old *camaraderie* days of Athens seemed to be renewing themselves. Tom found Maud stimulating in a way that May could not be, partly because he loved his wife, partly although he loved her. With May his responsibility asserted itself; he was always aware of an increasing anxiety as to what would happen to them all, crouching in his mind, ready to spring.

And he knew—he could not help knowing—that May did not really understand how essential his art was to him, how inexorable was his inner need of producing the best he could ; how bad, how immoral, the statuette of the boy with the rifle seemed to him. She had not an artistic nature, and she had never, except in him, known a man who served that most exacting of all mistresses, whose service is a passion to her slaves. For Manvers, as he often said himself, was not like those poets who sing because they must, but those who sing because they choose to sing. He was clever, diabolically clever, and he liked to exercise his intelligence.

With Maud then Tom could both throw off, or at least not be scourged by, his responsibilities, and also he knew that she understood how terrible the struggle he might have to go through would be. There was always the possibility ahead that no one would want to possess any of the shining gods and goddesses, and if so it was financially impossible for him to go on producing them.

The three were sitting on the balcony where Manvers and Maud had sat alone one night only a month or two ago, and, as usual in her presence, Tom's Promethean eagle had ceased pecking at him for the time, and had hopped away out of sight.

May was feeling a little out of it, and a little neglected, for Tom was talking to Maud in a way he did not talk to her. He was never anything but kind and considerate to her ; but the hurried luncheons which they ate together in their grilling little flat, were often rather silent affairs. If the morning's work had been satisfactory, Tom was only eager to finish and get to work again ; if he had got on badly, the Promethean eagle always seemed aware of it, and applied its claws and beak to the tenderest places with the accuracy of experience. But with Maud he was altogether different, partly, no doubt, for reasons stated above, and partly also because the most well-mannered and loving husbands do not trouble themselves to talk, if they are not inclined to talk, in the privacy of the domestic luncheon-table. Thirdly, as May knew herself, she was not, as Maud expressed it, a "dialogist," and it was of dialogists she and Tom were talking now. Incidentally, they were both behaving like dialogists.

"I think," Maud was saying, "that I'm about the best sort of dialogist. Not only can I talk quite intelligently and agreeably—can't I, May?—but I'm a first-rate listener."

"Good listening is not necessary for a dialogist," said Tom. "Dialogists enjoy themselves most when they both talk together, as we used to do at Athens."

"Oh, you're wrong," said Maud. "Each dialogist must know that the other is *sympathique*, and the easiest way of conveying that is by listening well."

"Yes ; but I know you are *sympathique* to me," said Tom, "so I don't care whether you listen or not. Besides, listening is rather a despicable quality. I don't think you've got it, you know, so I'm not being rude."

May got up.

"Well, we must go," she said. "I said I'd be back by three to take Mr. Thomas out."

"Oh, don't go yet," said Maud. "Why, you've only just finished lunch!"

"I must; but Tom can stop here."

May was conscious that it required a little magnanimity to say this, and at the same time that she threw a pinch of bitterness into her magnanimity. She wished Maud to know that she knew that it was Tom, not herself, Maud wanted to talk to; and though she had not spoken with any idea of her words conveying this, she was not sorry that they might bear such an interpretation.

But Tom did not dive into such feminine subtleties, though Maud suspected them.

"I shall stop a bit if I'm not in the way," he said. "I meant to take a holiday this afternoon, and I shall take it here."

Maud stood drumming with her fingers on the balustrade for a moment or two after May had gone. This was the first time she had been alone with Tom since her stay in Norfolk, and she revelled in her sense of security, for she felt all the old *camaraderie* feeling, and no touch of any more disturbing results from the companionship, and it was with the air and the words of a comrade that she spoke.

"I think you ought to have gone with May," she said. "I can say that to you, for you know how glad I am personally that you stayed."

Tom looked up.

"Why?"

"Because she wanted you to go. I am sure of that."

"I don't think so."

"But I do," said Maud. "Don't be banal, and say you ought to know because you are her husband. That's no argument. You are a man, and it is impossible for you to understand a woman as a woman can."

"But it's unreasonable."

"That, again, is no argument. Oh, good heavens, Tom, if we were all reasonable, what a simple world it would be! And how dull!"

"I'm not sure I don't prefer dulness to excitement," said Tom. "Wait till you've had a fright, and then see how you appreciate uneventfulness."

"Ah, but dulness is not a synonym for content," said Maud, speaking from her new experiences. "It is a great mistake to suppose that."

Tom flicked off the end of his cigarette ash. For the last few weeks he had deliberately stifled certain thoughts, but with Maud there was no need to stifle them.

"I am not sure," he said. "Of course one aims at content—one aims at nothing else. But one aims at it, I think, because one knows it is unattainable. There is no such thing as content for people who are alive—you know what I mean by alive. I think we have talked about it before. For human beings to be content is to be limited."

"Yes, and to be human is to be limited. I am talking like a maiden aunt, I know."

Tom looked up smiling.

"You have the distinction of having invented the least applicable definition possible of yourself. What's the opposite to maiden aunt? Married niece, I suppose. There is your label."

"But I am not married."

"No; but you unite qualities which are rarely united. You are experienced and you are fresh. How do you do it?"

"I might much more reasonably ask you that."

"Not at all. At present I feel like a *blasé* baby."

"You?"

Tom suddenly became overwhelmingly conscious of all he had stifled so long. His anxieties over petty money matters, the sordidness of the life in the little flat in Bloomsbury—all these were trifles ; but there were other things which were not trifles. He and May loved each other—that he believed ; but apart from their love to each other their passions lay as far sundered as the two poles. Each was invisible and incomprehensible to the other.

"It is this," he said. "I have felt and feel a passion for something which I shall, I am afraid, have to abandon. I am telling you things I have told to no one, hardly to myself. But, as you know, art is a passion to me. There is one art, so I think, and I am trying to realize it. But I have to face the probability that it will not be appreciated—already I call it a probability—and if so, I shall have to abandon it because I have other ties, and the need for bread and butter rightly outweighs all else. Not that I am less enthusiastic ; but one can neither live nor triumph by enthusiasm. There are claims which outweigh all enthusiasms or artistic convictions."

"Oh, but the two could not actually come in conflict," said Maud. "It is absurd to suppose that you will have to abandon your ideas of art at the very outset because they are not marketable. Besides, most purchasers are Philistines."

"That is exactly what I fear," said Tom. "Of course I don't say for a moment that I can produce good things, but I have an idea of beauty, and I must work for that as long as I can. Perhaps great encouragement from any one would mend my case, but the world regards me with disconcerting indifference. Manvers thinks me a delver after uninteresting survivals. He may be right, but again I may be. That the majority of purchasers think Manvers right is of course indisputable."

"But all this need not make you *blasé*," said Maud.

Tom was silent. What he hungered for was active, sincere sympathy from May, but that was not to be had. She seemed to regard the possible abandonment of his practice of art as she would regard any other change of employment, as if, for instance, Tom was a butcher and found it necessary to become a baker. He had, as he acknowledged to himself, taken an impossible view of all she might be to him. He was in love with her still, as much as, or even more than when they married, but he had realized that she did not and could not sympathize fully with his aims. At first it had seemed as if there was nothing she could not do for him, as if they two were wholly and inevitably one. But, without loving her the less, he had learned that it was not so. She had one passion, he another, and they had to support their passions singly. But the most rudimentary code of loyalty forbade his saying anything of the kind to Maud.

"No; you are right," he said. "I have a great many illusions left, and one can't be *blasé* if one has illusions. Of course I still have the illusion that the Demeter is going to be a masterpiece. But the necessity of wondering whether the masterpiece is marketable clouds the illusion a little."

"Oh, you are certainly not *blasé*," said Maud, with

conviction. "How can a man married to a woman he loves, working at what he loves, not only for its sake but to supply her actual needs, be *blasé*. You ought to keep young for ever."

"I am a quarter of a century old," said Tom, "and I should like to live till a hundred. It's a good thing to be alive. Do you know that line of Whitman's?— I can't quote it exactly—'Let us take hands and help each other to-day, because we are alive together.'"

Maud's eye kindled.

"I like great big common ideas like that," she said. "Mr. Manvers would think it was a sign of approaching *bourgeoisie* or old age. After all we are alive, and who is to help us except—except each other?" she added, with a fine superiority to grammar, and holding out her hand to Tom.

Tom smiled, and the dimples came. Just now it struck Maud that he was so like his cousin, instead of the other way about.

"I believe you understand me," he said. "And to understand any one is the greatest benefit you can do him!"

Lady Chatham returned before long from an unnecessary call, undertaken chiefly because the carriage had to go that way, and it was the most convenient thing in the world. She urged Tom to stop for tea, and it was consequently nearly six when he left the house.

His way lay across the park from the Albert Gate to the Marble Arch, and he loitered, for Maud had replenished his serenity, and when we are serene we are not in a hurry. It was a hot afternoon, and by the time he got to the Serpentine the banks were crowded with bathers. The grass underneath the big elm trees on the side of the Row was covered with heaps of clothes, and multitudes of boys and young men were standing about on the bank, or swimming. The soft persuasive colour of an English evening was there, and the warm languor of the south, and Tom stood watching them for some time, feeling rather as if a gallery of antique statues had come to life. Some of the bathers were very well made, one particularly, a boy of about eighteen, who was standing on the bank resting on his foremost foot, the other just touching the ground with the toes, his hands clasped behind his head. He was long in the leg, short and slight in the body, and his hair curled crisply on his forehead as in a Greek bronze. Tom told himself that he was Lysippian, and went on his way thinking what a fine subject for a statue Isaac would make—Isaac waiting with the faggots of wood on his shoulder, standing gracefully, unthinkingly, like the boy he had just seen, not knowing who the victim should be.

May meanwhile had taken Mr. Thomas out for his airing, had had tea alone, and was feeling a little ill-used. Maud had been quite right. Tom, she thought, ought to have come away with her. Why? Well, for no reason except the very important one that he wanted to stop. Then it occurred to her that a candid enemy might say she was in danger of becoming jealous of Maud, and the thought of that made her quite angry. But no one had suggested it except herself.

In Tom's mind the vision of Isaac was supplanted by other thoughts. He wondered whether he had said too much, whether by any chance Maud could guess his trouble, for he knew she was skilful at reading between the lines, and on his way down Oxford Street he determined to write her a line in order to counteract any such undesirable possibility.

May was not in the drawing-room when he got in, and taking up a postcard—for there was nothing private in what he meant to say—he wrote: " I am not *blasé* at all. Don't think I am."

He directed it, and leaving it with two or three others for the post, went to see if May was in yet. He found her with Mr. Thomas, who was a little fractious, and who, on Tom's entrance, began yelling in a way that shouted volumes for his lungs and larynx. Tom bore it for a minute or two, but as it did not subside he shouted out to May across the tumult—

" I've only just come in, and if I stop here I shall be deafened. I shall be in the studio till dinner."

Mr. Thomas condescended to go to sleep after a quarter of an hour or so, and May went to the drawing-room. Tom's post-card was lying address downwards, and not thinking what she was doing she read it. It was quite natural and innocent to see to whom he was writing, but when she saw the address she felt a little more ill-used than before.

About a week after this, Maud Wrexham came to see them in Bloomsbury. May was out, and Tom was in despair because the breezy model had taken it into her head to demand a higher wage for standing, and Tom could not afford either to pay her more, or to part with her. He had engaged her till the end of the week at the higher rate, but he knew he could not continue to do so indefinitely. He was walking up and down the studio when Maud was sloppily announced by the slip-shod maid—wondering what on earth was to be done.

"May not here," she said, "and you be-thunder-clouded! What's the matter?"

Tom related the woes of the afternoon, and commented bitterly on the rapacity of the human race.

"I really don't know what to do," he said. "I can't possibly keep her on at this rate. It's hard enough as it is."

Maud flushed suddenly, and seemed to have something to say.

"We are old friends," she began at length, "and I don't think you will be offended at what I am going to say. Will you do me a favour? Will you let me lend you some money?"

Tom stopped suddenly in his walk.

"How could I be offended?" he asked. "It is awfully kind of you. For myself I should say 'Yes' at once. Why not? But there is May."

Maud was silent a moment. A vague impatience came over her, for she had understood rather more than Tom had meant her to understand a week ago.

"Why should she know?" she asked at length. "It is a matter between you and me. I know some people would refuse such a thing at once. It is such a comfort that you are sensible. I have too much money, you have too little. There can be no reason why I should not lend you some."

Despite herself she felt a great anxiety that Tom should acquiesce. The thing was of no importance, but she could not help longing that Tom should take her offer, and not let May know. The feeling in her mind was too undefined to lend itself to analysis, but she was conscious of desiring this in some subtle manner beyond her control.

But Tom answered her at once.

"No, I must tell May. It would be out of the question not to tell her. You see that surely. But I thank you again for your offer. I will tell her to-night. Perhaps she will not object; on the other hand, I am afraid she may. I have no such feelings about it. Of course we can go on for a month or so, but what is to happen then? If I could get Demeter finished, and the clay sketch of the other done, I shall have done my best, and if no one buys them——"

Maud looked up inquiringly.

"God knows what next," said Tom. "If May and the baby keep well I can't bring myself to feel desperate. But if anything demanding expense happens to either of them I don't know what we shall do."

"You're fussed and worried this afternoon," said Maud, sympathetically. "It's this bother about the model, and the heat, and so on. This room is awfully hot. Why don't you have a new blind up?"

Tom laughed rather bitterly.

"New blinds!" he said. "I'm thankful we've got some old ones. Thank God May doesn't know about it all, how near we are to actual want! But I lie awake at night wondering if I ought to tell her. I am worried, I confess it ; and I thought I was so sure of myself. I aim at what I believe to be best. I would sooner have produced that"—and he pointed to the Demeter—"than all Manvers' things, for which he gets what he asks. It will be finished next week, and two or three dealers are coming here to look at it. They bought those miserable statuettes of mine readily enough."

"Of course you can't make any more of those," said Maud. "I understand that."

Tom flushed with pleasure.

"I believe you do," he said, "though I don't think any one else does. Manvers and Wallingthorpe think it is half out of sheer perversity that I make what they call heathen goddesses. But they are wrong. I do it because I must. I may be quite wrong about myself, but I believe I am an artist. If I didn't think that I should have taken to the statuettes again the moment we lost all our money. They might as well tell me to make plush brackets—which I could probably do tolerably well. If I am not an artist, of course I am wasting my time when I might be earning money, but I can't sterilize that possibility just yet. When you have a passion for a thing, it is not easy to give it all up because you have no bank-notes."

"It's hard," said Maud.

"I cannot serve two masters," continued Tom, earnestly. "I cannot use the gifts I believe I may possess in any other way than the way I believe to be best. If the worst comes to the worst, if I cannot get my living by—oh, it's impossible, impossible!" he cried.

Before Maud had time to reply the door opened, and May came in. She, too, saw by Tom's face that something had happened.

"Why, what's the matter, Tom?" she asked quickly.

"Nothing, dear," said he, getting up and recovering himself with an effort. "I have had a row with a model, and she says she won't sit for me any more at the present terms; and so we parted. May, give us some tea, dear, will you? I want tea badly, and so does Miss Wrexham."

May looked a little vexed; she felt she had not been told all. She shook hands with Maud, and remarked, a little curtly, that she did not know the Chathams were still in London.

"Only a few days more," said Maud. "How splendidly the Demeter has got on."

May was a little mollified.

"Yes, Tom's been working very hard—too hard, I think. He doesn't take enough exercise."

"Oh, there'll be plenty of time for that when she's finished," said Tom; "and it's exercise enough chipping away at that stone."

"I saw Mr. Holders this afternoon," said May. "Mr. Holders bought one of Tom's things last winter," she explained to Maud, "and he wants to know if you have anything else for him. I said there was one unfinished statuette, but I couldn't get you to finish it. Besides, you'd given it me."

Tom grinned and stirred his tea.

"No, dear, I should just think you couldn't get me to finish it," he said. "May means that little abortion on the chimney-piece in the sitting-room, you know. There's a horror for you!"

Maud Wrexham soon went away, and the two were left together. May's thoughts went back to the trouble she had seen on Tom's face when she entered, and presently she said—

"Tom, what was the matter when I came in?"

"We had been talking about what I told you," he said. "I can't possibly afford to give more than I do for models, and I am rather in a hole."

"Poor old boy!" said she. "But what can we do? You must have a model, you say, and you have to pay her."

"Unfortunately I have very little to pay her with. We must make the little we have last as long as possible."

"What did Maud Wrexham say?"

"She offered to lend me some."

May got up from where she had been sitting next to him with her cheeks blazing. The idea of borrowing at all had been distasteful to her, and the idea that Maud should have offered it was intolerable.

"She offered to lend you money—you? And you—what did you say to her?"

"May dear, don't behave like that. I said, of course, that I must ask you."

May was all on fire with indignation. The offer appeared to her an insult, and she smarted under it as a horse under a lash. She felt that her vague disquietude for the last week or so was explained and justified. What business had Tom to be on such terms with another? Her anger included Tom too. He had not rejected it with surprise and scorn.

"You said you would consult me?" she asked. "And what answer did you suppose I should give you? Did you think I should say, 'Take it'? Tom, you know me very little."

"May, do be reasonable," said Tom. "Perhaps I ought to have told you sooner, but the state is this: if no one offers to buy the Demeter, we have to face the fact that in a limited time we shall have no money left. What am I to do?"

But May hardly seemed to hear what he said.

"You accepted her offer provisionally!" she exclaimed. "Tom, how could you do it? And you said you would consult me? you told her that? And she knows that you and I are talking the matter over, discussing whether we should be her pensioners!"

Tom grew impatient.

"My dear, you really are talking nonsense," he said; "there is no question of being anybody's pensioners. It is to a certain extent always a matter of time before one is recognized. If I can manage to work on at the things I think worth doing, good. If not, what is to happen to us? Maud Wrexham is an old and great friend of mine. But you are unreasonable. Do not be unreasonable. It is not like you. You have given me your answer, and of course I accept your decision. Don't let us discuss it any more. It is no manner of use."

He walked to the door and paused, looking at her. But she made no sign, and he left the room.

Tom stood still for a moment on the narrow landing outside the room. A patch of ruddy sunlight came through the window which lit the stairs and struck on the narrow strip of oilcloth which did duty for a carpet. The window was bordered with hideous orange-coloured glass, and a ray through it fell on Tom's foot as he stood there, and the orange on the blacking made an abhorrent tone. He felt beaten and dispirited, and the whole place suddenly seemed intolerably sordid. The narrow strip of oilcloth was continued along the landing, and was bordered on each side by a foot or two of imperfectly stained board. The banisters were of that particularly flimsy build which is characteristic of cheap lodgings. There were two bad prints on the walls, one of King Alfred and the cakes, the other of the Duke of Wellington with an impressionist background of the battle of Waterloo. To Tom in his present mood the whole scene seemed to him to be a sort of spectre reflected on to space from his own mind. Everything was unlovely and impossible.

He felt sore and angry with May. She did not understand what his art was to him. She did not understand Maud Wrexham's offer. She did not understand him. More than once the impulse came on him to go back into the room and try to explain, but it seemed useless. She was angry and indignant, and anger is a bandage over our eyes. And he knew, and was honest enough to confess, that he was angry too, disappointed chiefly, but also angry. Maud's offer had come to him like manna. For himself he would as soon have thought of not drinking of a spring that suddenly welled up in a desert when he was dying of thirst, as of not accepting it. But May could not understand that. She felt it as an insult to him and to herself, and to disregard May's feelings was impossible.

He took his hat and went downstairs. It was a broiling August afternoon, and the world seemed dying of heat-apoplexy. The streets were breathless

and baked, and the sky was brass. At the corner
of the street a watercart had just passed, and Tom
stood still a moment inhaling a whiff of air which had
a certain freshness in it. It reminded him of the
smell of a morning in the country, after a rainy night.
He knew that he ought to go back and work, but it
was not to be done. His heart was heavy and his eye
was dull. Well, there was the British Museum only
a hundred yards off, and a man must be in a very bad
state, he reflected, if the Elgin marbles have nothing
to say to him. The place was nearly empty, and he
sat down in front of the eternal figures from the Parthenon pediments with a little sigh of relief.

He had made up accounts that morning with infinite
difficulty, for it was an operation to which he was
not accustomed. The rapidity with which twos and
threes added up into tens and twenties seemed to him
simply amazing. And really it was absurd that there
should only be twenty shillings in a pound. There
ought to have been at least twenty-five or thirty.
And the net result had been that at their present rate
of living they could go on for three weeks more, still
leaving the bill for the piece of Carrara unpaid. He
had faced the situation manfully. He had determined
to go on for three weeks more, giving his heart and
soul to what he thought best in art. But at the end of
those three weeks there stood a blank wall, separating
him completely and irrevocably from those shining
gods and goddesses who were of the golden age.
May's five hundred pounds he had determined quite
definitely he could not touch. More than once she
had wanted him to let her sell out, and though he had
thrilled all over with pleasure that she should make the

offer, it was impossible to say yes. There was too much at stake; he might die and leave her alone with the baby. Mr. Markham's tithes had been falling off lately, and if she went to live with him, as she would have to do, she must be able to help in household expenses.

But for the half-hour that he sat before the marbles he forgot it all. What did it matter after all if *he* produced beautiful things or not? Beautiful things had been produced; the high-water mark of art had been touched. A race of men had produced a race of gods, and he felt himself becoming sanely and healthily small in his own eyes. Meantime May was at home; they had parted in anger and indignation. Poor darling! perhaps she was unhappy, perhaps she thought he did not care—that he was angry with her. Tom smiled inwardly at the absurdity of the thought, and half unconsciously took off his hat as he looked his last at the still marble figures and thanked them for what they had taught him.

But into May's mind there had definitely entered that afternoon a certain subtle poison. For such a poison there is one unfailing antidote which Tom held, and it is pure love. But when that poison, which is as minute in dose as a drop of morphia injected from a silver syringe, has once entered the system, however plentifully the antidote is administered the body is never quite as healthy again as it was before. Where the syringe has pricked the skin there is a little sore spot, and now and again the nerves shrink instinctively at the thought that perhaps it may be introduced again. And the clear drop which it holds is called jealousy. For the last week, and once before that—one night soon after they had come up to London for the first time, when she and Maud and Manvers and Tom had dined together—she had seen the little green-eyed fiend hovering round her, and been vaguely disquieted at him. She thought that Tom felt more interest in Maud than he did in her. She could not talk smartly, she could not say those rather amusing things, which meant nothing, with which Maud was so glib, and which Tom apparently enjoyed hearing. But after that the baby had been born, and the little green-eyed fiend had put his syringe in his pocket and gone away. But for the last week he had been about, and this afternoon he had come again, and had said, " Allow me—or would you rather do it for yourself? " and had just pricked her with that fine point, and the poison was coursing through her veins.

Anger is blinding, but jealousy is blind : she could not be reasonable, and she would not. Tom had disgraced himself and degraded her, and his step was on the stairs. Her anger would have allowed her to throw herself into his arms, and say, " Forgive me, Tom, I was angry," but her jealousy forbade her. So she stood where she was with her back to the window, so that her face was in shadow, and when he came in she neither spoke nor gave any sign.

He sat down near her, and after a moment's silence held out his hand to her. May had long white fingers, and they often sat together talking, she twining her fingers into his, and the action was common with him. But she stood quite still, and his hand dropped again to his side. At length he spoke.

"May, how can you treat me like this?" he said. "What have I not done that I can do? It was not very pleasant to have you speak to me as you spoke this afternoon ; but I accepted your decision at once ; I did not attempt to persuade you ? ”

“ It would not have been much use trying,” said May in a high cool voice.

“ I should not have tried in any case,” said he.　“ I only wished to know what you thought, and I was content to abide absolutely by your decision.”

“ Why did you open the subject again, then,” said she with a sudden spasm of jealousy, “ unless it was to try to persuade me ? ”

Tom thought of the marble figures he had been looking at, and remembered what they had taught him.

“ May dear, please don’t speak to me like that,” he said quietly.　“ You know—you know that was not the reason.”

“ Then what was the reason ? ”

“ The look of your face and the tone of your voice was the reason.　You are not generous to me ; you will not meet me halfway or go a step towards me.”

“ No, you are right.　Do you expect me to come towards you on that road ? ”

“ On what road ? ” asked Tom, wonderingly.

Then quite suddenly and for the first time the real reason for his wife’s attitude struck him.　He got up and stood before her, and at that moment she was desperately afraid of him.　The anger which had possessed her seemed to have transferred itself to him.

“ May, how dare you think that ? ” he asked. “ Are you not ashamed of yourself ? ”

The least tremor passed through her, and she stood there not daring to meet his eyes.　The next moment he had turned from her and was walking towards the door. Once she tried to find her voice and failed, but before he had left the room she managed to speak.

"Tom, wait a minute," she said.

He turned at once. He had been longing with all his soul that she should say just that one word. He had been horribly wounded by her. Yet he felt that he had never cared for her before as he cared now. He crossed the room, sat down where he had sat before, and waited. The next moment she had flung herself on her knees by him, and her face was buried on his shoulder.

"My poor darling! what is it?" whispered Tom. "No, dear, don't tell me yet; wait a moment—yes, wait so. Come closer to me, May, closer. Your place is here."

In a few minutes her wild sobbing had become less passionate, and she raised her face to his.

"I want to tell you," she said. "I could never look you in the face again unless I told you. You know, but I must tell you. I thought—oh, Tom, Tom, what a brute I have been—I thought you cared for her, that she amused you, when I didn't. I can't amuse you, I know. I'm not amusing by nature, dear. And—and I thought your being willing to accept money from her, when you wouldn't let me sell out mine and give it you, meant just that. I wish you would take it, Tom. Tom, I can't tell you how I want to do something for you. Or take hers —that would be better. It will show that I know what a brute I have been, if I ask you to. Please do, Tom. But say you forgive me first. Oh, I have spoiled it all—it can never be the same again!"

She spoke with the fatal conviction of experience.

She had felt poisonous jealousy run through her veins—a poison that cannot but leave some trace behind. But of that Tom knew nothing.

And Tom forgave her from the fulness of his heart, and he believed that he could forget what had passed, hoping an impossible thing. All events and memories, as scientists tell us, write their record on our brains, as the sea writes its ripples on the sand, and there they remain till the sweet hand of death smooths the wrinkles out.

That evening Tom wrote to Maud, thanking her again for her offer, but refusing it. On that point he could not give way. He himself felt as acutely, or more acutely than May had done that afternoon, that to accept it now was impossible. And he began to learn at once that bitter lesson, even in the first glow of their reconciliation, the impossibility of forgetting. The thing had been like a thunderstorm which had passed over and left the air fresh and cool, but in the foreground stood the tree stripped and split by the lightning.

All that week Tom worked as he had never worked before. Doubts, fears, and disappointments left him when he took up his chisel. The statue was approaching completion, he had finished with the claw chisel, and was working only with the fine point. Sometimes as he entered the studio, his heart gave a sudden throb. Was his dream really coming true ? Was the Demeter really good—of the best ? An artist's conceptions are his religion, and when he sees his religion becoming incarnate before him how can he but be filled with joy and trembling ? He knew that he saw before him his conception. The thing was as he had meant it to be. He had realized his best.

And when she stood there finished, artists and others came and looked and admired, and went away again. The Academy, they thought, would be sure to take it; it was admirably conceived and wonderfully executed. But how on earth would Tom get it down those little front stairs? Ha, ha! he would have to take the roof off, or break off Demeter's arm and say she was an antique.

But Tom felt singularly content. It was done: he had touched his own high-water mark, and if no one else cared what cause was there for blame or regret? The moment which he had feared and dreaded had come and passed. Manvers was quite right; no one wanted the Demeter. They said it was beautiful; some one had said it was Praxitelean, and that was enough. And for the next three or four days he waited, doing nothing, walking out with May when the day grew cooler, going through any amount of baby cult, serene and content, knowing that in a little while the pause would inevitably be over, and that he would have to do something—what he knew not. He spent two days in shaping a little wax model of Persephone, which was to have been his next statue, lingeringly, lovingly, regretfully, knowing he would never make it.

About a week after Demeter had been finished, the end came. The baby had not been well, and May, who was not usually anxious, had sent for the doctor. Tom was out when he came, and she sat alone in the gathering dusk waiting for him to come in. The room was nearly dark, and her chair was in the shadow, so that when Tom entered the room he did not see her at once.

"May, are you there?" he said.

May's voice answered him, and he sat down beside her.

"I sent for the doctor this evening, Tom," she said; "baby's not well."

"What did he say?"

"He said there was nothing really wrong, but that we ought to leave town—to take baby to the seaside or somewhere. It's this heat and stuffy air. The nursery is terribly hot, you know; and I have to shut the window, or the noise in the streets wakes him."

Tom got up and walked up and down the room.

"There's hardly any money," he said. "I don't see how we can manage it."

"Mr. Holders was here again this afternoon," she said, "and he saw the statuette—that little half-finished one you gave me. He said it was so good, and told me to ask you to finish it at once for him. He said it was the best thing you had ever done."

There was a long pause. Tom stopped in his walk and stood with his forehead pressed against the window. The sun had just gone down, but the west was still luminous.

"She cannot understand," he thought to himself. "She will never understand."

And to confirm his thought, after a few moments May spoke again.

"I know how distasteful it will be to you, dear, because of course the other style is what you really like. But we must have money. Even if baby was quite well we should only be putting it off a little longer. And then if you will do that, and perhaps do one or two more, you will have money enough to go on with what you like. Mr. Holders admired it so awfully. He said it was the best thing you had ever done, and he is a very good critic, isn't he?"

But still Tom did not answer. His time had come, and he knew it, but he lingered a moment more by the window looking at the red colour in the west. At last he turned and sat down by her. She took his hand and twined her fingers into his.

"Yes, darling, you are quite right," he said. "I will finish it at once; and then we'll take baby off to some seaside place, and—and build sand-castles, and have a little jaunt generally."

*　　*　　*　　*　　*

May went to bed early that night, and when the house was still Tom took up the little rough sketch of Persephone, and with a candle in his hand went into the studio. Demeter stood shining there, her head bent in sorrow for her child. Tom looked at her long and steadily. The candle threw her shadow vaguely and distortedly on to the walls and ceiling, but the statue itself stood out radiantly from the obscurity round. He took hold of the cold marble hand and stood there looking up to the down-bent face.

"Good-bye," he whispered. "You are not wanted. And I—I have another goddess and another child."

EPILOGUE.

Tom and Manvers were sitting at the bottom of a punt in one of the upper reaches of the Thames on a September afternoon. Tom had taken out a fishing-rod, but it was too hot to do more than smoke. Smoke produces silence, and neither had spoken for some time. Manvers had arrived ten days ago, and was staying with Tom in a small house he had lately bought, in which he spent the summer months.

"It's only three years since I saw you last," he said at length, "but you look more than three years older."

Tom took his pipe out of his mouth and blew away a cloud of blue smoke.

"I feel eighty-four," he said. "Prosperity isn't so soothing as I was led to believe. I think worrying and fighting would have kept me young. You are the only person who always remains twenty-five. How have you managed it?"

"Growing old is absolutely a matter of will," said Manvers. "It is like Alice eating the mushroom to make her grow tall or short. You can eat which side of it you like: one side makes you old, the other keeps you young. No one need grow old unless he likes. The secret is to take nothing seriously. I only once took anything seriously, and it made me three years older in a single night. Consequently I am twenty-eight, not twenty-five."

"What was that?" asked Tom, listlessly.

"I took Miss Wrexham seriously. I asked her to marry me. That was just three years ago."

"Poor old boy! Why didn't you tell me? Are you going to try your fate again? She is coming down here in a week."

Manvers looked up.

"The deuce she is! No ; the incident is closed."

"Were you badly hurt ? "

"I found everything distasteful for a time, but I recovered. Life is so amusingly improbable. Fancy my doing that sort of thing ! However, it was very useful ; I learned several lessons."

"What did you learn ? "

"I learned that nothing can really damage one's capacity for enjoyment. Don't think I wasn't in earnest about it ; I was in deadly earnest. The second was that *homme propose.* It is a truism, of course, but it is useful to find by experience that a truism is true. I have yet to learn who disposes," he added. "I must say I have never personally experienced the last part of the proverb. By the way, I was talking to an old model the other day who was sitting to me for my 'Fourth Act'—the thing of the woman with the fan—and she said, 'Man appoints, God disappoints.' But woman usually disappoints. And the third thing I learned was that the most foolish thing in the world is to be serious. While one can certainly amuse one's self it is idle to forego that bird in the hand for a problematic bird in the bush."

"I wish I could learn one thing a year," said Tom, "as you have been doing. I should be getting confoundedly wise by now."

"You always used to be learning things," remarked the other. "I remember you used to discover the secret of life about every other day."

"I have unlearned a good many things, unfortunately."

"It's my turn to catechise. What have you unlearned ? "

"I have unlearned my theory that I could do all I wanted. I have unlearned my conviction that one made one's own limitations—that one could ever be certain about anything. In a way, I have all a reasonable man could want. I have May, I have three healthy children, I have fame—fame of a damnable kind, it is true—but there was a time when I shouldn't have been satisfied with anything. I longed to stretch out my arms round the whole world, to take the whole world into my grasp. But now I know I cannot do it, and, what is worse, I do not want to do it. I acquiesce in my own limitations. What can be sadder than that?"

"If you are happy nothing matters."

"I might once have been happier. I gave up what I believed I could do, and what I believed was supremely well worth doing. I am an apostate. Apostates may be very happy—they are rid of the thumbscrew and the boiling lead—but I wonder if they ever lose that little cankerworm of shame."

"My dear Tom, what nonsense! You tried to fly, and before you had succeeded some one took your apparatus away. Of course it is only natural for you to think that you might have flown if you had been left with your apparatus, but you never could have. Besides, you are rich now; you have your apparatus again."

Tom frowned.

"Cannot you understand?" he said, impatiently. "Good God, it is so simple! Stevenson says somewhere that three pot-boilers will destroy any talent. I must have made twenty pot-boilers at least. Don't you see that what I am regretting is that I no longer want to fly? The chances are a thousand to one that I never could have. But that blessed illusion that I could fly has gone."

"You took it too seriously."

"I did, much too seriously. I don't take things seriously now ; I have lost the trick. But how I long to be able to ! I was mad, no doubt : you often told me so. But it was a very sweet madness. All enthusiasm is madness according to you. But according to enthusiasts, enthusiasm is the only sanity. I oughtn't to complain. I sail closer to the shore. It is really much safer and pleasanter. Indeed, we are thinking of taking a house at Cambridge. It will be nice to have Ted near. If one wants to be happy, one ought to have no ill-balanced enthusiasms. They are very disturbing while they last, and they leave one as flat as a pancake. But when you have once tasted them, though you may have lost them entirely, you can never wholly forget their wonderful intoxication. One of those French enthusiasts says that one must be drunk on something—on life or love, or virtue or vice, it does not matter which."

"I, too, am very catholic," murmured Manvers. "I appreciate virtue as little as I dislike vice. It is all a question of temperament."

"Yes, temperament. That is another thing I have unlearned. There was a time when I was convinced that no man need be in the clutch of his temperament. I believed that one was free. One is not. One is in endless, hopeless bondage to one's temperament."

"You are pessimistic this afternoon."

"It is a relative term. I am really optimistic, though I allow my optimism would have seemed pessimism to me three years ago."

"I don't quite see from what standpoint you can be considered optimistic," remarked Manvers.

"I appreciate fully all I have got. I think the lines are laid for me in pleasant places. That is surely the whole essence of optimism. I believe that everything is for the best, and that if the best seems second-rate to me, it is I who am wrong. I love May more than I love any one in this world, and she is my wife. I have money, which is a hateful necessity, but as necessary as it is hateful. And I have a good digestion."

Tom leant back and beat out the ashes from his pipe against the side of the boat. They would not come out at first, but eventually the whole dottel of the pipe fell into the water with a subdued hiss. Some vague note of thought twanged in his brain, and he paused for a moment, frowning slightly, and trying to catch the remembrance which the sound had stirred. After a little he smiled rather sadly, and not with the completeness which a smile of pure amusement or of pure happiness has in it.

"I used to do that over King's bridge at Cambridge," he said irrelevantly; "and I thought it seemed so like what I was going to do myself. I meant to go through darkness, and then make a splash."

"The end of your pipe made a very little splash," said Manvers.

"Oh yes, a very little splash. All splashes are little; but splashes are rare. Most people slide into the water anyhow, and are content to be seen swimming."

"The world would count you singularly happy."

"Of course it would; it would be wrong if it did not. But—but what I mean is that I might have been happier, and May might have been happier."

Manvers looked up in surprise.

"I don't understand," he said.

Tom sat up and played rather nervously with the tassel of the cushion on which he was sitting.

"Surely it is simple enough," he said. "I have acquiesced in limitations. May is devoted to me— as much devoted to me as I am to her, I think. But don't you see there is less of me than there might have been. There is less of me to love and to be loved— God knows, it is all perfect enough in its own scale. But there might have been another scale. And now "—he dropped his hands and sat upright, looking at Manvers —"and now we are measured by yards, not by metres."

A little wind stirred suddenly in the elm trees by the bank and ruffled the surface of the water. A fish rose in mid-stream beyond the boat, and the current carried the concentric ripples down with it. Behind, the little rambling red-brick house stood sunning its southern front, and on the lawn, in the shadow of a tall copper beech, they could see the glimmer of a figure in a white dress sitting in a low basket chair. Tom turned as he spoke and looked half involuntarily at it.

"Come," he said ; "May will be waiting for us. We are going to have tea early, and then go for a row up the river. We are going to do many pleasant things."

The boat was anchored among some flowering rushes ; a few strokes of the punt pole sent it back to the bottom of the lawn. They strolled up together to where May was sitting, and she welcomed them with that brilliant smile which was so natural to her.

"Tom has been so sombre this last day or two," she said to Manvers. "I hope you have been cheering him up."

"I don't think there is much the matter with him," said Manvers. "He says he feels optimistic."

"Manvers called me pessimistic," remarked Tom; "but that is only a most flagrant instance of his own pessimism. He sees everything through his own spectacles."

May raised her eyebrows.

"What frightfully contradictory accounts," she said. "Oh, Tom, by the way, there is a man here who has come from the station to have the carriage of the Demeter paid. It is fifteen pounds. Surely that is an awful lot. I thought I had better ask you before I paid it."

Manvers looked inquiringly at Tom.

"Have you the Demeter here?" he asked.

"Yes; I bought it back from Lord Henderson. He was very nice about it. He saw I really wanted it, and he let me have it for what he had paid for it. He bought it, you know, as a piece of cultured lumber, perhaps also as a species of charity, and he has sold it for charity. It came two days ago. I told them to unpack it this morning. Where have you had it put, May?"

"In your study, dear, where you said you wanted it. They unpacked it to-day. But surely fifteen pounds is too much for the carriage, Tom?"

Tom's eyes wandered over the lawn, but came back to May.

"Yes, it seems a good deal. But I wanted it, you know, and one pays anything for what one wants; in fact, one often pays a good deal for what one doesn't want."

"You can't say that that speech is optimistic," said Manvers, triumphantly.

"No, I don't defend it," said Tom. "May dear, let's come in and have tea now. It is getting much cooler, and then we can start in half an hour."

May rose and walked with Manvers towards the house. Tom strolled on a few steps ahead of them. As they reached the terrace which ran along the front of the house he turned.

"I don't think you ever saw the Demeter finished," he said to Manvers. "Come with me and look at it."

"Yes, let's all go and see it," said May. "It looks so nice in that corner, with the dark red paper behind, Tom. I went to see it just before I came out."

Tom's room opened out of the hall, opposite the drawing-room. Just as they got to the door he stopped and spoke to May without looking at her.

"Then will you have us told when tea is ready, dear?" he said.

May had intended to come in with them, but something in Tom's voice made her hesitate.

"Yes; don't be long," she said; "and don't get to talking shop about it. We shall never start if you do."

Tom opened the door for Manvers and shut it again after they had entered. The sun was already getting low, and a great blaze of light came in almost horizontally through the open window and shone full on the statue. Tom sat down opposite it, and Manvers stood near him. In the ruddy glow of the evening the white marble was flushed with delicate red, and for the first time Manvers really appreciated the noble conception of it—about the execution he had never had any doubt.

They sat there in silence for some time, and then Tom got up.

"Do you see," he said rather huskily, "do you see what I mean when I say that I might have—might have—— "

He turned abruptly. On the floor was lying the

sheet in which the statue had been wrapped.　He took it up quickly and flung it over it.

"We all have ghosts in our houses," he said ; "but we can at least veil them a little.　Besides," he added, " to go back to what I was saying about my optimism, I have had three crises, three revelations—unimportant little revelations no doubt—in my life.　I think I told you and Maud Wrexham about them one evening, oh, ever so long ago!"

"I remember," said Manvers.

"Well, to have had a crisis is in itself a most delightful experience, but if your crisis remains, so to speak, critical, you ought to be perfectly happy.　Two of my crises were still-born.　The crisis I had when I saw the Hermes at Olympia has come to nothing."

"Do you call that nothing?" said Manvers, pointing to the shrouded Demeter.

"Worse than nothing.　It is a dead child.　It had better never have been born.　And the crisis I had, or thought I had, when the baby was born is—is yet unfulfilled. But my third crisis remains critical.　I met May, I loved her, I love her.　But the ghosts, the ghosts—— "

They left the room.　In the hall was the three-year-old Thomas, being towed sideways across the hall by his nurse, going out for a walk.　Tom took the youngster up in his arms and turned to Manvers with a smile.

"I am a fool if I cannot lay my ghosts," he said.

THE END.